Cahill Cowboys

Texas's Finest

In the heart of America's Wild West, only one family matters—the legendary Cahills.

Once a dynasty to be reckoned with, their name has been dragged through the cattle-worn mud, and their family has been torn apart.

Now the three Cahill cowboys and their scandalous sister reunite.

With a past as dark as the Texas night sky, it's time for the family to heal their hearts and seek justice….

CHRISTMAS AT CAHILL CROSSING
by Carol Finch October 2011

THE LONE RANCHER
by Carol Finch November 2011

THE MARSHAL AND MISS MERRITT
Debra Cowan December 2011

SCANDAL AT THE CAHILL SALOON
Carol Arens January 2012

THE LAST CAHILL COWBOY
Jenna Kernan February 2012

Author Note

Welcome to Cahill Crossing! Settle back and let yourself be drawn into the lives of four proud Texas siblings torn apart by tragedy and reunited by a common devotion to their late parents. As a reader, I always thought a Western series like this would be great, so I eagerly accepted the offer to participate.

Brainstorming ideas about characters and setting and story was a fun and rewarding challenge. One of our easier decisions was choosing the Texas Hill Country as our setting, because we all thought the area beautiful. Determining a family name? Not so easy. But once we decided that, our characters began to take on their own personalities. Thanks to my fellow authors, Carol Finch, Carol Arens and Jenna Kernan, for a great experience.

In this book, you'll meet lawman Bowie Cahill, the second Cahill sibling, and Merritt Dixon, his widowed landlady. Bowie has returned home for one reason only: to find out who murdered his parents. But along the way, he reclaims his place in the family and finds his future with a woman who convinces him there are still some things worth trusting.

Happy trails.

For all you Western fans—you're the best!

DEBRA COWAN

THE MARSHAL AND MISS MERRITT

Harlequin®

TORONTO NEW YORK LONDON
AMSTERDAM PARIS SYDNEY HAMBURG
STOCKHOLM ATHENS TOKYO MILAN MADRID
PRAGUE WARSAW BUDAPEST AUCKLAND

Recycling programs for this product may not exist in your area.

ISBN-13: 978-0-373-29667-5

THE MARSHAL AND MISS MERRITT

This edition published by arrangement with Harlequin Books S.A.

For questions and comments about the quality of this book please contact us at Customer_eCare@Harlequin.ca.

www.Harlequin.com

Printed in U.S.A.

DEBRA COWAN

Like many writers, Debra Cowan made up stories in her head as a child. Her BA in English was obtained with the intention of following family tradition and becoming a schoolteacher, but after she wrote her first novel, there was no looking back. An avid history buff, Debra writes both historical and contemporary romances. Born in the foothills of the Kiamichi Mountains, Debra still lives in her native Oklahoma with her husband.

Debra loves to hear from readers. You can contact her via her website, www.debracowan.net.

Prologue

Central Texas, early 1880s

Bowie Cahill ripped off his black string tie and undid the top button of his starched Sunday shirt, cussing under his breath. His parents, Earl and Ruby Cahill, had perished in a wagon accident and would never see the land they had sold to the railroad become a town named Cahill Crossing. It wasn't bad enough that he and his siblings had just buried their parents, but now Quin, the oldest, had called a meeting and was throwing out orders like it was his God-given right.

"I have a job, in case you've forgotten, brother," Bowie snapped, peeling off his dark suit coat. "I can hardly oversee the horse operation, the livestock and hired hands if I'm already working as the county sheriff in Deer County."

Quin kept talking, now directing his comments to Leanna.

"Annie, you'll be in charge of the meals, our house and its staff, just like Ma."

Bowie's baby sister narrowed her eyes. Lips pursed, she glared at Quin. She looked a lot like Ma when she did that, Bowie thought.

He wasn't sure about his sister, but he knew his brothers were feeling the same guilt he was. Any one of them could have prevented the wagon accident if they had been with Ma and Pa.

"Why do we have to change things right now?" Leanna asked, looking pale in her black silk mourning dress. "We haven't even dried our tears yet. I need to go upstairs and bawl my eyes out, not go fix you something to eat."

She rose from her place on the couch, smoothing her skirts as she told Quin she wouldn't order the staff around. "Honestly, I'd rather move out on my own than let you take advantage of me."

"This isn't about what you want, Annie. It's about what's best for the 4C. We are family and we stick together."

Quin turned to face his youngest brother, who was looking out of the window toward the place where their parents had been buried. "Chance, you're working with me. You'll be helping with the breeding and cattle, and you'll give the orders to the cowboys while I'm gone on roundup come spring and fall."

"So, I'm your hired hand?" Chance asked.

"Now, just hold on, Quin," Bowie said. "We should all have a say in what we want to do. I have my hands full as a lawman and I can't do that job—from a county away, I might add—and mess with the ranch. You may have bossed us around as kids, but we're not kids anymore. Ma and Pa are dead. That's the end of an era."

"How ungrateful can a man get?" Quin fumed. "You think you're honorable and responsible enough to draw a lawman's wages? You can't even own up to your family responsibility."

He looked Bowie up and down, his lip curling. "Just because you wield your gun and use it to control others who don't behave any better than you do doesn't make you a model sheriff. You need to resign and take your rightful place on the ranch, as Pa wanted."

Temper starting to boil, Bowie advanced on Quin. It had taken a brutal jilting for Bowie to get the guts to leave the ranch and try something different, but he had done it. "I'm good at what I do."

"You should be using your supposed talent to round up the bandits and rustlers that threaten the 4C and your own family. Do I need to remind you that Pa was none too thrilled when you walked away from here to defend people you didn't even know?"

Bowie didn't need his brother telling him that Pa hadn't liked it when Bowie had left the ranch for the law. Earl Cahill had been clear about that.

"You disappointed Pa." Quin glared. "He grumbled to me plenty of times. And who do you think got stuck with the extra chores? It damn sure wasn't Annie or Chance."

"Is that why you're so mad? Because of the work?" Bowie snorted. "Hell, hire another hand or two. It's not like we can't afford it."

"How do you know what we can afford? You haven't been around for two years and I'm fed up covering for you. Hell, I'm surprised you bothered to attend today's funeral. Better late than never, I suppose."

Jaw clenching tight at the snide remark, Bowie growled.

Quin growled back. "You hightailed it outta here after Clea North jilted you. She decided you weren't good enough for her, right? Can't blame her for thinking that."

Bowie couldn't believe his brother was bringing up one of the worst events of his life.

"You thumbed your nose at family obligation, pinned on a badge and refused to compromise for anyone."

"All I've ever done is compromise!" Bowie yelled. "And walk in your shadow for all of my twenty-nine years. Well, I'm sick of it! I'm not quitting my job to become your errand boy!"

Before he even realized he'd taken a step, he shoved Quin against the wall, sending Ma's treasured porcelain wedding bowl crashing to the floor. The pieces skittered away and Bowie saw that Quin had cut his hand.

Annie cried out behind them. Quin lowered his shoulder and knocked Bowie into Pa's big leather chair.

"Accept your responsibility," Quin commanded. "Let someone else get his head blown off defending law and order. I need help with this ranch. It belongs to all of us. Our first obligation is here, and here you'll stay."

Bowie scrambled to his feet. "Go to hell and take your orders with you. Nobody put you in charge."

"Someone has to take charge. You aren't around often enough to do it."

"You're not Pa and you'll never be able to fill his boots, no matter how hard you try."

Quin's shoulders went rigid. "At least *I've* been here to fulfill Pa's dream of expansion."

"Yeah," Bowie jeered. "Until you went to the spring cattle sale in Dodge City and got way*laid* by a couple of whores. 'Scuse my language, Annie."

Quin jabbed a finger at Bowie. "I covered for you more times than I care to count while *you* chased after one skirt or another! You *knew* I might not be back in time. *You* should've been here to take up the slack, *for once.*

"Especially when *you* got word that Pa had broken his wrist. You knew he would need help driving to and from Wolf Grove to meet with the railroad executives."

"I was working that day," Bowie gritted out. "There was a dangerous prisoner in my jail." Still, he could've, and should've, left that responsibility to his deputy in order to meet his parents in Wolf Grove and drive them home, but he hadn't. He had assumed Quin would be with their parents; he was always where he was supposed to be. Except this time.

Bowie hadn't been there, either, and guilt had chewed at him ever since he'd gotten word about the wagon accident.

Chance stepped between his brothers. "I'm not staying to take orders from either of you anymore. If I do, I'll never be anything but your kid brother. Pa's gone and I'm through being a ranch hand."

"You're part owner of this ranch," Quin gritted out. "As such, you have to work just like the rest of us. We are doing what is best for the 4C."

"Ranching isn't in my blood, Quin, and I only stayed this long for Pa."

Quin exploded. "Ma and Pa are barely in the ground and you two are turning your backs on this ranch? Pa wanted us to be the most influential ranching family in Texas and, by damned, we will be!"

"That's what *you* want, Quin," Bowie snapped.

Chance nodded. "I'm going."

"Me, too," Annie said firmly.

Quin stared at their kid sister as if she had betrayed him. "This is our home, our way of life, our *birthright!* You aren't going anywhere and neither are Bowie and Chance."

"You just watch," Bowie said.

Fists clenched, Chance got right in Quin's face. "I damn sure am."

"Stop fighting and yelling at one another," Annie demanded, moving between them. "Don't do anything you'll regret!"

"That goes for you, too, little sister." The eldest Cahill sibling shoved a hand through his dark hair. "You have plenty of regrets already."

Bowie knew his brother was referring to Leanna's last heated words to their parents.

Quin looked disgusted. "What a shame that Ma's last thoughts were probably about your childish tantrum for a new dress."

Despite the tears filling her blue eyes, Leanna's spine locked and she tilted her chin at Quin. "I'm not playing maid to you and I don't want to be isolated on this ranch!"

"You spoiled brat! You'll do as you're told."

"No one made you ruler over us all, Quin!" she yelled.

"Grow up! You're not fit for anything other than looking pretty and playing games. You couldn't come close to filling Ma's shoes even if you were willing to try."

Anger flushed her pretty features as she went toe to toe with their eldest brother. "You can try to hold the ranch together, but you won't be able to do it alone. Bowie has his own life. Chance doesn't want yours and neither do I."

"You're going to find a job?" he asked scornfully. "There's only one place I know where a woman like you can get by doing nothing more than smiling and looking pretty for pay. I can't picture you as a saloon girl."

"If that's where my dreams lead me, then so be it. I think we should sell the ranch and each take our share."

Chance froze, his shocked gaze going to Leanna.

Bowie's head jerked toward his sister.

Quin looked as if he might faint dead away. "Are you out of your damn mind? Sell off chunks of the ranch?"

Bowie took an involuntary step back. Thanks to his once-busted nose, he knew exactly what Quin's quiet, steely tone meant. His older brother had been pushed to his limit.

"Over my dead body!" Quin bellowed. "Ranching is our way of life. It's who we are. We just buried Ma and Pa on this land."

But Annie just kept on. "Making a bigger name for the 4C, for the Cahills, won't bring back Mama and Papa."

Bowie wanted to take up for Leanna, but her suggestion sounded irreverent somehow, downright disrespectful. Still, he had no interest in hanging around to work the ranch when he already had a job he liked. Besides, Quin was much better at 4C business.

Bowie could hold his own at the ranch and he had a love for the horses, but Quin had more than his fair share of ranching in his Cahill blood.

"This ranch is our destiny," Quin declared.

"Yours, maybe. Not mine," Chance shot back.

"Fine! Follow your dreams and see how far you get without your family to back you up. I'll be here to see the 4C grow and prosper, doing what Ma and Pa wanted, *expected*."

He leveled a hard stare on all of them. "All profits from cattle and town properties go into expanding this ranch. If you leave, you're walking away with no more than the clothes and belongings Ma and Pa bought for you."

Chance scoffed. "More than what I expected."

"Take your favorite horse and get the hell out of my sight!" Quin yelled.

Bowie didn't need his brother's permission to take his gelding with him, and he was done asking anything of Quin.

His older brother stabbed a finger toward the front door as if the three of them were too dense to know where it was. "Go! Defy your legacy if you want. You might as well walk over our parents' graves on your way by, too.

"You think leaving here will help you find out who you are?" he asked scathingly. "I can save you the trip. You're *quitters* and I'm ashamed to call you family."

Chance muttered something foul as Bowie lunged.

Leanna grabbed his arm. "No, Bowie. Don't make this worse."

"Stay out of it Annie," he snarled, shaking off her hold.

"None of you are worthy to bear the Cahill name." Quin sneered. "Maybe you should take an alias to hide your shame for defying Ma and Pa. I sure as hell don't want to claim any of you!"

Bowie started forward again, wanting to plow his fist into his brother's face, but he stopped. Quin could argue with a rock night and day, and still never say "uncle." It just wasn't worth it to Bowie. He was burning daylight.

He turned on his heel and strode out of the door.

"Don't come back!" Quin yelled. "Do you hear me?"

Chance and Leanna followed Bowie. Quin's boots thudded loudly on the porch as he stalked out behind them, cursing them up one side and down the other.

Bowie mounted up, staring soberly at the big house where he and his family had lived well before the railroad had come, before a town named after the Cahills had sprung up. For years, it had been only Ma, Pa and the four of them, and now it was all gone. His gaze met Quin's.

His brother's eyes were stormy with anger. Well, Bowie was blistered up, too.

He didn't like the thought that he couldn't return to the 4C whenever he wanted. And he'd never seen his brother this lathered up about anything. For a moment, a fleeting second, Bowie thought about trying again to reason with Quin.

Until the other man shouted, "Don't think I'll beg you to come back, because I won't."

Quin spun, stomped into the house and slammed the door.

Bowie hated the thought of walking away from his family, but he wasn't going to give in to Quin, either. Not this time. He glanced at Annie and Chance, angry at them, at the whole damn situation. "You know how to reach me if you need to. Y'all might want to let me know the same once you light somewhere."

His brother and sister nodded, their faces flushed with the same fury Bowie felt.

With one last look at the sprawling ranch house atop a lush green treed hill, Bowie kneed his horse into motion and rode away.

Chapter One

Central Texas, two years later

Bowie had figured he would return to Cahill Crossing someday, but not for the reason he had. A reason he flat didn't like.

He stepped inside the Morning Glory Boardinghouse, his shadow cutting off the June sunshine as the screened door clattered shut behind him. He palmed off his hat and ran a hand over his sweat-dampened hair. Once he had turned in his sheriff's badge at White Tail, he'd ridden straight out, west across the hilly countryside. His older brother's telegram had lit a fire under him.

The last time he had ignored a request from home, his folks had wound up dead. Now Quin had come into some information that led him to believe their parents had been murdered and not the victims of a wagon accident, as the four siblings had believed since Earl's and Ruby's shocking and sudden deaths two years ago.

Bowie glanced around the entry of the boarding-house. The two-story pine structure still looked fairly new. The golden wood floor was warmed by a colorful rug and against the wall stood a dark wood coat tree. A parlor to his right had a cozy arrangement of chairs in front of the fireplace.

Cahill Crossing had changed drastically since his last visit. Mostly for the good, some bad. Like the red-light shanties that sat north of the railroad tracks. The town now boasted lawyers, a bank, a newspaper. And right next to this white frame home, there was even an opera house, for cryin' out loud! The swish of skirts had him turning to his left toward the dining area. Across the room, a petite woman with dark hair came through a connecting door, wiping her hands on the apron tied around her tiny waist.

A white shirtwaist and yellow gingham skirt skimmed her sleek figure like a glove. Rounding a long dining table, she stopped a few feet away. "I'm Merritt Dixon. May I help you?"

She was a small but curvy package. A spot of flour dusted one cheek and her pert nose. Sable-dark hair was pulled back in a braid, her face flushed. Wisps of hair curled around her oval face and drew his attention to her clear green eyes. Spring-grass green. They were the prettiest eyes he'd ever seen, but it was her warm, open smile that sent a sudden and unexpected kick of desire through him. She watched him expectantly.

Irked at his reaction, he gave her a polite smile. "I was wondering if you had any rooms to let."

"For how many people?"

"Just me."

Was the sudden wariness that clouded her eyes due to him being a single man? Or a stranger? Either way, Bowie volunteered, "Quin Cahill will vouch for me."

He hoped.

At mention of his brother, the woman's lips curved. "Very well. I have a couple of rooms available. All of the rented rooms are upstairs."

She walked in front of him to the bottom of a pine staircase and he couldn't help a smile at the flour still on her face.

"How many rooms do you rent?"

"Four." Putting a foot on the first step, she glanced back to see if he was following.

Still holding his hat, he did, unable to keep his gaze from sliding down her trim back to the gentle flare of her hips. She was small, but every bit a woman. With that satiny curtain of dark hair, her rose-and-cream skin and her regal bearing, she was a fancy piece.

Well, he'd learned his lesson about fancy women. At the top of the stairs, she turned right. He shifted his attention to his surroundings, noting the three closed doors they passed on the way to a room at the end of the hall. Bowie wanted to know who would be living so close to him.

"Are the other rooms occupied?"

"Only one. Hank Wilson is a widower and often helps me around here."

Bowie nodded, intending to meet the man for himself.

She stopped in front of a closed door with a porcelain knob, just like the others. "Here's your room."

She opened the door and Bowie stepped up to look inside. When his arm brushed her shoulder, she eased away. Drawing in her fresh, light scent, he moved into the room, noting the cleanliness of the floor, bed frame and window. A red-and-white quilt lay folded at the foot of a bed that looked as if it might just accommodate his six-foot-three frame.

He walked to the window that looked west over the opera house and marshal's office and the thickly treed hills beyond. "This will do just fine."

"How do you know Quin?"

It wasn't a secret, but Bowie didn't like giving out information about himself. He glanced over his shoulder. "He's my brother."

Recognition flared in her pretty eyes. "I knew Earl and Ruby had four children. You must be Bowie."

He turned to face her, biting back a smile at the flour still on her face. "Why do you say that?"

"I've met Leanna and Chance." Though her tone was still polite, he thought there was an edge to it. "You're the lawman."

"Not currently." He'd given up his badge to answer his brother's call home.

"Did you come back to help Quin and Addie?"

Addie. The new wife Quin had mentioned in his wire. Bowie wondered what kind of woman his brother had married. His gaze skimmed the room, noting the sparkling white basin and pitcher atop a sturdy pine dresser. "Help with what?"

"The fires and cattle rustling, the horse thefts."

He looked at her sharply. This was the first he'd heard of any trouble like that.

"It's been going on for a couple of months. A lot of people call it the Cahill Curse."

Was his brother having recently been framed for murder part of that curse? He tapped his hat against his thigh. "Is that what you think? That there's a curse?"

"I don't hold with that nonsense." She pushed back a wisp of dark hair, still wearing the flour.

Barely stopping himself from reaching out to brush it away, he couldn't stop a grin.

Irritation flickered in her eyes. "I think someone wants to cause your family problems, although I don't know why. Your parents were fine folks, as are your brothers and sister."

"You knew my parents?"

She nodded, her green eyes darkening. "I'm very sorry for your loss. I admired them both a great deal."

He wondered if she knew of Quin's suspicions. If anyone did.

"Are you sure you still want the room?"

"Yes." He frowned. "Why wouldn't I?"

"I thought you might stay at the 4C."

He studied her for a moment, wondering if she was fishing for something else, like information about the rift between him and his siblings. Was she a gossip? The steadiness of her gaze had him deciding he was too suspicious by far, a by-product of being a lawman.

His gaze lit again on her flour-dusted face. Before he could bring it to her attention, she gave him a barely disguised look of exasperation.

"May I ask why you keep smiling at me like that?"

"You have flour on your cheek." He barely brushed his finger against her satiny skin, but it was enough to send a jolt of electricity shooting up his arm. He pulled back. "And your nose."

She colored slightly, lifting the hem of the apron to wipe her face. "Is it gone?"

He nodded.

She let the apron fall and gave her cheek one last swipe. "I guess it makes sense you'd want to stay here."

"How so?"

"I hadn't taken into consideration your brother being a newlywed. I imagine you'd want to give them some privacy."

Bowie saw no reason to set her straight. As charmed as he was by the delicate pink in her cheeks, it was none of her business why he was here or why he wasn't staying at the ranch.

The fact was Bowie didn't know if he wanted to stay at the 4C. Or if he was even welcome. A room here would do until he decided if he was staying in Cahill Crossing. That would depend on whether there was anything to Quin's claim that Ma and Pa had been murdered.

"What's the first week's rent?"

She named a fair price and he handed over the money.

"You'd probably like to wash up. I'll bring some water."

"Don't bother." The idea held appeal, but he still had to ride to the ranch. He was ready to get his meeting with Quin over and done with. "I have some things I need to do. I'll take you up on that later, though."

She nodded, sweeping past him into the hall. He quickly caught up and they started down the stairs. He let her walk ahead, watching the sun play in the dark strands of her hair. His gaze was drawn to the creaminess of her skin and the delicate curve of her neck where it met her shoulder.

He wondered what her story was. He saw no ring on her delicate hand. She hadn't mentioned a husband or any other family. Was she alone?

He hadn't been so curious about a woman since Clea and look how that had turned out. He didn't need to know Merritt Dixon's story. He had only returned to Cahill Crossing because of Quin's wire. He wasn't interested in anything else. He wouldn't let himself be.

"Breakfast is at six every morning, lunch at noon and supper at six in the evening."

"Okay."

They reached the first floor and she turned, her subtle scent wafting to him. "There's a key for your room, if you'd like."

"I would. Thanks. I'll get it when I return."

"All right. I'll see you then." She moved through the dining room toward the kitchen. Bowie settled his hat on his head and reached for the front doorknob.

"Mr. Cahill?"

"Bo," he said automatically, glancing over. "Or Bowie."

"Bowie." She gave him a warm smile. "Welcome home."

The sentiment struck him hard. Home.

He stood unmoving for a moment, until he realized she was giving him a puzzled look. "Thank you."

The hell of it was he did feel welcome. He hadn't expected that. Neither had he expected to have such a strong reaction to Merritt Dixon. Any reaction, for that matter. He didn't like it one damn bit.

Even so, Bowie would rather deal with her than his brother and the reason he'd come home.

Bowie had no hesitation about helping find out who had murdered their parents, if indeed they had been murdered. But he was of two minds about seeing his older brother.

Quin's pretty chestnut-haired wife, Addie, had greeted Bowie at the door. After introducing herself, she urged him inside.

Without giving him time to even wash his hands, she had marched him up the stairs to their parents' room, which now belonged to Quin and his new missus. Bowie bet Ellie Jenkins's folks hadn't liked Quin getting hitched; they'd made no secret of wanting him for their daughter. Actually, they had pushed Ellie at Bowie, too. Chance had escaped.

Bowie stopped in the bedroom doorway as Addie swept inside, skirts rustling.

Though it was strange to see Quin in their parents' bed, what gave Bowie a jolt was the sight of his rawhide-tough brother slumped against the headboard, eyes closed, with a bandage wrapped around his middle.

Quin had said in his wire that he'd been injured, but it looked more serious than he'd let on. Had he almost died?

Addie walked to the foot of the four-poster bed and lightly touched the big man's leg through the sheet. "Quin?"

He opened his eyes, the softness in his gaze shifting to wariness when he spied Bowie.

The new Mrs. Cahill stepped back. "I'll bring up some water, if you're thirsty."

"Yes," the men replied at the same time.

Addie gave her husband a look. "Talk."

Bowie stood there with his dusty hat in his hand until the click of her heels faded.

In his mind, he could still hear the echo of angry words from the last time he and his siblings had been together. His harsh accusation that Quin would never be able to fill Earl Cahill's boots. Just standing here plowed up all kinds of guilt and resentment. Tension pulsed in the room and Bowie dragged a hand across his nape.

Quin's steel-gray eyes were piercing. "Wasn't sure you'd come."

The clipped words got Bowie's back up. "Well, here I am. Did you send word to Annie and Chance, too? Annie's in Deadwood."

"I know that. I also know she's working as a saloon girl," the other man growled. "How could you let her do that?"

"Let her! I had no idea what she was doing." He paused. "Are you sure?"

"My information came from Preston Van Slyck."

"You trust that? He's probably still sore at her for spurning his advances."

"I don't like him much, but he's seen Leanna, and the saloon ain't even the worst of it. He said she has a baby, too."

A baby? Annie? "Who's the father?" Bowie demanded.

"Van Slyck didn't know."

"Do you really believe she has an illegitimate child?"

"I don't want to, but I don't know the truth, either."

Bowie's gut clenched. His baby sister had been in trouble and had obviously felt she couldn't contact him. Dammit. He turned his attention to their other sibling. "What about Chance?"

"I don't know where he is, but Annie will hear from him before either of us and she can tell him what's going on."

Bowie figured Quin's wire to Annie would have his sister heading home, just as it had Bowie. "What exactly *is* going on? Why do you think Ma's and Pa's deaths weren't an accident?"

"Over the past couple of months, I've gotten two anonymous notes claiming Ma and Pa were murdered. Both times, I was promised 'the truth' if I paid two thousand dollars. When I arrived at the first meeting, I was knocked unconscious. I came to with a dead man lying beside me, my gun in my hand."

"And the money was gone," Bowie said flatly.

"Yes." Quin paused as Addie walked back into the room carrying two glasses of water.

As she handed one to Bowie and the other to his brother, he thought about asking for something stronger to drink, but he needed a clear head.

Quin gestured toward his wife. "Boston followed me and heard three men riding away from the scene. In different directions."

So Quin called his wife Boston for the town where

she'd come from. "Any guesses as to who those three men might be?"

"No." She walked over to stand beside the bed. "We don't know who the dead man is, either."

Who had taken that money? Bowie wondered as he drained his glass of water. "When Marshal Hobbs told us about the wagon wreck two years ago, he said he found nothing at Ghost Canyon to indicate foul play. He believed the wreck was caused by a loose wagon wheel or hub."

Quin shook his head. "If that were true, why would someone kill the man who claimed to have information about Ma's and Pa's deaths?"

Bowie had to agree.

"And frame Quin for the murder." Addie put a hand on her husband's shoulder. "Hobbs even arrested him."

"Thanks to Boston, that didn't stick." Quin smiled up at his wife and his whole face softened.

Bowie blinked. He had never seen his brother look at a woman that way. And she was looking back at him the same way.

"Tell him the rest, Quin," Addie urged.

"After being released for the murder *I didn't commit,* I received a second anonymous note also offering the truth in exchange for money. This time, the meeting was at Triple Creek. Both notes were delivered by a lanky Mexican kid riding a burro."

Bowie tucked that away in his mind. "So you went to the meeting?"

"Boston intercepted the note and went." Quin gave his wife a stern look. "When I realized what she'd done,

I hightailed it to Triple Creek and saw two men wearing black hoods holding her at gunpoint."

Questions whirled through Bowie's mind, but he let his brother continue.

"When they saw me, a gunfight broke out."

Addie nodded. "Quin fired to protect me and that's when he was shot."

"But I did hit one of those bastards and Boston stabbed the other one."

Bowie arched a brow.

"She carries a blade in her boot," his brother explained.

"Is that right?" It seemed his new sister-in-law could hold her own with anyone, including his gruff brother. She had already softened Quin's blunt edges.

"I got the skunk in the neck and arm," Addie confirmed. "But he still got away with the money, blast it."

"The other one didn't get away. He died." Quin took up the story. "But before he did, he told me our parents had been murdered and we had no idea how deep the scheme went."

Scheme? Bowie frowned. That sounded as if someone had *planned* to kill Earl and Ruby Cahill. Who would want to do that and why?

"You don't know who either of these dead men are?" Bowie asked.

"No."

Bowie wanted to get everything straight. "So at your first meeting, you found a dead man, still unidentified. And Addie heard three men ride away from there."

"Yes." The chestnut-haired beauty nodded.

Bowie directed his comments to his brother. "And

at the second meeting, another man was killed by you when he shot at Addie?"

"That's right," Quin said. "And the second hooded man who was there escaped with the money."

"He may or may not be one of the three men who rode away from your first meeting."

The other man nodded.

Bowie walked over to the window, staring out at the oversize barn, the bunkhouse and corrals. Lush wooded hills stretched as far as he could see.

He recalled the information Merritt Dixon had shared with him. "I stopped in town on the way out here. The lady at the Morning Glory Boardinghouse mentioned a Cahill Curse."

"What hogwash!" Addie dismissed. "It wasn't a curse. It was two ranch hands."

Bowie almost smiled as he recalled the petite brunette saying the same thing. "Miz Dixon said there were fires set out here and cattle stolen."

"Yes," Quin and Addie said at the same time.

"Do you think that has anything to do with what happened to Ma and Pa?"

"We aren't sure, but we don't believe so." Quin's face darkened. "Those things were aimed only at Boston and me."

Addie nodded. "4C livestock were moved over to McKnight land to make it look as though I was stealing Quin's cattle. And my cattle were moved over here so I'd think Quin was responsible for the thefts."

"We knew it had to be somebody with access to both ranches," Quin said.

"We caught them." Addie's green eyes sparked with

anger. "One was a man from McKnight Ranch named Chester Purvis."

"And the other was a ranch hand from the 4C named Ezra Fields."

"Fields? I don't know him," Bowie said.

"That's because I had to hire him after the three of you took off." His brother's even tone told Bowie that Quin still resented the fact that his siblings had left.

He wasn't sorry for striking out on his own, but sometimes he regretted that he'd done so in anger.

"These two men also set fire to the addition Boston was building on to her ranch house."

"They tried to blame that on Quin, too," Addie said indignantly.

Bowie focused on one of the corrals. "And you're sure these ranch hands, Purvis and Fields, had nothing to do with the anonymous notes you received about Ma and Pa being murdered?"

"We questioned them pretty hard and they said no." Quin shook his head. "I'm of a mind to believe them. They're sittin' in Ca-Cross's jail right now."

"What about the man you were falsely accused of killing? Did you find a connection between him and these ranch hands?"

"No. They swear they got orders and were paid by anonymous notes left at a remote ravine where they hid cattle on the 4C. They claim to know nothing about our folks' wagon accident."

"They're no-account, but I don't think they could murder anyone," Addie said.

"So, what do you think?" Quin shifted, favoring his left side. "Do you agree Ma and Pa were murdered?"

Bowie glanced over his shoulder. "I'm not inclined to dismiss it. What I can't figure is *why* someone would want them dead."

He turned to face his brother and sister-in-law, resting his backside on the window frame. "Who could profit from their deaths?"

"Or who had a grudge strong enough to do murder?" Quin asked.

Bowie nodded, staring absently at his mother's walnut dressing table and mirror. The marble-topped piece matched the dressers in the big room and had been her favorite. Pa had given it to her one year for their anniversary.

He tapped his hat against his thigh. "I would say Ma and Pa were victims of a random attack, but the man you shot and killed told you their murders were part of a scheme. That isn't random."

"Right."

Bowie's gaze kept going to his mother's dressing table, bare now of her silver brush and comb, her small bottle of perfume. His attention lingered on the two-poster mirror where she always hung her only necklace when she took it off. He didn't recall burying her with it.

He straightened and walked to the dressing table, frowning. "Did you do something with Ma's jewelry when you moved in here? Maybe put it somewhere for safekeeping or give it to Addie?"

"No," Addie said.

Quin's eyes narrowed. "There wasn't any jewelry. Ma was buried wearing her wedding band. That's all she had."

"What about her ruby necklace?"

The other man's gaze went to the mirror. "I forgot about that. She only ever took it off at night."

"That trip to Wolf Grove was for a special occasion. She would've worn it that day." Bowie dragged a hand across his nape.

"I haven't seen it around here. Haven't seen it since before they died." His brother scowled. "Hell, I didn't even notice!"

It wasn't really surprising given the fact that he had been single-handedly trying to keep the ranch going while dealing with trouble after trouble.

"Her necklace wasn't anywhere around Ghost Canyon when we went back to see where the wreck had happened," Bowie recalled. "We looked over every inch of that place. The only things we knew had been stolen were their supplies and money."

"That means the necklace had to have been taken when the wagon was wrecked," Quin said gruffly.

Bowie clenched his fists as he fought to control the anger burning through him. "It looks that way."

"Do you think robbery was the reason your parents were killed?" Addie asked.

He intended to find out. "If so, maybe the men who contacted Quin were involved. How else would they know about it?"

"The man I killed said the scheme went deep," his brother said slowly. "Don't need much of a scheme to steal a piece of jewelry."

"Good point." He shook his head. "Why would someone wait for two years after Ma's and Pa's deaths to come forward with information?"

Quin studied Bowie. "So you believe it was murder?"

"I believe it needs to be looked into." He dragged a hand down his face. "If it was murder, we'll find whoever's responsible. And they'd better have that necklace."

A look of relief crossed his brother's face. "So you'll stay long enough to help?"

Hadn't he just said so? Bowie's jaw clamped tight. "I'm not going anywhere."

"Glad to hear it."

"Well, you're in no shape to find out anything."

Quin's eyes flashed with resentment.

Bowie was already forming a plan. "One of the first things I'm going to do is find out who those dead men are."

As he walked to the door, Quin moved as though to stand.

"Stay put," Bowie said. He glanced at his new sister-in-law. "Nice to meet you, Addie. Congratulations to you both."

"You're not going to stay here at the ranch?" Quin asked. "Your room's sitting empty."

Bowie hesitated. Just because his brother had asked him to come home didn't mean the invitation extended to the ranch.

"I thought you newlyweds might like to have your privacy. I got a room at that boardinghouse when I stopped earlier."

"Lovely!" Addie said. "Merritt will treat you right."

Quin nodded. "She's a friend. She was to Ma and Pa, too."

"She came to Ca-Cross after her husband died," Addie put in.

"It was after you left, four years back." Quin's pointed words brought back Bowie's humiliation over Clea North's jilting.

Quin had been poking at Bowie since he'd arrived. Just another reason he wasn't staying here.

"So she said." Again, he found himself wanting to know more about the petite woman with the quick smile, like *why* she had come to Cahill Crossing, but he didn't ask. He had enough questions to deal with if he was going to find out who had killed his parents.

"I'll let you know if I learn anything."

Just as he stepped into the hall, Quin said, "Bo?"

He turned.

"Thanks," his brother said gruffly. "I appreciate it."

Bowie started to say he wasn't doing it for Quin, but he stopped himself. His brother was making an effort; Bowie could do the same. "You're welcome."

He bid his brother and new sister goodbye, then made his way downstairs. Stopping in the doorway of the parlor where hot tempers and careless words had sent him and his siblings scattering, he was hit with twin waves of regret and a burning urge to leave again.

He didn't want to stay, but he owed Ma and Pa. He'd let them down the day they'd died. He wouldn't do it again.

Chapter Two

W hy was Bowie Cahill really back in Cahill Crossing? Merritt was still wondering that just before dawn the next morning as she stoked the cookstove, then walked across the kitchen to the small room built on the side of the house. The single bunk in there was available to whoever might need it.

It was none of her business why Mr. Cahill had returned, but still she wanted to know. Maybe he had come home to patch things up with his older brother. She had half expected Bowie to stay at the 4C last night, despite what he'd said about not doing so, but she'd heard him return late.

His sister-in-law, Addie, had told Merritt that there had been a family fight after Earl and Ruby's funeral that had driven a wedge between the siblings. It must have been a humdinger.

Thanks to her friendship with Bowie's mother, Merritt already knew quite a bit about the man. So why did she want to know more?

Maybe because she'd felt a tug in the pit of her stomach when she'd first laid eyes on him. And when he had touched her cheek to tell her about the flour she had on her face. Merritt hadn't had a reaction like that to a man, a *connection* like that, since her marriage.

She frowned. That was enough of Mr. Bowie Cahill. She opened the door to the small room off the kitchen where Lefty Gorman sometimes slept off his overindulgence of liquor, but not last night. The bed was empty.

She walked out of the kitchen and crossed the dining area, moving down the short hall to the back of the house. She carefully opened the door in case Lefty had chosen to spend the night on her stoop. He had done so before, though more often than not, he spent the night in an empty bunk at the jail.

Pushing open the screen door, she stepped out and was hit immediately with the strong odor of whiskey on the summer air. Lefty was slumped against the adjacent wall, his long legs sticking out in front of him. His graying brown hair stood up at the back, testament that he had been in that position for some time.

He had once told her he had owned a successful business back in Missouri, but the financial panic that had swept across the country in 1873 had ruined him. He'd begun drinking and over a period of years had lost his wife and children, his home. So he had headed to Texas, arriving in Cahill Crossing about the same time Merritt had.

Occasionally, he did jobs for her. But he still had frequent nights when he drank himself into oblivion.

The liquor didn't make him violent or cruel, just helped him forget for a while.

"Oh, Lefty," she murmured. She couldn't turn him away and didn't want to. She could have been in his same situation.

She knew from bitter experience that a life could be destroyed in the blink of an eye. After Seth was killed, she had wanted to lose herself in a bottle every single day for two years. The prisoner he was escorting—a murderer—had escaped when his friends ambushed her husband and the two Texas Rangers who were in charge of getting the man to Austin for trial.

Seth had been a Texas Ranger, too, but his commanding officer hadn't ordered or even requested that he go. Her husband had volunteered, despite being told it wasn't necessary. And he'd been killed protecting some outlaw who wasn't his responsibility. Instead of liquor, Merritt had lived on anger for two years.

She knelt in front of Lefty and shook his shoulder.

The older man opened one bleary blue eye, peering at her. "Miss Merritt."

"Come inside and have some coffee."

"'Kay," he whispered, trying to get to his feet.

She slid a shoulder under his arm, propping the door open with her foot. Getting him upright was a slow process, but she did it. With a lot of turning and shifting, she got him inside.

"Sorry." The word was slurred. It seemed a major effort for the man to put one foot in front of the other.

She tightened her hold around his waist, staggering under his weight. They veered toward the wall.

"Sorry to dis'point you, Miss Merritt."

"You haven't disappointed me," she said, her voice labored as she struggled to keep the man upright. "Keep moving toward the table."

He took a step, his heavy booted foot coming down on her toes.

She winced.

"The jail was full," he said.

She nodded, concentrating on keeping her balance and trying to steer him in a straight line. Suddenly, he turned toward her and stumbled, dislodging her hold.

She grabbed for his arm. "Hang on to me, Lefty."

His feet tangled with hers and they both crashed into the wall.

A dull pain shot through Merritt's hip. She would have a bruise, but it was nothing serious.

"Ooomph," Lefty grunted, sliding to the floor. Kneeling in front of him, she held on to his wrists and pulled until he sat up.

"Sorry, Miss Merritt. You okay?"

"I am. Now come on. Once you have some coffee in you, you'll feel much better."

She wasn't sure how she was going to get him to the table if he couldn't make it on his own. "Can you stand?"

"Yes." But all he managed was to get to one knee.

Merritt moved to his side, trying to figure out how to get the man on his feet. "Brace yourself against the wall. I'll count to three, then you lean on me and use the wall for support to stand."

He nodded.

She bent to slip her shoulder under his arm. "One, two— Oh!"

A pair of strong, hot hands clamped around her waist and lifted her effortlessly to the side, setting her on her feet.

She whirled to see Bowie Cahill.

As he released her, he glanced at Lefty. His gaze sharpened as it came back to Merritt. "You bring in drunk men often?"

Not liking the way he said that, she lifted her chin. "If necessary."

"Hmph." His blue eyes glinted. "Looks like you could use some help. What are you trying to do?"

"Get him to the table and get some coffee in him."

"Is this your boarder, Mr. Wilson?"

"No. This is Lefty. He…sometimes sleeps here. This morning I found him on the back stoop."

The older man squinted up at Bowie. "I'm not liquored up all the way."

Bowie nodded, stooped and helped Lefty to his feet. Draping one of the man's thin arms around his neck, Bowie practically carried him to the dining table.

Merritt followed, unable to tear her gaze from Bowie's broad back. The muscles in his shoulders and arms strained against the seams of his white shirt. My, he was big.

Giving herself a mental shake, she hurried around him and pulled out a chair, pressing back against the table to keep out of the way.

He lowered the older man into the chair.

After a mumbled "Thanks," Lefty put his head in his hands.

Merritt smiled at Bowie. "Thank you."

"You're welcome."

"I'll get that coffee." Intending to go to the kitchen, she turned and was pulled up short. Frowning, she looked back to find her skirts caught beneath her intoxicated friend. She tugged, to no avail.

Looking as though he was hiding a grin, Bowie tipped Lefty forward slightly and gathered Merritt's skirts in one hand, freeing them.

She expected him to drop them straightaway, but instead his gaze lingered on her exposed ankles and calves. His eyes darkened. Despite her stockings, her skin tingled as if he had touched her bare skin.

Feeling her cheeks burn, she tugged at her skirts.

This time, he released her garment. "Here ya go."

"Thank you." She hurried into the kitchen, anxious to get away from him. The man had eyed her as if he could see all the way up her skirts!

It irritated her that merely his looking at her stocking-clad limbs could affect her so strongly. She hadn't felt a stir in her blood like that since her marriage and she didn't care for it. Why was it happening? Had she been oblivious to men for the past three years? She certainly wasn't oblivious to Bowie Cahill.

She checked the coffee on the stove. Wrapping a cloth around the handle of the percolator, she returned to the dining area and poured a cup for Lefty.

"Would you like some?" she asked Bowie, staring at the hollow of his strong throat.

"Please." He pulled out a chair at the opposite end of the table and sat.

Taking another china teacup from the cupboard behind her, she went to him and poured. She moved to Lefty's far side and shook his shoulder.

He lifted his head and struggled to focus his red-rimmed blue eyes on her.

She pushed the cup toward him. "Drink some coffee, Lefty. Just a little."

He studied the steaming brew, then carefully picked up the delicate dish. She waited until he had taken a couple of sips before she filled her own cup.

She set the coffeepot on the table. "I'll start the biscuits. Breakfast will be ready shortly."

Fighting the urge to escape, she moved into the kitchen and began to roll out the dough.

"You've got a nice place here."

"Oh!" Startled, she almost dropped the rolling pin. "Thank you."

Bowie braced one broad shoulder against the door frame, his gaze scanning the room with its long counter and currently dormant fireplace.

He had the same hard angle to his jaw as his brother. "I left your room key on your washstand. Did you find it?"

"Yes, thanks."

"I hope you slept well."

"I did." His voice was deep, causing a flutter in her belly.

Using a tin cup, she cut out biscuits and placed them in a pan. Why had he followed her to the kitchen? "How was your room last night? Was everything okay?"

He nodded. "The window wouldn't stay up, but it didn't keep me awake."

"Were you uncomfortable?" Last night's temperature hadn't been much lower than that of the daytime. "It was hot."

"I was fine."

"I'll get the window fixed."

"It probably doesn't need much work. I'll take a look at it."

Merritt didn't believe in having her boarders take care of repairs. Or meals or chores.

As he took a sip of coffee, she noted that he had big hands. Except for the delicate handle, the china cup was completely hidden in his grasp.

"How many are you feeding this morning?"

"The three of us and Mr. Wilson." She felt the need to fill the silence. She smiled. "Do you cook?"

"A fair bit. Being a bachelor, I have to."

Merritt remembered his mother telling her that Bowie had left the family ranch four years ago because of a woman.

She slid him a look under her lashes. The man seemed about as movable as a mountain. Merritt wondered what any woman could possibly have done to make him leave.

"Yesterday, it sounded as if you knew quite a bit about the goings-on in town."

"I guess." She threw him a puzzled look, moving to slide the biscuit pan into the cookstove. Its heat added to that of the humid morning and Merritt wiped her damp face with her apron.

She then placed a big skillet on the stove top.

"Do you get many visitors or do most people stay here permanently?"

"I get visitors from time to time. Sometimes people can't afford to stay in the new Château Royale or Porter

Hotel." Wondering why he asked, she reached for the bowl of eggs she'd set aside earlier.

"When I spoke to Quin yesterday, he filled me in on some of the things that have been happening, including that he'd been framed for murder. Did you know the man he was accused of killing?"

"No." She cracked several eggs into the cast-iron frying pan, then began to scramble them. "Undertaker Druckman had a viewing, but I didn't recognize the man. Have you asked Marshal Hobbs?"

"Not yet, but I will."

"You're Quin Cahill's brother?" Lefty's scratchy voice barely carried from the dining room.

Bowie looked over his shoulder at the man. "Yes."

Merritt said quietly, "Lefty usually sleeps it off in the jail, but he didn't this time because there are two prisoners there. They were arrested for stealing cattle and setting fires on your brother's ranch. And Addie's, too. Maybe they know something that could help you?"

"Quin talked to them already and they swear they had nothing to do with that man's murder." Bowie's blue eyes settled on her face. "Do you know anything about them?"

"Only that one worked for your brother's—I mean, your family's—ranch and one worked at Addie's."

"I plan to pay them a visit. Someone, somewhere, has to know the identity of the man my brother was accused of killing."

"His name's Pettit," Lefty said, his voice a little stronger.

Bowie turned, stepping back toward the table. Merritt took the eggs off the cooktop and followed.

"How do you know the man's name?" Bowie asked Lefty. "Were you acquainted?"

"I overheard Marshal Hobbs say it."

Bowie frowned. "Are you sure the marshal was talking about the man my brother was accused of killing?"

"Well." The older man stared hard at the table. "It was the night the marshal let your brother out of jail. Right after he left."

"Are you sure?"

"I…think so."

Bowie moved closer. "I need you to be sure."

Bowie Cahill might not be wearing a badge, Merritt thought, but he still acted as though he were. She gave him a look before turning to her friend.

"Think hard, Lefty," she urged.

"Are you sure the marshal was talking about the man my brother was accused of killing?" Bowie pressed.

Seconds ticked by as the other man sat silent. Tension stretched in the room.

"Mister?" Bowie asked impatiently.

"I couldn't swear to it. Maybe I dreamed it." His face fell. "I do that sometimes."

Bowie showed no emotion, but Merritt could feel his disappointment. Still, he didn't berate the older man. Instead, he said, "Well, it's something to go on."

"How will that information help you?" Lefty asked.

"If I have the dead man's name, I might be able to find someone who knew him."

"And," Merritt said, "you might be able to learn why he was at Phantom Springs at the same time as your brother."

Bowie's gaze sliced to her. "What do you know about that?"

"Only what Addie told me. That she and Quin believed the man he was accused of killing was the one who sent a note asking to meet with your brother."

He seemed to relax slightly. Was that why he had come home? she wondered. To delve deeper into his brother's trouble?

He looked at the mantel clock atop the cupboard. "When does the marshal usually start his day?"

"Around eight."

"Good. I can be there when he arrives."

Remembering breakfast, Merritt returned to the kitchen and put the eggs back on the cooktop to finish cooking. She checked the biscuits and determined they were done, sliding the flaky golden bread onto a platter.

She glanced up. "Once you learn what you can about the dead man, will you be going back to White Tail?"

His jaw hardened, and for a long moment he just stared at her. "I don't remember telling you that I came from there."

"Your mother did." She frowned at his set features. "Is it a secret?"

"No. I guess my ma talked to you a lot?"

"Yes." He didn't appear to like that fact.

"I'm not sure yet what I'll be doing. It's unlikely the town of White Tail will keep the job open."

Without thinking, she said, "Ruby would have been relieved to see you stop wearing a badge."

"And take my place at the 4C?" he bit out.

The hard edge in his voice had her studying him.

"Not necessarily. I believe she wanted you to do something that didn't put you in a gun's sights."

"Hmph."

Even though he seemed to relax a bit, Merritt could tell he didn't like talking about his chosen profession. Or maybe he didn't like talking to her. He probably didn't want to be reminded of his mother's death. She couldn't blame him for that.

"Breakfast is ready." She swept past him with the platter of biscuits and another of eggs.

He followed, sliding the coffeepot to one side so she could set the food on the table.

"Thank you." She smiled.

"You bet."

He pulled out her chair and she sat, feeling the same rush in her blood she'd felt earlier when he had stared at her legs.

What was wrong with her? The fact that he could affect her so easily was beyond vexing. It was downright aggravating and she determined to ignore it.

Bowie couldn't stop thinking about Merritt's pretty blush when he'd caught her skirts.

He reckoned he should've dropped them as soon as he'd freed her and maybe even pretended that he hadn't seen her neat ankles and sleek calves. But he *had* seen them. And he would have liked to see even more.

He bet her legs were that shapely all the way up, but he wasn't going to find out.

Bowie pushed thoughts of her away as he climbed the steps to the jail and marshal's office. The summer day was already heating up and he rolled back his white shirtsleeves as he stepped inside the sturdy pine structure. He removed his hat, getting a flash of quick impressions—a wide scratched oak desk with a potbelly stove in the corner, a pair of wanted posters on the wall behind the desk.

A dark-haired man wearing a badge pinned to his gray vest came toward the door. Tobias Hobbs looked more like a gambler than a lawman. "Nice to see you, Bowie. What brings you to Ca-Cross?"

Bowie shook the marshal's hand. "I came to check on my brother."

"How's Quin doing? I haven't been out to see him since he was shot."

"He's coming along. Actually, he's the reason I stopped by."

"How's that?" Hobbs gave an easy smile. "If there's anything I can do, I'm always willing to help a fellow lawman."

"Quin didn't know the name of the man he was accused of killing, but I have learned it might have been Pettit. I thought you might want to know."

Something flickered in the other man's eyes, but it was gone too quickly for Bowie to identify it.

"That's fast work," he said. "I only just learned the same thing. Full name is Vernon Pettit."

So Lefty had heard correctly. Bowie wondered why the marshal hadn't informed Quin, but before he could ask, Hobbs explained, "I planned to ride out to the 4C and tell your brother. Just haven't had a chance yet."

"No need. I can tell him." He tapped his hat lightly against his leg. "I was also hoping you might have learned the identity of the man Quin killed in self-defense, the one who shot him a few days ago."

Hobbs nodded. "I did learn it, in fact. It's Huck Allen."

"Thanks. I'll pass that along to Quin, as well. How did you find out these men's names?"

"Started asking around. Sid over at Hell's Corner recognized Pettit from being at the saloon and one of the regulars knew his name. I thought Allen looked familiar and found him on a wanted poster. It was a couple of years old."

"That's good information. Thanks. Quin said you have two men in jail."

"Yes, the ones he and your sister-in-law caught."

"I wonder if I could talk to them."

"About why they caused trouble for Quin and Addie? Or if they know anything about why your brother was contacted for a secret meeting?"

Bowie frowned. "You know about that?"

"Just that Quin received two notes, each asking to meet him at a different place. Your brother had no idea why he was contacted and I haven't been able to learn anything about that."

Bowie wondered how hard the marshal was trying to find out, but he didn't ask. He and Quin were in agreement that they wanted to keep quiet concerning Quin's suspicions about their parents being murdered.

If Bowie was going to investigate his brother's suspicions, then he would check out everything for himself. "I'd still like to talk to your prisoners."

For a moment, Hobbs looked as if he might refuse,

then shrugged. "I think it's a waste of time, but I guess it's your time to waste."

The marshal led him through a door in the corner separating the cells from the office area, then indicated the bearded man in the first cell. "This is Ezra Fields, the one who worked for the 4C."

Hobbs hooked a thumb toward the next cell where a stocky brown-eyed man stood. "And that's Chester Purvis."

Fields unfolded his lanky length from where he lay on a cot beneath the lone window. Keeping his distance, he stroked his stringy beard. "Who're you?"

"This is Sheriff Cahill," Hobbs said before Bowie could answer. "He wants to talk to the both of y'all."

Bowie saw no reason to tell the marshal that he wasn't currently a sheriff.

"Cahill?" Fields eyed Bowie warily. "Are you part of the 4C family? Them Cahills?"

"That's right. I understand you worked there for a while."

"Yeah."

"So why did you cause so much trouble for my brother?"

"Like I told him, it was the money. We got a lot more for following those anonymous instructions than working our fingers to a nub on the ranch."

Bowie's gaze moved from Fields to Purvis. "Did either of you know the man my brother was accused of killing or the one he killed in self-defense?"

Both men said no.

In hopes of startling a reaction out of them, Bowie tried asking the same question in a different way.

"Either of y'all know a man named Pettit?"

"No," they answered in unison.

"What about Huck Allen?"

Fields gripped the bars and stared balefully at Bowie. "What's this about? Who are these men?"

"Is that a 'no'?"

Fields gave a sharp nod.

"I don't know him, either," Purvis said.

Neither man had shown any reaction to the names Bowie had given them. It appeared they really didn't know either man.

Purvis shoved his unruly hair out of his eyes. "What did these two fellas do?"

Bowie didn't answer, just glanced at Hobbs and said, "That's all."

The marshal nodded, following Bowie out the door, then closing it.

"Thanks for your cooperation," Bowie said.

"I'm sorry you didn't learn anything. It's been pretty frustrating for me, too."

He had confirmed Pettit's identity and learned the name of the man his brother had killed in self-defense. That was more than he'd had when he began his morning.

"I appreciate it." He started for the door and the marshal accompanied him.

"I heard you took a room at the Morning Glory."

Bowie nodded, wondering where Hobbs had gotten the information.

"Merritt is a fine woman. Really has a way about her."

"She seems to." Bowie was willing to admit that. Was this conversation going somewhere?

"She's quite generous and a wonderful cook."

His eyes narrowed as he studied the man standing with him at the door. Maybe he could get Hobbs to share what he knew about Merritt Dixon. "You know the lady pretty well?"

"Not as well as I'd like, if you get my drift." Hobbs winked.

Bowie did get it and he didn't like it.

"She's easy on the eyes."

There was no arguing with that. Was Hobbs sweet on the petite beauty? Bowie didn't like that, either, although he couldn't have said why.

"She's a beautiful woman, inside and out. Especially out. She has some very nice assets up top."

The coarse observation had Bowie tensing and he gave the marshal a steely look.

The other man appeared to get the message and opened the door.

Bowie didn't know much about Merritt Dixon, but he knew she was a good woman and he didn't want to hear that kind of talk about her.

Even if you had noticed yourself? a little voice taunted.

That wasn't all he had noticed. Earlier when he had picked her up to move her out of the way so he could help Lefty, it had been plain she hadn't been wearing a corset. And judging from the way her skirts outlined her legs, she had on only two petticoats at the most.

But thinking about her…assets was different from talking about them.

Resettling his hat on his head, he bid Hobbs goodbye and jogged down the steps. He passed the opera house, then the Morning Glory. Crossing the street, he headed for Town Square. He angled between the Porter Hotel and Café and Doc Lewis's office, making his way to the boot and saddle shop.

He had actually managed to keep Merritt Dixon out of his thoughts for a while there, but Hobbs bringing up her name put her right back in Bowie's head. He might as well satisfy his curiosity about the woman.

Besides, if he was going to live in her house, he needed to know as much as possible about her, didn't he? The fact was he didn't like her knowing more about him than he did about her. He had learned one thing. The fool woman took in drunks.

How well did she know Lefty? Bowie had seen his share of violent drunks and Lefty didn't seem dangerous.

Bowie's friend who owned the boot and saddle shop would have information about Merritt and possibly her older friend.

He and Ace Keating had become friends four years ago when they'd met in White Tail. At the time, Ace was the Deer County sheriff and Bowie had applied for a job as deputy. Ace had been the county sheriff there for almost ten years and Bowie counted himself lucky to learn from the man.

Two years after they began working together, Ace decided to retire from being a lawman and open a saddle shop, something he had long wanted to do.

Through Bowie, he knew of Cahill Crossing. A new and growing town established beside the railroad tracks had seemed like the perfect place for him to start a business. Ace had moved here and Bowie had become Deer County sheriff.

He hadn't really kept in touch with his friend. After he and his siblings had fallen out, Bowie had returned to White Tail and tried to put some distance between him and his guilt over his parents' deaths.

Last night after leaving the 4C, he had stopped to visit with Ace and his blond-haired wife, Livvy. Today, the big man was in the shop alone.

Though he'd told Ace that he was here to stay for a time, he hadn't shared Quin's suspicions that their parents had been murdered. He wanted to wait until he had more information.

The smell of rich leather greeted him as he walked through the open door. A new dark brown saddle sat atop a sawhorse in the corner. On the wall, a hook held a visibly worn bridle. Ace also did repairs and made boots. Wooden boot forms in different sizes stood neatly against the back wall.

Ace looked up from a boot he was carefully sewing, a broad smile creasing his sun-bronzed features. "Didn't think I'd see you so soon. Are you needin' something for your gelding?"

"No. I actually came by to see what you might know about Lefty Gorman."

"Lefty? Why?"

"According to Miz Dixon, he sometimes sleeps off the drink at her boardinghouse."

The other man ran his forearm across his forehead. "He's harmless."

"That's the impression I got, too."

"It's a sad story. Several years ago, he lost everything, including his family, and left his home in Missouri. He ended up here."

"How did Miz Dixon come to be his caretaker?"

"That, I don't know."

"What *do* you know about her?"

Ace studied Bowie for a moment. "She and Livvy became fast friends when we first moved here. She was in Cahill Crossing almost a year before we came."

"Where did she come from?"

"Down by Austin." Ace laid down his curved awl and needle, his shrewd gray gaze sharpening. "Why all the interest?"

"Just want to know about the lady."

"Why don't you ask *her?*"

Bowie scowled. "She knows things about me, things I didn't tell her."

"And you feel at a disadvantage. You want to find out more without her knowing you asked."

"Yes."

His friend grinned, dark eyes full of humor.

Bowie thumbed his hat back. "Quin and Addie told me she's a widow."

"Her husband was a Ranger, killed by an outlaw."

"That's rough." Was that why she had asked if Bowie planned to put down his badge forever? Resentment had bubbled up at that and he had assumed she felt the same way Clea had about his being a lawman. He had learned a second later that he was wrong. "Did you know Miz Dixon's husband?"

"No, he never made it to White Tail while I was sheriff." Ace pulled a rag from the pocket of his britches and wiped his hands. "You sure are curious."

"I think I should find out as much as I can about the woman whose house I'm living in."

His friend grinned. "If I weren't married, I wouldn't mind getting to know her better."

Bowie shot the other man a look. "Well, you *are* married."

"Doesn't mean I'm blind."

Neither was Bowie and that was the problem. It was all too easy to recall the fine porcelain grain of her skin, the way her eyes had darkened to emerald when she'd caught him looking at her legs.

After another couple of minutes of conversation, Bowie bid Ace goodbye and headed for Hell's Corner. The saloon was one place that every man in town visited at some point. The bartender might remember more about Pettit than just seeing him. He might also know something about Huck Allen.

Bowie angled toward the church, then crossed the dusty street. The saloon sat on the other side of the railroad tracks along with two other saloons, a dance hall, a gambling house and a few other businesses. He would visit them all to learn what he could about Pettit and Allen.

This was what he should be doing, not thinking about his fancy landlady and her clean soap scent. Or how he could still feel the lithe tautness of her waist beneath his hold.

From now on, he planned to keep his mind on his investigation and his hands off of Merritt Dixon.

Chapter Three

Bowie spent the rest of the day talking to people in town. Sid at Hell's Corner Saloon said he had never seen Pettit and Allen together. After that, Bowie questioned all of the neighboring business owners on that side of the railroad tracks—the Whistle Stop Café, the billiard hall, Hobart's Hotel, two more saloons, Monty's Dance Hall and Pearl's Palace.

A man at the dance hall who remembered Pettit turned out to be the same man who had also met him at Hell's Corner.

By suppertime, Bowie was hot, grimy and as frustrated as a gelding in a mare corral. He may not have learned anything further, but he had done a darn good job of keeping Merritt Dixon out of his thoughts. He hadn't thought about her once. Well, maybe once.

He was thinking about her now as he walked up the boardinghouse steps because he was hungry. If supper was as good as what she'd fixed for breakfast, he was in for a treat.

As he moved inside, he checked the mantel clock across the dining room. He had plenty of time to wash up before the evening meal.

Starting up the stairs, he heard a bang and a clatter. Then a cry. A woman's cry.

He bolted up the steps to the second floor and turned right. The door to his room was open and he could hear something from there. As he neared, he realized the sound was a feminine voice. Muttering. What the hell?

He rushed to his room, stopping in the doorway. Miz Dixon sat on the floor beneath the window, her blue calico skirts pooled around her.

"Mr. Cahill." She looked up, her voice angry. A tear rolled down her cheek.

What was going on? Then he saw the blood on her temple. His chest tightened. He reached her in two strides and went to one knee in front of her. "What happened?"

"The stupid window slammed on my hand."

A hammer lay beside her as well as a few twopenny nails. The back of her delicate hand, all the way across, was marked with a cruel red welt and beginning to swell. The blood on her temple was his immediate concern.

She shifted as though to get up.

"Don't move." He gave her his best lawman glare, then rose and went to his washstand, bringing back the basin filled with fresh water.

He fished his one clean bandanna from his saddlebag

and dipped it in the water. Wringing out the cloth, he knelt and reached toward her head.

She drew back. "What are you doing?"

"You're cut."

"I am?" Her hand went to her temple and came away with a smear of blood. She was trembling and pain clouded her green eyes. "I didn't know."

"I'm going to clean it."

She didn't answer.

"Merritt? Okay?"

She nodded.

He carefully moved a wisp of her dark hair back from her temple. Even though he was as gentle as possible, she winced at the first contact. He dabbed at the cut, glad to see the wound wasn't deep enough to need stitches.

With one knuckle, he angled her face toward him, keeping his touch light as he cleaned the wound. A sigh shuddered out of her and he felt the wash of her breath against his wrist. The day's heat swirled around them.

"Where's Lefty?" Bowie asked.

"He's out back peeling potatoes for supper."

"And Mr. Wilson?"

"I think he said he was working at the newspaper today."

Bowie didn't need to ask what she had been doing. The hammer and window made it plain enough. He tried to keep his irritation in check. He'd told her *he* would fix the problem.

She looked up at him, the wet green of her eyes dissolving his temper.

"How bad is it?" she asked.

"It's not too deep, but your head's gonna hurt like blue blazes, if it doesn't already."

She nodded.

"I'm concerned about your hand, too." He dropped the bandanna into the water, then gingerly lifted her wrist, hating that she winced. "Can you wiggle your fingers?"

She did, features taut with distress.

"It doesn't appear to be broken, but it's going to bruise badly."

"Stupid window," she muttered.

The stark pain on her face had his gut knotting. "I don't know what to do for your hand. I'm sending for Doc Lewis."

"That isn't necessary."

"It's a good idea." He didn't wait for her to agree, but got to his feet and opened the window all the way. He leaned out, spying a blond-haired boy sweeping the porch of the opera house next door.

"You there, boy!" When the young man looked up, Bowie waved. "Could you fetch the doc? Miz Dixon has hurt her hand."

"Yessir!" The kid propped the broom against the wall and tore across the street toward the doctor's office.

Lowering the window, Bowie turned back to Merritt. "Clancy can at least tell us if your hand is broken."

"I don't think it is."

"It won't hurt to be sure."

She looked dazed and he wondered just how hard that window had hit her head. Easing down on the floor in front of her, he braced his shoulders against the bed and draped one arm over his raised knee. "Sit still for a minute, okay?"

"All right." She stared down at her hand, her forehead creasing in pain.

Seeing that blood on her head had nearly made Bowie's heart stop. Now that he had tended to her, he noticed other things. She was flushed, and a few tendrils of dark hair had come loose from her braid to curl against her elegant neck.

He took in the tracks of tears drying on her face, the sweat-dampened collar of her dress and—

He smiled.

"What?" she grumbled.

"You have some dirt on your face."

She sighed, reaching up with her uninjured hand.

"I've got it." He caught her hand and lowered it back to her lap. With his thumb, he wiped away the grime on the end of her pert nose, then the smear on her chin.

Beneath his work-roughened hand, her skin felt as soft as down, tempting him to stroke her cheek.

He pulled away. "There. All gone."

"Thank you."

"You were trying to fix the window."

"Well, yes, I was."

"I told you I'd take a look at it when I got back." Her face had regained some color. "I certainly didn't expect you to handle it."

"It's my house and you're my boarder." Her jaw took on a mulish slant. "I don't hold with my boarders doing repairs to their rooms."

"I don't hold with my landlady getting her head and her hand slammed to bits."

"It was an easy repair."

He gave her a look.

"Well, it was supposed to be." Irritation flickered across her fine-boned features. "The window just needed to be fastened to the frame, which is what I was trying to do when the thing hit me in the head. Before I could grab it, the window slammed down on my hand."

"You should've let me take care of it."

"I already told you—"

"Yes, you did." Lord save him from stubborn women. "Your color's better. Think you can stand?"

She gave a little snort. "The window didn't fall on my foot."

"Okay." Grinning, he rose and held out a hand to her. She slid her much smaller one into his, slowly getting to her feet.

"See? I'm all right. Thank you."

His gaze dropped to her mouth and he wondered what she would taste like. When he realized what he was doing, he quickly released her.

She wobbled and grabbed for the wall behind her.

He caught her, curling one arm around her waist to steady her. "You got up too soon."

"I was dizzy for a second. I'm fine."

He wasn't so sure. Or maybe he just wasn't ready to release her. He liked the way she fit against him, her soft curves against his hard frame. Liked the way her breasts brushed his chest and the gentle swirl of her skirts around his legs.

Looking suddenly nervous, she licked her lips. "I'm really fine."

Her face was pale, the raw cut standing out in stark relief against her flawless skin. She still didn't look steady. When he loosed his hold so she could step back, she swayed.

He gently grasped her upper arm, urging her toward the bed. "Sit."

"But—"

"Just until you get your bearings."

She eased down on the mattress, looking at once irritated and relieved. "I think I can walk."

"Maybe two steps," he drawled.

Her mouth tightened.

"Wait there while I check the window."

She opened her mouth—to argue, he knew.

"Please," he said.

There was a long pause. "All right, but I do so under protest."

He couldn't stop a smile. "Noted."

A quick look at the window showed that the problem was with the track that guided the window. A portion of the wood strip had split and a nail had popped loose on the front. There was nothing to support that side.

Bowie searched for a spot on the track where the wood hadn't split. He found one and hammered in a new nail.

When he glanced back to see how she was doing, she gave him a wan smile.

"Almost finished," he said.

If he hadn't mentioned this to her, she wouldn't have been in here and wouldn't have gotten hurt. At present, the window would raise only partially, but it went higher than it had last night.

Steamy June air pushed into the room. Later, he would go to the general store and get a new strip of wood to replace the damaged one. Until then, the repair he'd made would hold.

"Thank you," she said softly. "I'm sorry you had to do that."

"I'm not. And from now on, if you need help with something, you should ask."

"I didn't know I needed help." She sounded irritated as all get-out.

"Once I replace this strip of wood, the window should work just fine."

"Buy what you need at the general store and tell Mr. Stokes to put it on my account."

"I'll take care of it. Are you still dizzy?"

"No. I'm fine." She got slowly to her feet.

He looked her over, relieved to see she was steady.

Still, if it weren't for him, she wouldn't be hurt. What if that window had knocked her out? Or broken her hand?

"I really need to start supper." She started for the door.

He caught up to her in two strides and lightly cupped her elbow. He wasn't supporting her, but he planned to stay close in case he needed to.

"Thanks for doctoring me." The sweet smile she gave him had his mind blanking for a moment.

"Glad I was here," he said gruffly.

And he was. But it didn't escape him that he'd only been able to keep his hands off her for all of an afternoon.

* * *

Merritt had definitely needed Bowie's help and she was grateful for it, but her resolve to remain unaffected by him was shot. It was difficult to not be affected by the man when he was close enough for her to feel the heat of his body and smell the purely male scent of him.

By the time they reached the first floor, Dr. Lewis had arrived. After examining her hand, he gave her a smile, his brown eyes reassuring. Only a couple of years older than she, he agreed it wasn't broken, but ordered her to wear a sling to limit the use of her hand for a few days. He checked the cut on her temple as well, seconding Bowie's prediction that her head was going to hurt like the devil for a bit.

Once he left, Merritt and Bowie made their way across the dining area to the kitchen.

He stopped beside her in the kitchen doorway, glancing around. Late-afternoon sunlight filtered through the screen door, dotting the floor. A black Dutch oven sat on the cooktop and a skillet waited on the counter next to a covered plate.

"Tell me what needs to be done and I'll get busy," Bowie said.

Her head jerked toward him. "That isn't necessary."

"You need help," he pointed out.

She didn't want to need help, but she feared he was right.

The fact that she had also needed assistance to fix the window vexed her.

"It's my fault that you're hurt."

"It certainly isn't. I don't think of it that way."

"Well, I do," he said stubbornly.

She took a few steps into the kitchen, glad for the slight breeze coming through the screen door. "I may move a little slower, but I can manage just fine."

"Would you rather I get someone else to help?"

"There's no need to get anyone. There will probably only be four for supper. Mr. Wilson, you, me and maybe Lefty. I can handle that."

"Looks like you get me, then." He spoke as if she hadn't said a word.

"Mr. Cahill."

"Miz Merritt, you don't want me scrounging up something for supper," he warned.

She blew out a breath. "You're my boarder. Meals are provided as part of your rent."

"Hmm, I think we'll have collard greens and onions. Liver."

"Mr. Cahill."

"Hardtack, beans—"

"Very well!" Despite the throbbing of her hand, a smile tugged at her mouth. "There's chicken to fry and potatoes to mash."

"Done. I've never fried chicken. Successfully, anyway."

"Oh, dear," she murmured.

"You'll have to supervise."

"All right." She moved to the cookstove and checked the Dutch oven. "Lefty cubed the potatoes and put them in here. We'll need to cover them with water, then add a little salt."

Bowie filled a large bowl with water, then poured it into the big pot.

She added the salt. "Put that on the left cook lid and cover it."

He did as instructed.

"While we're waiting for the water to boil, we can batter the chicken." She turned to get two medium-size bowls from the shelf above the counter. "Beat a few eggs in one bowl, adding some salt and pepper. Pour flour in the other bowl. I've already cut up the meat and it's been soaking in a seasoning mixture. Roll the chicken in the flour, then the egg mixture and again in the flour."

After beating the eggs, he speared a fork into a piece of chicken. He rolled it in flour, then in the egg mixture. As he moved back to the flour, the meat slipped off the fork and plopped into the bowl, sending up a puff of white.

He gave her a relieved look. "Good thing that didn't fall on the floor."

As he continued, she watched a muscle flex up his strong bronzed forearm. Her gaze moved over his wide shoulders, then to his corded neck, lingering on the dark hair curled damply against his nape.

Her skin was damp, too. The heat from the cookstove turned the summer air even hotter. She plucked at her bodice, staring at the way Bowie's white shirt clung to the supple muscles in his back.

She realized with a start that he had turned and asked her something. The glint in his eye told her that he had caught her staring.

"Am I doing this right?" he asked.

"Yes." Looking away, she lifted the lid on the pota-toes. They weren't boiling yet so she moved to the pantry. Stepping just inside, she picked up a jar of green beans.

"What are you doing?"

She started, nearly dropping the glass container. "You're entirely too quiet, Mr. Cahill!"

"Bowie." He took the jar from her. "You're not supposed to be doing anything."

"One of my hands works perfectly fine."

"Does it still hurt?"

She pursed her lips. "Yes."

"What about your head?"

"A little, but I don't need to be coddled."

He looked as though he might argue that, but instead asked, "How many jars of beans do you want?"

"Just one more."

He carried the vegetables to the long counter, which was within easy reach of the stove. After opening the glass containers, he went back to battering the chicken.

Merritt poured the green beans into a pot, then set it on one of the empty cook lids.

"Okay, chicken's done." He sounded proud of himself.

She nodded, peering into the Dutch oven. "The potatoes are ready. I can fry the chicken if you'll take care of mashing the potatoes."

She spooned an amount of lard into the skillet. As she waited for it to melt, she glanced over just as he poured the drained potatoes into a bowl.

"You'll need to add butter and some milk." She pointed him toward the crockery dish of butter on the shelf above him, then the milk jug in the pantry.

Once the grease was hot enough, she forked in the

chicken. She watched as Bowie mashed the potatoes. When she caught herself staring at him again, she knew she'd best focus on something other than the man's physical attributes.

"Did you learn anything from Marshal Hobbs?"

"Lefty was right about the name of the man Quin was accused of killing."

"Pettit?"

Bowie nodded. "And the marshal had also just learned the name of the man Quin killed in self-defense."

"I guess you learned everything you wanted." Did that mean he would be leaving soon?

He finished the potatoes and covered the bowl with a cloth. He moved closer and leaned over her shoulder. "That chicken smells good."

His words tickled her ear, put a flutter in her stomach. She drew in a deep breath, inhaling the scents of man and musk and savory meat.

"How does your hand feel now?"

"It's still all right. And so is my head," she added before he could ask about it again.

"What next?"

"The beans, please." Using a pair of tongs, she turned the chicken to their other side to cook.

He stepped around her and picked up the spoon she'd laid to the side. "How long should I stir?"

"Just enough to make sure everything's being heated."

His attention went from the green beans to the skillet. "Do you recognize the name Huck Allen?"

She frowned. "No. Is that the other man you were interested in? The man Quin killed in self-defense?"

She couldn't hear his answer over the crackle of

frying meat, but she saw him nod. "What will you do now?"

He turned his head to look at her.

"Now that you've learned what you wanted to," she explained.

"Well, those names give me a starting place."

Oh, yes, she remembered now. He wanted to know why those men had both wound up dead at a meeting with his brother.

He put down his spoon and took a step away from the stove's overbearing heat. "Are you going to make some of those biscuits like we had this morning?"

"We'll eat what was left."

"Those were mighty tasty."

"I'm glad you liked them." It looked as though something was on his face. With the sunlight streaming through the window, she couldn't be sure, but she thought…

She laughed.

"What?" A half smile tugged at his mouth. "What's funny?"

"You have flour on your face."

"Me?"

"Yes."

"Where?"

"Your jaw. You must've gotten it when you were battering the chicken."

"That proves I was slaving away in the kitchen." Grinning, he swiped at it, but there was still a spot the size of a fifty-cent piece on the hard line of his jaw.

"Here, I'll get it."

Resting the tongs against the side of the skillet, she

brushed her fingers against his bristly jaw. Most of the white powder came off. Using her thumb, she wiped away the rest, her hand lingering against his whiskered face.

Her pulse hitched at the flash of heat in his eyes. She slowly lowered her hand, her heart racing.

His blue gaze searched her face. Just as an acrid odor drifted to her, Bowie grabbed for the tongs.

"Chicken's burning!"

"Oh!"

He quickly grabbed a cloth and wrapped it around the skillet handle, removing the pan from the stove.

He set it on the counter and began turning the pieces over.

Merritt leaned around him to check it. "It's not burned too badly."

"At least it isn't black, just a very dark brown." He grinned. "Nothing wrong with that."

"I'm glad you think so since you'll have to eat it."

"I'm hungry. It won't be a hardship."

"Good." Shifting her attention from him, she took a large platter from the shelf above the sink. "I'll finish the chicken if you'll get everything else to the table."

He nodded, picking up the bowl of potatoes. "And I'll come back for that platter."

"It's not heavy. I can carry it with one hand."

"I don't want you dropping any of my chicken on the floor."

"All right." She smiled at his teasing as she arranged a cloth on the platter to absorb some of the grease.

As she put the chicken on the plate, he returned for

the green beans. Having his help hadn't bothered her as much as she'd thought it would.

In fact, she had enjoyed having someone to talk to.

It had been a long time since she had shared so much time with someone of the opposite sex. It made her wonder what it would be like to have a man in her life again.

This man.

Chapter Four

T here was no way Bowie could keep his hands to himself. As long as Merritt needed his help, there would be times when he might have to touch her. Like today.

Two days after her injury, they were washing the boardinghouse windows. He had filled a pail with water and measured in the amount of vinegar she specified. The windows upstairs and in the parlor were finished. Now they were tackling the large window in the dining room.

His gaze moved over her fine-boned profile, pausing at her temple before sliding down one slender arm. The cut on her head was healing nicely, more quickly than her injured hand, which was still swollen. The bruise had gone from bluish-black to a sickly purple.

She still wore the sling, which forced her to limit the use of her hand.

She shifted, her soft scent drifting to him. "How's your brother? Is he healing up all right?"

"He is," Bowie said. "He and Addie left for Dodge City this morning. Cattle drive."

"Addie went, too?"

"According to Quin, she's not one to miss out on anything that might be an adventure."

Merritt smiled. "I would agree with that."

Bowie had ridden out to the 4C last evening and told Quin he'd learned the names of the two men who had each wound up dead at their respective meetings with him. He'd also told his brother that he, too, now believed there was a strong possibility that their parents had been murdered.

Determined to learn anything else he could, he had questioned Ace about Huck Allen, the man Quin had killed in self-defense. His friend hadn't heard of Allen. So far, only Marshal Hobbs had. His claim that he'd seen Allen on a wanted poster had Bowie wiring the sheriffs in the surrounding counties to ask if any of them could share any information on Huck Allen or Vernon Pettit.

If Bowie could establish where the men came from, it might give him some answers about why they had crossed paths with his brother. So far, he had heard from the county sheriff in San Saba, who had no knowledge of either man.

Merritt glanced at him. "Thanks for your help since the accident. If it weren't for you, I'd be behind on my chores."

"You're welcome." He rubbed at the film of red dust coating the window.

"I also appreciate you fixing the window in your room. Not everyone is so handy."

"It's nice to know I can do more than wear a badge, huh?"

She smiled as he'd intended, dipping her rag in the pail and wringing it out. After a moment, she turned to him with a sober look. "May I ask you something?"

"Sure."

"Why did you become a lawman?"

There was genuine curiosity in her voice. He slid a look at her, wondering what had brought on the question. He started to give her his standard answer—that he believed in order and justice. Instead, he found himself telling the real reason.

"I'd like to say I always wanted to wear a badge, but at first I hired on as a lawman because I wanted to get out of Quin's shadow."

She tilted her head. "I can't imagine you in anyone's shadow."

"I was." He gave her a half smile, pushing the bucket closer to her with his foot. "He was the firstborn, always ahead of me at roping, herding, knowing good stock. I wanted to do something he never had. So when my—" He broke off. "Something happened and I left Ca-Cross."

"Something?" She frowned.

"I was engaged and it didn't work out," he said flatly.

Pausing in her work, her gaze slid to his. "Your mother said you left because of a woman. I guess that's what she meant?"

How much had Ma told Merritt? "I ended up in White Tail and Ace hired me as his deputy. I liked it and I was good at it."

"And then you became the Deer County sheriff after Livvy and Ace moved here."

He nodded.

"Do you think you wouldn't have made a good rancher?"

"I'd be okay at it now, but not then. The fact is I can't imagine what my life would be if I hadn't pinned on a badge."

"I've known men like that," she said quietly.

He recalled what Ace had told him about her. "I heard your late husband was a Ranger."

She paused, her good hand crushing the cleaning rag she flattened against the window. "Yes, and he was good at it, too. Very good."

She made the compliment sound like an insult.

Despite telling himself not to take her attitude personally, his voice tightened. "You didn't approve?"

"Well, I didn't want him to be bad at it," she said smartly. "What I meant was he was so good at it, there was no room for anything else. Or anyone, like a wife. Did you know that most Rangers retire when they marry? It's encouraged because otherwise they'll be gone too much."

"But your husband didn't." Bowie watched her closely.

"No, not Seth." Her voice was steady, her face calm, but bitterness drummed beneath her words. "He was always a lawman first, a husband second."

"And you resented him for not choosing you," Bowie said evenly.

"Sometimes, yes."

Thanks to Clea, he knew about being chosen last.

He himself had chosen his job over his family and they had paid the price with their lives. It was why he had no intention of ever getting close enough to anyone to have to make the choice.

She moved to the next section of window. "Don't misunderstand. I respect the law and admire those who enforce it. But Seth always put his job ahead of me and it got him killed."

She rubbed hard at the same place on the glass over and over. Bowie felt an overwhelming urge to comfort her, to touch her. Instead, he asked, "What happened?"

She dunked her rag in the pail, wrung it out and went back to the window. "Though he wasn't ordered or even asked to go, he rode out with two other Rangers who were escorting a prisoner to Austin. They were ambushed by the outlaw's friends and all three Rangers were killed."

"Did they leave wives behind, too?"

"No, neither was married. And Seth shouldn't have gone at all."

"Do you resent him for dying?"

"At one time, I did. He didn't *have* to ride along."

Bowie didn't point out that the man had obviously felt there was a reason. He understood Merritt's resentment, to a degree. "Did your husband ever talk about leaving the Rangers?"

"No." Her tone was subdued. "It wasn't as though I didn't know who I was marrying. I knew how important his job was to him and I was aware of the dangers, but he put himself in harm's way when there was no need."

"Did you try to talk him out of going on that particular trip?"

"It was more that I demanded he not go. He had missed both of our birthdays and our wedding anniversary, and I was angry. I told him I wanted him to stop being a Ranger, but I really didn't. I just wanted him to put me first sometimes."

The way Bowie should have done with his parents.

"I know now that I'm not cut out to be a lawman's wife."

And Bowie knew if he ever decided to marry, his wife would have to accept that he was a lawman, for better or worse.

Merritt glanced at him sheepishly. "I'm sorry. I don't usually talk about him."

"That's all right. I'm glad to know." And he was.

Just as he pushed a dining chair closer to the table, the front door opened. Glad for the interruption, Bowie looked over to see Dr. Lewis step inside.

"Hi, Clancy."

The fair-haired man swept off his hat and placed it on the dining table, looking at Merritt. "I came to check your hand."

"All right."

He pulled out a chair and motioned her over. "Have a seat."

When she did, Bowie moved to Clancy's other side. Merritt slipped her arm out of the sling so the doctor could examine her.

"The swelling is down slightly," he said. "Wiggle your fingers for me."

She winced and Bowie watched her face as she followed Clancy's orders.

"Straighten your hand for me if you can."

She tried, but couldn't flatten it.

"How's the pain?"

"It's like a dull throb unless I try to pick something up, then it hurts."

Clancy gave her a reassuring smile. "It's coming along. You can use it, but if it pains you, stop."

Merritt nodded.

The doctor turned, scooping up his hat. "I'll be back in another couple of days."

"Thank you," she said.

As Lewis started out the door, he paused, saying to Bowie, "Have you thought about our conversation?"

Merritt looked from the doctor to him.

"I have," he said.

"I bet Merritt would agree with us."

"About what?" she asked.

The other man inclined his head toward Bowie. "Ace and I, along with a couple of others, want Cahill to run for town marshal."

"Oh? Is there a problem with Marshal Hobbs?" Her tone was mild, but tension coiled through her words.

"Not a problem, exactly," Clancy said. "He hasn't done anything bad. He just doesn't do much of anything good."

Merritt nodded, turning to Bowie. "Have you made up your mind? Are you going to run?"

His gaze searched hers as he tried to get an idea about her thoughts. He could read nothing. "Yes. I've decided to do it."

Clancy clapped him on the shoulder. "That's good news."

A small smile flashed across her face. "Well, you're certainly qualified."

It wasn't exactly a vote of confidence.

"You'll be good for Cahill Crossing." Clancy resettled his hat on his head.

"Don't jump the gun," Bowie cautioned. "The election is still a week away."

"I have a good feeling about it," his friend said, walking to the door. "I'll see you both later."

"All right." Bowie lifted a hand in farewell as Merritt murmured goodbye.

Once they were alone again, he dipped his rag in the water-and-vinegar mixture, and continued to clean his side of the window.

She had grown quiet since the doctor had taken his leave. Bowie told himself her opinion didn't matter, but he wanted to hear it. "So, what do you think? About me running for marshal, I mean."

"It sounds like you've given it a lot of thought."

Which told him nothing. "I don't reckon I'll win. I've been away too long and a lot of people don't know me."

She nodded. "You could be right."

He moved farther down the window. If he did win, it could help his investigation. It would also mean that he would be staying in Ca-Cross for a while. At least four years, unless he decided to resign. Was he ready to do that?

Frustrated, he slid a look at her. She made him question his decision and he didn't know why.

She'd agreed he had the qualifications, hadn't shown

any disapproval or even asked if he was sure. Even so, there was now a tension between them that hadn't been there before.

She hoped Bowie lost the election. It was utterly self-ish and Merritt would never say it aloud, but she hoped for it all the same. A week after learning he planned to run for marshal, she sat in the opera house surrounded by almost every resident of Ca-Cross waiting for the voting results.

The town hall had been proposed as the first gathering place, but the opera house was bigger. Even so, there wasn't room for everyone and a crowd of people gathered outside the entrance. The double front doors as well as the single one in the back were open, and late-day sunshine flowed inside over the dark wood floors.

The buzz of voices rose and fell around her. She inhaled the mingling scents of beeswax and various perfumes and dirt.

The gold-trimmed red velvet draperies had been raised to provide more standing room. Bowie and Hobbs waited at center stage while lawyer Arthur Slocum counted the ballots.

"Can you see?" To her left, Rosa Greer Burnett touched Merritt's shoulder. "Lucas said there are some seats up by the stage."

"I'm fine." Not wanting to sit closer than their seats in the middle of the room, Merritt smiled at the blond-haired woman and her tall half-Comanche husband.

Rosa had been a good friend since moving here a few months ago, although Merritt hadn't gotten to know

Lucas until he and Rosa had married. The former Texas Ranger had typically kept to himself on his ranch.

Merritt patted Rosa's hand. "You two can move if you'd like."

"We'll stay here. Dog's already settled."

A glance down showed Lucas's constant four-legged companion stretched out in front of her and her friend's feet. When he lifted his head to stare at her with black eyes, Merritt scratched the wolf-dog behind the ears.

Her gaze went to Bowie, whose rugged build was imposing even beneath the high velvet curtains. As he spoke with Ace Keating and Dr. Lewis, the other candidate worked his way through the crowd, greeting and mingling with people. After visiting with rancher Don Fitzgerald, who had publicly endorsed him, Tobias Hobbs headed in Merritt's direction, weaving through the crush of people.

Fitzgerald was second in power and influence only to the Cahills. Maybe his support of Hobbs would swing the votes in the current marshal's favor.

The mustached lawman paused beside Merritt's row and shook Lucas's hand. After greeting Rosa, Hobbs leaned toward Merritt. "Mrs. Dixon, how's your injury?"

He had checked on her a few times since the accident. "I'm healing nicely. Thank you for asking."

"If you need anything, anything at all, you send for me."

"I will. Thank you." There was no need, though. She knew Tobias was more than willing to help. He had offered for other reasons in the past, and this evening he had taken it upon himself to escort her to a seat.

His help wasn't what she wanted.

A smiling Ellie Jenkins walked by, pausing to speak to the Burnetts. Although Merritt didn't care much for the girl's pompous mother, Minnie, she did like the charming young woman whose parents owned the new Château Royale Hotel.

Feeling as though she was being watched, she scanned the room, her attention finally landing on the stage. Bowie's blue eyes were focused on her with razor-sharp intensity, and a tingly heat moved under her skin.

She couldn't tear her attention from his bronzed features, softened by the golden light. His neck was strong and corded. A white cotton shirt molded broad shoulders and arms, hinting at the definition of muscle beneath the fabric.

The weight of his gaze had her smoothing a few stray wisps of hair out of her face. Her heart pounded so hard she could hear it over the low din of the crowd. One of the men next to him spoke and he looked away from her.

Merritt stared down at her flower-sprigged skirts, hoping again that Bowie wouldn't win. They had become friends, maybe more.

To wit, she had surprised herself by telling him so much about Seth and their marriage. She didn't know if Bowie had understood her resentment, but he hadn't dismissed her feelings.

Becoming aware that Rosa was talking to her, she shifted her attention to her friend.

The other woman's unusual amethyst eyes sparkled. "I think Bowie might win."

Everything inside Merritt went tight. The week leading up to the election had scraped her nerves raw. After she had learned of his plans, they hadn't spoken of it again. That suited her just fine.

"It could happen," Lucas rumbled in a voice loud enough for her to hear. "He has just as much experience as Hobbs, plus a good reputation."

Rosa nodded. "And he's part of the family responsible for the existence of Cahill Crossing."

"He's been gone four years." Didn't anyone care about that? Irritation burned through Merritt. "He only came back to check on his brother. If Quin hadn't been shot, I doubt Bowie would be here."

Rosa eyed her thoughtfully. "If he weren't planning to stay, I don't think he would have run for marshal."

"Probably not," she admitted, shifting uneasily in her chair.

"Don't you think he would make a good marshal?"

"I'm sure he would. Probably better than good."

At Merritt's dry tone, her friend tilted her head. After a long moment, she said, "He's been helping you since your accident."

What did that have to do with anything? "Yes."

"A lot."

Merritt flicked her a look. "Only when I need it."

Rosa leaned in. "I think you're sweet on him."

Her pulse jumped and she fought to keep her features blank. "We're friends. That's all."

"If that were all, you'd want him to win. You obviously don't."

"I never said that." She plucked at her skirts, staring avidly at the pattern of tiny pink flowers sprinkled on the white dimity background.

"No, you didn't." Rosa drummed her fingers on her leg. "But you did say you would never get involved with another lawman. If you weren't sweet on him, you wouldn't give a fig if he won."

Her friend knew her too well, but Merritt admitted nothing. She reached down to stroke Dog's thick dark coat.

Arthur Slocum stood and walked to the edge of the stage, holding a piece of paper. After a series of attention-getting whistles, the crowd quieted.

The slight man adjusted his spectacles. "And the results are…" He let the words hang, the anticipation build.

Oh, forevermore! Merritt's stomach knotted.

"Cahill wins by more than one hundred votes!"

Some cheers erupted and a healthy amount of applause broke out.

Heart sinking, she only now realized she had been holding her breath. Her gaze automatically sought Bowie. He looked stunned as Hobbs walked over to shake his hand.

People swarmed the stage around him. Before he was enveloped by the crowd, his gaze met Merritt's. She forced a smile. She wouldn't ruin this for him, even though she wished it hadn't happened. At some point, she should congratulate him.

Over the past week, he had made himself available for whatever she needed—cooking, laundry, cleaning. She had wondered what it would be like to have him in her life and now she knew. In fact, it hadn't taken two shakes to get used to having him around and liking it.

They were friends and would only ever be friends.

She wouldn't let herself want more. She might be ready for a man in her life, but not a lawman.

For several minutes after the announcement, people crowded around Bowie, congratulating him. He certainly hadn't expected to win. Hopefully, Quin would be fine with the fact that Bowie would once again be serving as a lawman, now in Ca-Cross. At least until the next election. Four years.

He looked around for Merritt. After scanning the large room, he realized she was no longer inside. And neither was Tobias Hobbs.

Bowie's muscles seized up. He hoped the two of them weren't together, but it was possible. Merritt hadn't seemed that interested in the former marshal's attention back when he'd been the law. Now, though, Hobbs was no longer marshal. Bowie was.

He hoped that wouldn't change things between him and Merritt too much, but after what she'd told him about her husband, how could it not?

Three days later, Bowie unlocked the door to the jail. He walked inside, palming off his hat and running a hand through his sweat-dampened hair. Midafternoon sunshine streamed through the window. The whistle of the daily train sounded as the locomotive rolled into town.

He hadn't seen much of his landlady over the past few days. The morning after being sworn in, he had gotten a steady stream of threats against the two prisoners who were waiting in Cahill Crossing's jail. Seemed everyone—from their former ranch-hand friends to

Stokes, the general-store owner—was angry about the trouble Purvis and Fields had caused Quin and Addie.

Bowie decided the men might be safer if they were moved to Wolf Grove to await trial. Ace had agreed and ridden along to help Bowie transport the prisoners.

Before leaving, Bowie had asked Merritt if she needed help with anything, but she had said no. Her hand was healing well. While he was glad for that, she didn't need him around now and he sometimes wished she did.

He had only just returned from Wolf Grove. It appeared Hobbs had taken his coffeepot and mug with him. The guns, wanted posters, desk and stove were all in place.

Grabbing the broom, Bowie began cleaning out the cells. The dust wouldn't stay gone for long, so he was more concerned about getting rid of the food and pebbles and anything else that had wound up on the floor. Sweeping reminded him of helping Merritt clean rooms at the Morning Glory.

The two times he had seen her since the night of the election results, she had been friendly, though she hadn't lingered. And he couldn't ignore a now-tangible limitation to their friendship. Though he tried to resist thinking about her, he missed seeing her, spending time with her.

As he dumped the last of the trash from the dustpan out the cell window, he heard the front door open.

"Be right with you," he called.

"Okay."

He froze at the soft feminine voice he recognized immediately. Merritt.

Had she noticed his return from Wolf Grove? Surprised at how glad he was to see her, he propped the broom against the wall and walked out to greet her, unable to keep from grinning. "Hi. How are you?"

"I'm fine." The smile she gave him came and went in a flash. "How was your trip?"

"No problems at all."

"That's good." She looked relieved for about a second, then walked to the window and stared out.

What was going on? Bowie eased down onto one corner of the oak desk, admiring the sleek line of her back and gentle flare of her hips. Her silky braid fell to the middle of her spine.

She turned to face him in a swirl of blue skirts, her hands clenching and unclenching in the fabric.

Noting the worry in her pretty green eyes, he got to his feet. "Has something happened?"

"Yes. No." Anxiety vibrated from her.

He frowned.

"I need to tell you something."

"All right." Bowie took a step toward her.

Seconds ticked by. She looked as though she was bracing herself for something.

Concerned, he said softly, "Whatever it is, it can't be that bad, can it?"

She looked at him then and he saw tears in her eyes. Jolted, he reached for her, but she inched back.

"Merritt?"

"Your parents' deaths weren't an accident." Her words rushed out and he struggled to make sense of them. "They were murdered."

Chapter Five

"What!" The word exploded from him. "What are you talking about?"

"I don't have proof—"

He cupped her shoulders, his grip firm, though not rough. "Tell me what's going on."

"I'm trying!"

His hold loosened, but he didn't release her. "Why would you say my parents were murdered? Why would you even think so?"

She peered around him. "Are we alone?"

"Yes," he said impatiently. "Get to it, please."

Very aware of his big hands on her, her gaze lifted to his. She didn't want to share this, although he needed to know. The news had saddened her. And frightened her. She could only imagine how it would make him feel. She blinked back tears. "Lefty overheard Hobbs telling someone that another person besides them knew the Cahills had been murdered."

Bowie frowned. "Lefty?"

Hadn't he heard her say his parents had been *murdered?* Feeling shaky, she said, "He was at the jail one night."

"Sleeping one off in a cell."

"Yes." Why was he more concerned with Lefty? "The sound of voices outside the window woke him and he recognized one of them as belonging to Hobbs."

He released her, his eyes narrowing. "How many voices?"

"Two, both male." She missed the reassuring weight of his touch.

"And he had no idea who the other speaker was?"

She shook her head. Had it been only three days since she'd seen him? Whiskers shadowed the hard line of his jaw and his skin was even more burnished from his recent days in the saddle. Red dust filmed his pale blue shirt and well-fitted denim trousers.

"Even though I have no proof, I did the right thing by telling you, didn't I?" She searched his stormy eyes. "Seth always said that any bit of information, even if it didn't seem relevant or trustworthy, helped him do his job better."

"Yes, you did the right thing."

She wished Bowie would tell her there was no possibility that his parents—her friends—had been murdered, but he didn't. In fact, he didn't seem surprised. Though he was obviously concerned, he hadn't scoffed at the information and had gone straight into asking her questions.

Cold dread spread through her and a fine trembling began in her legs. "You aren't the least bit shocked. Or jostled up at all. Did you suspect your parents had been murdered?"

His mouth tightened. "This isn't the first time I've heard it."

"And you think it's true?" Her voice cracked.

"Yes."

The somber word arrowed right through her. Her stomach roiled and a wave of dizziness hit. "Oh. Oh, my goodness."

His hand closed around her upper arm. Muttering something, he hooked one booted foot around the leg of a straight-backed chair and pulled it over, urging her down into it. "Sit. You look like you might pass out."

Dazed, she stared up at him, noticing the flex of muscle in his lean jaw. Earl and Ruby had really been *murdered*? "Why would someone want to kill your parents?"

"I'm trying to figure that out." He shoved a hand through his hair, leaving furrows in the dark, thick mass.

"There could be a murderer in Ca-Cross." Her voice wobbled as she got to her feet. "What if other people are in danger?"

"Hey." When she swayed, he closed one hand on her waist, holding her steady. "What befell my parents happened two years ago. If others were in danger, I think something would have happened by now."

"I suppose."

"I'm not just saying that." Sliding a knuckle under her chin, he tipped her face up. His blue eyes were earnest. "I believe it."

She nodded, her nerves somewhat soothed. "Do you have any idea who might have done it? Hobbs?"

The possibility chilled her, especially since the man came around the Morning Glory more often than she liked.

"It's possible, or at least he knows who did kill them. I plan to find out."

"Tobias could be involved in any number of things. Do you think the same person could have killed Pettit and framed Quin for it?"

"Could be. Those notes Quin received promised the truth about the wagon wreck in exchange for money. Pettit could've been killed because he knew something incriminating. Quin and I know for a fact that Allen, the man Quin killed in self-defense, had information about the murders. He confirmed it before dying."

"What did he say?"

"That our parents weren't killed in an accident. That it was murder and Quin had no idea how deep it went."

"I'm so sorry," she said, trying to gather her thoughts. The entire business unnerved her. "Why do you think those men waited two years after your parents' deaths to contact your brother?"

"I have no idea." Bowie's eyes narrowed. "And I don't want anyone else knowing about this."

"I won't say a word and I'll tell Lefty the same."

"Let him know that I'll check into what you told me." When she nodded, he continued, "When did he overhear Hobbs talking about my folks?"

"About a month ago."

"A month ago. It's obvious why he didn't say anything to Hobbs, but why didn't he tell Quin? Or me when I arrived in Ca-Cross?"

"He wasn't sure he heard what he thought he did. He didn't want to make an accusation like that. There had been no talk, not even a whisper, of your folks being murdered. When you became the new marshal, Lefty decided he should give you the information."

"Then why didn't *he* come to see me?"

Merritt hesitated. "He's really in no shape."

"Drunk," Bowie stated flatly.

She nodded.

"The election was three days ago. He could've told me then."

She gave him a pointed look. "You were surrounded by people, then you left town."

"True," he acceded.

"Is that part of the reason you came home? To find out if your parents were murdered?"

"Yes."

"Is that why you ran for marshal?" Did it matter? she asked herself. Knowing why he had chosen to put himself on the ballot wouldn't change the fact that he was a lawman.

"I figured if I won, it might help my investigation." He dragged a hand down his haggard face. "It sure couldn't hurt. I *will* find out who's responsible."

She nodded, wanting to touch him, though she wasn't sure if that was to comfort him or herself after the upsetting news.

She couldn't let herself do that. Besides, as soon as she left here, he would forget about her and shift all of his focus to his job. Just as Seth had always done.

She turned for the door. "Well, I guess you have things to do. I'll be going."

"Wait." He gently caught her elbow. "I haven't had a chance to talk to you since I got back. How's your hand?"

"Getting better, thank you."

Before she knew what he was about, he took her hand in his much larger one, making her pulse thud. He examined it closely, his body heat wrapping around her. The scents of male musk and leather and the outdoors slid into her lungs.

He held her hand carefully, his thumb barely brushing over her knuckles. Her stomach dipped and she stepped back, pulling her hand away.

His gaze roamed over her face in a way that made her toes curl and she found it hard to get a full breath. Though she wanted to blame it on her stays, she knew it was because of the lean, rugged man in front of her. The *lawman* in front of her.

"If you need help, I want you to let me know."

She didn't want to do that, didn't want to spend more time with him than she had to. In fact, it would be best if he weren't around at all. That sparked a thought. "With your brother gone on that cattle drive, will you need to move out to the ranch?"

"No. I need to stay in town." He gave her a crooked grin. "Are you trying to get rid of me?"

"Of course not." She might want to, but now she realized she shouldn't. Though she didn't like the effect he had on her, this information about Hobbs made her grateful that Bowie would be nearby.

He opened the door for her. "If Lefty learns anything else, have him come see me directly."

"I will. And if I come across anything on my own, I'll let you know."

He stiffened, stopping her by bracing one arm across the open doorway. "What do you mean, come across anything on your own?"

She tilted her head, wondering at his protective tone. "Hobbs comes by the boardinghouse often."

Bowie scowled. "How often?"

"Almost every day."

After a long moment, he said tightly, "Don't get any fool ideas about trying to get something out of him. The last thing I need to worry about is you poking around."

"I won't do anything, but I would like to know what you find out."

He nodded in agreement. She couldn't believe she was asking to be included in an investigation, but Earl and Ruby had been her friends.

Just like Bowie was.

As she left the jail, she glanced back. He stood on the top step, the sun glinting off his dark hair. She couldn't see the look in his eyes, but she could feel his gaze on her.

Her urgency to get to the jail hadn't been only because he needed to hear her unsettling information as soon as possible. She had wanted to see him.

In the days since the election, she had managed to steer clear of him. Of course, it helped that he had been gone.

She had told herself that she wouldn't let herself want

more than friendship, but she did want more. Still, getting involved with a lawman was a mistake she didn't intend to make again.

Black fury pulsed inside Bowie. Hobbs had passed off Earl's and Ruby's deaths as an accident for two years. Bowie barely kept from plowing his fist into the wall.

If the lie hadn't been enough to tangle his guts like rusty barbed wire, the fact that Merritt had been the one to bring him the information certainly was. He didn't like seeing her upset. The pain in her eyes when she learned about his parents had punched him right in the chest.

And reminded him that she had been friends with his folks. Bowie hadn't wanted to add to his petite landlady's anxiety by showing how angry he grew with each passing second. Hobbs had lied about what had happened to Bowie's parents and who knew what else? Bowie wanted answers.

It was a good fifteen minutes before he felt calm enough to walk to the ex-marshal's house down the street from the Morning Glory.

Stepping onto the porch of the small log home, Bowie knocked on the front door. The town of Cahill Crossing didn't provide housing for their marshal like some towns did, so this place belonged to Hobbs rather than the town.

The former marshal answered the door, sans suit coat, hat and vest. It was the first time Bowie had seen the other man without a full suit.

Rolling up his shirtsleeves, the other man's eyes widened at seeing Bowie. "Hullo, Marshal Cahill. What brings you by?"

Bowie shoved down the swirl of fury inside him, knowing he needed to stay calm if he wanted answers. "I came across some information that I wanted to talk to you about."

"Of course." The man's face was blank as he opened the door wider and motioned Bowie inside.

As he palmed off his hat, he stepped over the threshold, fighting the urge to pound the ex-marshal to a pulp.

The house was small but nice, with a large front room that comprised the kitchen, dining and sitting room. The cookstove squatted against the wall to Bowie's left. In front of him was a small sink with a pump, then a table and chair. Straight ahead, a large tin washtub leaned against the wall adjacent to the bedroom entrance, where he could see the foot of a bed and an open window.

"Nice place," he observed. His attention returned to the other man, who stood near the still-open door with an expectant look on his face. A faint breeze stirred the heavy summer air.

"Thanks," Hobbs said. "What can I help you with?"

Bowie wanted to see Tobias's face when he told him why he was here. "Some information I've gotten leads me to believe my parents were murdered and that you knew their deaths were no accident."

"Me?" Anger flushed his face. "I know nothing of the sort. Why would someone murder them?"

"I'm asking the questions."

Something flickered in Hobbs's eyes, but was gone

before Bowie could identify it. The other man glared. "Earl and Ruby were killed in a wagon wreck."

"My source overheard you talking to someone, telling them that another party knew the Cahills had been murdered."

"Who's your source? I have a right to know who's accusing me."

As if he would say. Bowie just gave him a flat stare.

"They must have misunderstood," Hobbs said coldly.

"They're certain." Bowie felt no compunction about the lie.

"You've been given false information."

The man's refined features were still fixed in the same blank mask he'd worn since Bowie's arrival, but a subtle tension vibrated in the room. Of course, that could've been because Bowie was calling the man a liar.

"I was at the scene of the wreck," Hobbs said. "Nothing there pointed to murder. Does this anonymous source have any credibility? Or are you just fishing?"

Bowie wasn't answering that. Instead, he asked, "Exactly what did you find at the scene of the accident?"

Folding his arms, the other man matched Bowie's level stare. "You already know. I told you and your siblings."

"Tell me again." His hand clenched tightly on his hat.

"There were clear signs that the wagon had gone over the road's edge into Ghost Canyon. I looked around thoroughly." Hobbs's words were clipped, precise. "The wheels were busted. Three were with the wagon, but one was up on the road. From what I could determine, it came off and caused the accident."

"You saw no footprints, nothing to indicate that someone might have been there? That there might have been foul play?"

"Nothing." He met Bowie's gaze unflinchingly. "The four of you went out there yourselves. Y'all didn't find anything suspicious. Or if you did, none of you said anything to me about it."

Bowie had thought about the scene of that wreck more than once. And there hadn't been signs of anything other than an accident. Of course, Hobbs could've removed any evidence that might point to murder or look incriminating.

"I don't know why you're giving this so-called information any credence. Either someone misunderstood or they're making it up. When did this conversation supposedly take place?"

"A little over a month ago."

"Well, I don't know what to tell you."

"Are you denying that you spoke to someone about my parents' murders?"

"I am." Hobbs gave nothing away. The man wasn't perspiring or shifting frequently. There was nothing in his person to suggest he was lying or nervous. Just angry.

And right now there wasn't a damn thing Bowie could do about it. His gut said Lefty had indeed heard what he believed he had. The notes Quin had received backed that up.

"When did you find my parents?"

"You already know this," the former marshal said impatiently.

"I want to hear it again."

"I discovered them on my way back from Wolf Grove. Like a lot of people, I had gone over for the big announcement that your parents had donated land to the railroad. Earl and Ruby left Wolf Grove about an hour after the announcement. I left about two hours behind them. They couldn't have been dead very long when I found them."

Even though the visit from Hobbs to inform Bowie and his family had happened two years ago, every word was burned into Bowie's brain. The ex-marshal's story was consistent with what he had told all of them back then, but that didn't mean Bowie believed it. Not anymore.

"Was my mother wearing a ruby necklace when you found her?"

"There was no jewelry on her."

Probably because the bastard had stolen it.

Bowie had hoped to startle a reaction out of the ex-marshal and he hadn't. Bowie realized he wasn't going to get anything out of Hobbs. At least not today.

Hobbs gave him a dark look. "Is there anything else, Marshal?"

"I may have questions later, but that's all for now."

"Fine."

Giving a curt nod, Bowie settled his hat on his head and stalked out.

Bowie's temper hadn't abated during the discussion; if anything, it just burned hotter. His parents had been murdered and that bastard knew it. Just how involved was the ex-marshal? Had he done more than keep it quiet? Had he been the one who had killed Earl and Ruby? It was possible. Hobbs said he'd been alone when he found their bodies and no one had ever disputed that fact.

Bowie had wanted a reaction when he told Hobbs he was onto him; he hadn't gotten one. But he wasn't finished. He was just getting started.

Bowie wanted to talk to his brother about his visit with Hobbs, but Quin was away on the cattle drive. Merritt and Lefty were the only other people who knew Earl and Ruby had been murdered. Bowie supposed he could talk to Merritt, but he didn't want to involve her further. And talking to Lefty was just a plumb bad idea. He would talk to Ace. The saddle maker had good judgment and could keep things to himself.

A few minutes later, his friend laid down his curved awl, his gaze sober. "Are you sure about this? Your parents were really murdered?"

Bowie nodded, just as blistered up now as he'd been since hearing from Merritt.

"What makes you think so?"

Bowie explained about the anonymous notes Quin had received and the man Quin had killed in self-defense who confirmed it. He ended with the information Lefty had overheard.

Ace grimaced. "Lefty isn't the most reliable."

"No, but I believe him. He was right about Pettit's name and he thought he dreamed that, so I'm willing to give him the benefit of the doubt."

"How did Hobbs react when you told him what you'd learned?"

"He was angry. Denied everything."

"What does your gut say?"

"That Lefty really did hear what he thought he did."

"Anything you remember from when your parents were killed?"

"Just what Hobbs said the day he talked to all of us, which is the same story he just told me. But he could've been acting suspiciously that day. I was in shock, maybe too much to really be aware of what was going on. My brothers and sister were the same. He could've lied about everything. He was involved from the beginning. He found the bodies. He's the one who told us it was an accident."

"He was the marshal then. It makes sense that he would be the one to talk to the victims' family."

"True, but it's pretty convenient that he was the one to find them, the *only* one to see them." Bowie's thoughts raced. "Don't you find it strange that no one passed by before or during the time he was at Ghost Canyon? There were plenty of people that day who would've been returning on that same road from Wolf Grove to Ca-Cross."

Bowie hadn't been there, of course. He'd chosen to remain at White Tail with a prisoner, assuming Quin would be with their parents. "Plus Hobbs was the one who falsely arrested Quin for killing Vernon Pettit."

"Pettit was the dead man Quin woke next to after receiving the first note?" Ace asked.

"Yes. Then when Quin responded to the second note, things went south quick and he shot Huck Allen in self-defense. Before he died, Allen confirmed that our parents were murdered."

"So, you're thinking Hobbs could've killed Pettit and framed Quin."

"It would be a way to get rid of both of them."

"And if Hobbs found out about Pettit's intention to sell information to your brother, Hobbs could've told whoever he's working with that someone besides the two of them knew that your parents had been murdered."

"Which is what Lefty overheard." Fighting back savage emotion, Bowie gripped the edge of his friend's worktable. "Hobbs could also have stolen Ma's necklace and that possibility makes me madder than hell. Quin and I know she would've worn it to Wolf Grove for the announcement from the railroad. It's the only piece she had."

The opening of the front door had both men turning. Muddy Newton, who operated the ferry that navigated the South Kiowa River, clomped inside. The bite of liquor hung over him like a cloud. The ferryman, whom the Cahill family had known for years, smelled like the inside of a whiskey bottle.

"Bowie." The short, skinny man pulled off his ever-present slouch hat. His long gray hair lay plastered to his head. "Ace."

"Hello, Muddy."

The man's bloodshot gaze went to Bowie. "There's a problem over at the Hard Luck Saloon. Sid sent me over to fetch the new marshal."

"What's going on?"

"It's Preston Van Slyck and those Fitzgerald boys."

"Are guns involved?"

"No. Not yet, anyway. They're just botherin' Monty's dance girls. Sid was hoping you could come before they cause worse trouble."

"Sure." Bowie shook hands with Ace. "I appreciate the conversation. See you later."

Ace nodded as Bowie followed Muddy to the door. Once the other man stepped outside, Ace asked, "What are you gonna do about Hobbs?"

Bowie glanced at Muddy to see if he had heard anything, but the ferryman didn't act as though he had.

In a low voice, he told his friend, "I'm going to watch the bastard."

"Let me know if you need help with anything."

"Thanks." Glad he'd confided in his friend, Bowie closed the door and started for the Hard Luck with Muddy.

Hobbs wasn't the only one Bowie planned to keep an eye on. He would also keep track of Lefty. Now that Hobbs was aware that someone had overheard him, he might easily figure out Bowie's source was Lefty Gorman. If he thought about it very long, he would figure it out. If that happened, Hobbs might hurt Merritt's friend. Bowie didn't want that to happen.

After he handled this business at the saloon, he planned to speak to Lefty. Bowie wanted to hear from the man in his own words. But right now, he had to deal with three of the most obnoxious whelps in town.

Preston Van Slyck and the Fitzgerald boys were bad enough on their own. Together, they could cause serious trouble. The son of banker Willem Van Slyck, Preston was the one who had been telling people that Bowie's sister, Leanna, worked in Deadwood as a saloon girl and had an illegitimate son.

Whether that was true or not, Bowie didn't know. How could he when his baby sister had contacted him only once to let him know where she was after the Cahill siblings had gone their separate ways? And the thought that Leanna might have confided in Van Slyck ratcheted Bowie's jaw tighter.

Bowie had never liked the weasel, but he liked the Fitzgerald brothers, Ira and Johny, even less. Their father, Don, was the second most influential rancher in the area, behind the Cahills.

As Bowie and Muddy neared the saloon, Bowie spied Van Slyck first. The dark-haired man was handsome, but inside he was as rotten as a wormy apple. Ira and Johny were nearby. All three men took what they wanted, when they wanted, taught they could by their fathers. Like blisters, they never showed up until the work was done.

As Bowie approached, they were circling around a girl wearing a garish red-and-black dress short enough to reveal her legs.

An hour later, Bowie headed to the Morning Glory. He'd gone around and around with Van Slyck and the Fitzgerald boys. They denied harassing anyone, despite Bowie seeing them intimidate the girl and her reporting that they had taken her reticule.

After the bullies finally returned the young woman's purse and scattered, Bowie checked with Monty to make sure the rest of his girls were fine and that none of them had further complaints. He would just as soon not have to deal with such nonsense every day, but he knew jackasses like Preston, Ira and Johny were in every town.

Bowie squinted against the late-day sun as he neared the boardinghouse. Someone stepped off the front porch. In the blinding glare, he could determine only that it was a man. As he got closer, he recognized Tobias Hobbs.

What was he doing here? Bowie wondered as Hobbs strode down the street and out of sight. Obviously not eating, since he was leaving just before suppertime.

Bowie had just enough time to wash up before making his way to the dining room. There he spotted Merritt. She was flushed, attesting to her time in the kitchen. Tendrils of hair escaped from her loose braid to curl against the creamy flesh of her elegant neck.

He was glad to see she still wore her sling. Mr. Wilson and Doc Lewis carried food to the table. She followed behind, checking everything.

Clancy looked over as he pulled out a chair for Merritt. "Hey, Bowie."

"Hey, Doc, are you joining us for supper?"

"I am. I came to check on Merritt's hand and she was kind enough to invite me."

Bowie's attention shifted to his landlady. Golden light played in her dark hair. Her pale blue dress, the same one she'd had on earlier in the day, molded perfectly to her breasts and nipped in at her trim waist. The neckline was square, showing a patch of velvety skin above her collarbone. "Evenin', Miss Merritt."

"Hello." She gave him a warm smile.

He moved toward the chair at the end of the table,

leaning forward to shake Mr. Wilson's hand before he sat. "Professor, nice to see you again."

"You, as well, young man."

Not feeling all that young, Bowie grinned at the portly man on his right. Along with Ace, Clancy and Undertaker Druckman, Wilson had been a key supporter of Bowie running for marshal.

A burst of color caught his eye and he turned his head to see a bouquet of wildflowers on top of the sideboard. Next to the yellow, orange and purple blooms was a thin hardback book. Where had those come from?

His gaze went to Merritt.

She smiled. "How was your day?"

"It was fine." He caught a hint of worry in her green eyes. She probably wanted to know if he'd learned anything from Hobbs and would likely ask when they were alone.

Bowie didn't particularly want to tell her anything, but he would if it might help put her mind at ease.

Once everyone had finished supper, Merritt brought out an apple pie. While she poured fresh coffee, Mr. Wilson served the dessert. Bowie noted the fatigue etching her delicate features. She took a bite of pie, then dabbed at her mouth with a napkin. He tried not to stare at the curve of her lips or her rose-and-cream skin.

He helped Mr. Wilson clean up while she finished her pie and visited with the doctor. After telling Merritt he would look in on her in a couple of days, Clancy took his leave. Mr. Wilson excused himself, stating that he had an article to write for the next edition of the newspaper.

Bowie helped himself to another slice of pie and

eased down into the seat next to her, then poured fresh coffee for both of them.

He grinned. "This is good pie."

"I'm glad you like it." Keeping her voice low, she leaned closer. "Did you talk to Tobias? Did you learn anything?"

"I saw him leaving here just before supper." The words came out more sharply than he had intended. "What did he want?"

She eyed him speculatively. "Some things I ordered from the general store arrived on today's train and Tobias brought them over. Apples, baking powder, muslin for new sheets."

Bowie glanced at the flowers and book on the sideboard. "And those?"

She followed his gaze and nodded. "He brought those things, but I didn't order them."

His jaw tightened. "He's bringing you gifts? Is he courting you?"

"Goodness, no!" She looked indignant. "And if he asked to, I would refuse. I didn't want to accept the flowers or the poetry, but I was afraid he might guess what I know about him."

"That was smart," he admitted reluctantly. "If you start acting differently around him, especially so soon after I practically accused him of murder, he might start wondering if you know something."

She drew back. "Why would he think so?"

"You and I share a house. He might think that I told you that I thought my parents had been murdered and he knew it."

"Instead, I'm the one who told you," she said quietly.

"Yes." He wished she weren't involved in this. "If you can treat him the same way you always have, that would be good. But if not, just try to limit your time with him."

"All right," she murmured, looking uncertain.

"You were here before my folks died and you knew Hobbs."

She tilted her head.

"Did you notice him acting out of character after their deaths?"

"No."

"Did you notice if he began or stopped spending time with someone he typically didn't?"

She thought for a long moment, then shook her head. Her eyes were a stormy green. "I'm sorry. Did you find out anything when you talked to him?"

"Nothing I can use against him. He denied ever saying anything about my parents being murdered. He flat-out dismissed what I told him, although he wanted to know where I'd got my information."

The worry came back into her pretty eyes. "Did you—you didn't tell him about Lefty, did you?"

"Of course not." He told himself that she didn't mean to insult his intelligence. She was only concerned for her friend. "I do want to talk to Lefty on my own, just to make sure he told you everything he might know."

"You think he might have kept something back?"

"Not on purpose, but maybe there's something in his memory that he missed."

"As much as I hate it, I think he really overheard what he thought he did."

"So do I."

"Does that mean you aren't going to dismiss what he told me?"

"It does. I believe him and I'm going to dig until I can prove it."

Merritt looked pleased, so pleased that he felt compelled to warn her. "That doesn't mean you should do any digging on your own."

"What if I learn something else? Do you not want me to tell you?"

"I want you to tell me." Frustrated at the situation, Bowie ground his teeth. "But I'm also going to hope that you don't learn anything more."

"So am I," she said, half under her breath.

Good, because the last thing he needed was her getting in the middle of this hornet's nest.

Chapter Six

Over the next several days, Merritt and Bowie settled into a routine. They saw each other at meals and most evenings after supper. He spent time with her and Mr. Wilson in the parlor, cleaning his guns, sometimes playing checkers as they all visited.

Though still unsettled over learning Earl and Ruby had been murdered, she was reassured by Bowie's presence and his vow to catch their killers. She believed he would. Whether she liked it or not, he was a lawman and, from what she'd observed, a good one.

They didn't see each other as much as they had straight after her injury and that was for the best, but she missed him. Missed his help, although she no longer wore the sling and could do most things on her own. Until now, she hadn't realized how much time they had spent together. He put all of his energy into his job. Besides investigating his parents' murders, he was trying to get to know the new people in town as well as handling other duties. Everything from tracking down a chicken thief to finding a little girl's lost doll.

Merritt stayed busy with the boardinghouse—cooking, cleaning, washing, mending. Sometimes she caught his gaze on her. When she did, he gave her a slow smile of frank male appreciation that put a curl of heat in her belly.

She still wanted more than friendship, but that wouldn't be smart. And although she didn't want to get drawn further into his investigation, she was definitely interested in it.

Each night he came in, she asked the same question with her eyes. *Had he learned anything new about Hobbs or his parents' murders?* And he would shake his head no.

That was the extent of her association with the investigation and Merritt knew she should be glad about that. Him doing his job, her going about her business. Which was exactly what she was doing when she found the note.

A week after she had shared Lefty's information with Bowie, she went into her bedroom to change the sheets. She was immediately hit with a wall of stuffy air. Dumping the sheets on the mattress, she went to the window, which she clearly recalled having left open.

As soon as she pushed up the window, she saw a piece of paper stuck there and grabbed it before it could blow away.

Her foster brother, Saul Bream, used to leave her notes this way. When she caught sight of the sketch of her profile on the folded paper, she knew it was from him. He had been taken in by her family when he was orphaned at ten years old. She was six.

Over two years had passed since she or her parents had heard from him and she had no idea where he'd been. Her affection for him was dimmed by a familiar mix of concern and irritation.

Opening the note, she quickly scanned it. He wanted her to meet him after dark at Triple Creek. Disappointed, Merritt stared at his neat handwriting. If Saul wanted to meet in secret, it must mean he was in trouble. Again.

He had been flying with one wing since he had turned sixteen and left the home her parents had provided when his sole parent, an abusive father, had died.

The rest of the day she went about her work with a nervous feeling in her stomach. Thank goodness Bowie didn't show up at lunchtime or supper. She would've been even more anxious with him there.

After Mr. Wilson fell asleep in the parlor, Merritt changed into her gray split skirt so she could ride astride. She wrapped up leftover ham and biscuits, then made her way to the livery to borrow the mare Mr. Wilson boarded there. He had graciously told Merritt she could use the animal whenever she needed to. The mare quickly reached Triple Creek, a place north of town named for the junction of three creeks.

No one was in the clearing beside the water so Merritt stayed on her horse, pulling her small pistol from her skirt pocket.

"Merritt?"

She jumped at the familiar voice that came from just ahead. A looming shadow separated itself from the line of trees along the bank of the creek. She recognized the tall frame on horseback dressed all in black, but it wasn't until he moved into the moonlight that she could make out Saul's lean, hawklike features. In the shifting shadows, he looked gaunt, his cheeks even more hollowed than usual.

His charming grin and boyish face had gotten him out of numerous scrapes, but in all the years she'd known him, Merritt had never considered him boyish. He was the product of a cruel upbringing yet he wasn't cruel himself, probably because he had been treated kindly by her family and their friends.

"Are you alone?" she asked in a low voice, peering through the dim light.

"Yes." He dismounted, and as he moved to help her do the same, she slid her gun back into her pocket. She had brought the weapon for her peace of mind, not because she feared her foster brother.

He didn't smell like liquor. Or dirt. In fact, he seemed to have bathed recently. He hugged her before setting her on her feet.

"How are you?" He tugged at her braid as he always had.

"I'm fine. I brought some food." She pulled the wrapped meat and bread from her saddlebag.

He took the bundle, sliding it into a canvas pouch on his saddle. "Thanks."

She took stock of him, from his limp straw cowboy hat to his dark shirt with the sleeves rolled up. In the silvery light, she spied a scar on his left forearm and touched it. "What happened?"

"I had…an accident with a knife."

"Do you need salve or bandages?"

"It's healing up." He smiled crookedly, anxiety vibrating from him as his gaze darted around.

"Where have you been the past couple of years, Saul? What have you been doing?"

His gaze dropped and he asked in a low voice, "Remember what you said last time you saw me?"

"Stay out of trouble," they said together.

It was what she always told him and what he never did.

From the ages of ten to sixteen, he had been fine, but once he'd finished his schooling, he began associating with the wrong crowd. As a result, he had been in trouble with the law more than once.

He looked up, unmistakable fear in his eyes.

"Saul?"

He glanced over his shoulder. "I've been in jail."

Merritt blew out a weary breath. She wasn't surprised.

Sadly, she expected the worst of him, although she never stopped hoping he would change his ways. "Why were you there?"

"I threw in with a couple of fellas and we robbed a train," he whispered. "Got caught."

"Oh, Saul."

He glanced around, stepping closer. "That's not the worst of it."

She was distantly aware of the chirp of crickets and the occasional croak of a frog. Moonlight rippled across the grass, carving out the planes of his face.

Seconds ticked by. When he still hadn't spoken, she prompted, "What happened?"

"Is Hobbs still the marshal here?"

"Hobbs?" Surprised, she studied him as her mare moved restlessly behind her. "How do you know him?"

"Is he?"

"No. As of two weeks ago, we have a new marshal."

"Good, because Hobbs has no business being a lawman at all."

"Why?"

His head jerked toward an outcropping of rock across the creek bank. Trees swayed in the breeze. "Did you hear something?"

She stilled, catching the push of the wind through the trees and the gurgle of the creek. "I don't hear anything. What do you mean about Hobbs?"

"You can't tell anyone you got this from me."

She frowned. "Saul."

"Promise."

"And if I don't?"

"I can't tell you and…" Looking tortured, his gaze met hers. "I really need to tell you."

She contemplated strangling him. He was obviously in trouble and she had no idea what she was conceding. Still, she knew he wouldn't confide in her unless she gave him her word. Dread ticked against her nerves. "All right, I promise."

He shifted from one foot to the other, reaching out to lay a hand on his horse's neck. The animal was skittish, too. "I should probably just ride off. It's over and done with. There's nothing I can do about it now."

"About what?"

He was silent for so long that her palms became

clammy. Finally, he said, "Hobbs hired someone to kill the people this town was named for."

Her heart stopped, then restarted with a painful kick. Horrified, she stared at him, barely able to push the words through her tight throat. "The Cahills."

"Yes."

Pain squeezed her chest until she couldn't breathe. Anger and disbelief and panic bubbled together.

Saul stepped toward her, concern creasing his handsome features. "Merritt, you okay?"

"No!" Tears blurred her vision and she roughly swiped them away with one hand. "Those people were my friends!"

Bowing his head, he cursed, then cursed again.

"How do you know this?" she cried. "Please tell me you weren't there!"

He grabbed her recently injured hand and she winced. He released her. "It was supposed to be a robbery. That's what I was told, but it ended up in murder."

He had been there. Saul had been involved. The words circled in her brain. Another tear spilled down her cheek. "How do you know Hobbs was behind it?"

"The fella he hired to do it was a friend of mine. Vernon Pettit." Saul's gaze moved again over and around the area where they stood. "He was only supposed to rob them."

Pettit. The man Quin had been framed for murdering.

"So, why are the Cahills dead?" she demanded, her voice thick with emotion.

"Pettit planned all along to kill them, but we didn't know." His voice shook. "I swear we didn't."

"We? Who else?"

"My friend Huck Allen."

The man who had told Quin that Earl and Ruby had indeed been murdered.

Cold dread slashed through her. "Please tell me you didn't kill those people."

"I didn't." He wouldn't meet her eyes.

Heart breaking, she said quietly, "But you were there when it happened. You didn't stop it."

He didn't answer, which confirmed her fears. She exploded. "Tell me right now what happened!"

Saul swallowed hard. "When Huck and I stopped them on the road, Pettit spooked their horses and ran them off the road over into Ghost Canyon. It was supposed to look like an accident."

Clenching her fists, she tried to keep her wits about her. Lefty had been right. Hobbs was involved in the Cahills' murders. And so was Saul. It infuriated her. And broke her heart.

Merritt felt sick to her stomach. "I want you to come with me and talk to the new marshal."

"Hell, no!" he yelled, then lowered his voice, looking apologetic as he began to pace. "I can't do that, Merritt. He'll slap me in irons."

"Yes, but if you turn yourself in, he will treat you fairly." She hoped. She wasn't going to tell him the new marshal was the son of the murder victims.

Saul snorted. "I've been around enough lawmen to know that probably isn't the case."

She recalled the tension between her late husband and her foster brother the few times they'd been in each other's company. "Seth was fair."

"He still wanted to put me behind bars."

"You broke the law, Saul." He'd stolen horses and cattle and who knew what else? He was a smart, educated, handsome man. She had given up trying to understand why he had chosen such a dark path. "I'll stay with you the whole time."

"No."

"You know what you did was wrong. That's why you contacted me. Because you still have a conscience."

"I just wanted someone to know who was really behind what happened." He continued to prowl the small piece of ground where they stood. "If I go see this new lawman, the whole thing will be laid on me."

"No, it won't." She wasn't sure about that. Bowie was furious about his parents' murders, as she would be if in the same position. She wanted to believe he could be fair, but would he be? Could *she* if she were in that situation?

"C'mon, Merritt, you know it's true. Besides, who's going to take my word over that of Hobbs?"

"I believe you. I think Bowie would, too."

Saul gave her a sad smile.

"Besides spooking the horses, did you have anything to do with it?" She didn't want to ask, but she had to. Bile rose in her throat. "Did you help murder the Cahills?" *Please say no.*

"No, but—"

"You can help Bowie prove that Hobbs did. The marshal will hold you responsible only for your actions and you might be able to help bring Hobbs to justice. That could count for something."

"Like what?"

"Like you might not hang," she snapped.

He winced and she fixed him with a stare. "Please."

He stilled next to his horse. Even in the half-light, she could read the uncertainty in his eyes. For a moment, she thought he might relent.

Then he swung into his saddle and gathered the reins.

"Saul, please come with me."

He shook his head, his bay mare shifting restlessly.

"What if Hobbs finds out about you?"

"He already knows. Pettit told him."

"What?" Alarmed, she moved closer and put a hand on his leg. "You're not safe out here alone."

"Pettit didn't give Hobbs my name, just told him there were other people who knew he had murdered the Cahills."

"If he finds out you told someone—"

"He can't find out, sister."

A sob caught in her chest. "Please come back to the boardinghouse with me."

"I'm sure as hell not going to put you in that position. This is for the best."

"Will I see you again?"

"I don't know."

"Don't disappear. Please." There was more he wasn't telling her. She knew it. "There's a spare room off my kitchen."

"I don't want you in the middle of this."

"It's a little late for that," she bit out.

"I shouldn't have told you."

"It was the right thing to do. Please come back to Ca-Cross with me."

"I can't." His bay danced impatiently, mirroring the

anxiety swirling in the air. He turned his horse toward the trees.

"If you need food or anything, come to the boardinghouse."

"I will."

"Promise me you won't disappear. That I'll hear from you again."

He shook his head.

"Promise," she ordered fiercely, her hand tightening on his leg. "I can help you."

She wanted to scream at him never to contact her again, but if she did, he would vanish. She would be left to wonder if he was dead or alive. She would likely never hear from him again. That would be the worst thing for the two of them. And for Bowie.

"You have to contact me again," she said. "Don't put me through another two years of wondering if something bad has happened to you."

His gaze softened. "All right. I'll get in touch with you soon. I've got to go. I love you, little sister."

"I love you, too." Throat tight, she watched as he turned his horse into the trees, then melted into the night.

She wanted to scream, to hit something. Heart sinking, she mounted up.

She had managed to stay out of Bowie's investigation for a week. He would not be happy to hear that she had learned something else, but the information she had was too important not to share.

She choked back a sob. She didn't want to tell Bowie what she had learned, but she really had no choice.

* * *

It was almost midnight when Merritt heard Bowie finally come in. She had just brushed out her hair and was starting to rebraid it when she caught the measured tread of his boots on the stairs. Since seeing Saul, she had done her share of crying and raging. She was calm now. Or at least more so.

She was still furious at him for being involved in the Cahills' murders, but she knew he wasn't the one behind it.

No. That was Tobias Hobbs and whoever Lefty had overheard talking.

Her anger was punctuated with fear for her foster brother and a growing dislike of the former marshal. So far, Tobias had gotten away with killing her friends. What if he had killed someone else? What if he were searching for Saul to kill *him?*

On edge, unsure of the welcome she would receive, Merritt pulled on her button-up shoes and quietly made her way to Bowie's room.

A fringe of light showed under his door. Good, he was still awake. Shadows shifted in the hall, her path lit by a lamp she'd left burning at the foot of the stairs. The open window at the end of the hall allowed in some air, but it was warm and heavy.

Dreading what Bowie would say when she told him why she'd come, she knocked lightly.

The door opened and he stood there bare-chested, framed in the glow of the lamp behind him.

His hair and shoulders were damp and she caught a whiff of soap. The sight of his taut muscled flesh sent a rush of desire through her. Her gaze moved from his brawny shoulders to his lean waist and down his long legs. The breath backed up in her lungs. *Oh. My.*

His look of surprise faded and he frowned. "Merritt? Are you okay?"

"Mm, yes. If you weren't able to eat supper, there are some leftovers in the kitchen." She couldn't seem to tear her gaze from the dark hair on his chest, the way it thinned down the hard plane of his stomach to disappear beneath the waist of his denims.

He braced one shoulder against the door frame, muscles flexing down his arm with the movement. "I ate at the 4C. I rode out there to check on things for Quin and Addie. Their cook, Elda, fed me."

Merritt struggled to gather her wits. It wasn't as if she hadn't seen a man's bare chest before. Or bare other things. She was a widow, for goodness' sake. But as always, anything to do with *this* man seemed to knock her silly.

"Have you heard from your brother and sister-in-law?"

"Not yet." His gaze searched hers, lingering briefly on her mouth. "Are you sure there isn't something wrong?"

She might as well get it over with. She glanced down the hall to make sure the other doors were closed. "I need to talk to you about your parents' murders."

He snapped to attention, catching her wrist and pulling her inside. He closed the door. "No one else knows about that."

"I tried to be quiet."

His open window let in a draft of summer air and she drew in the scent of leather and male musk. As he released her, his thumb brushed the sensitive skin of her wrist, sending a tingle up her arm. "What's going on?"

She saw no reason to tiptoe around. "I spoke to someone who confirmed that Hobbs knew your folks were murdered."

His eyes narrowed. "Why in the hell would you be talking to anyone about that? I told you not to—"

"Did you hear what I said?"

"Yes. Answer me."

"A man contacted me and asked me to meet him at Triple Creek."

Bowie stilled, smoky amber light washing over his bare torso.

"And you went?" he asked roughly.

"Yes."

"Did it occur to you that might have been dangerous?"

"Yes. I took my gun."

He didn't look relieved.

"This is important, Bowie."

He pinched the bridge of his nose. "Why would he contact *you*?"

She started to give Saul's name, but something held her back. Tears stung her eyes. "This man said his friend Pettit was hired by Hobbs to kill your parents."

"How does he know that?"

"Because Pettit hired him to help."

Bowie's shoulders went rigid. "So, this mystery man is one of the people responsible for my parents' murders."

"Not directly." That seemed a fine line to draw.

"Pettit told this man that they were to rob the Cahills. He never said anything about killing them. My...friend's part was to stop the wagon. When he did, Pettit spooked the horses and ran them off the road."

"And then they killed my parents?" Bowie's eyes turned to steel.

The stark words gave her a jolt. "You don't think Earl and Ruby might have died when the wagon crashed?"

"No. Hobbs said their injuries were caused by the wagon wreck, but Pa's skull looked—" Bowie broke off, his voice hoarse. "It looked like it had been bashed in, by a rock or a rifle butt. Quin agreed with me, but we had no reason to think murder back then. Druckman tried to fix Pa's head for the funeral, but he couldn't. Not all the way."

She winced, remembering how she had barely been able to look at Earl or Ruby. Earl's head wound must have been horrible if the undertaker hadn't been able to smooth it out.

Savage emotion flashed in Bowie's eyes. "Did your new friend tell you if he and Pettit stole anything?"

She shook her head. She hadn't thought to ask that. She'd been too stunned by the things Saul had shared with her, by his confessed involvement. "Were some things stolen from them?"

Bowie didn't answer, which caused a pang of hurt in Merritt's chest. What else had Saul done? She could barely stand to think there might be more he hadn't told her.

"So, this man you met. He was there when the wagon went off the road at Ghost Canyon?"

"Yes."

"What else did he tell you? That Hobbs killed Pettit?"

"No."

"That Huck Allen was also in on it?"

"Yes, he did say that."

Seething with anger, Bowie stepped closer. "You're upset."

"Of course I am!"

"Because this information confirms my folks were murdered?"

"Yes."

A shrewd look came into his blue eyes. "And because this person you met with means something to you."

She drew in a sharp breath. "Why do you say that?"

"If he didn't, you would've already given me a name."

She had intended to do just that, but now she didn't want to. Not until she could determine how Bowie would treat her foster brother.

Bowie shifted, his big body forcing her back a step. Then another. Flickering lamplight swirled on the floor and walls. "Who is it?"

"Bowie."

He crowded her against the door. His muscular chest brushed hers, his legs spread wide to cage her in. "So, this mystery man just randomly chose you?"

The suspicion in his voice had her spine going stiff. "What are you implying? That I had something to do with what happened to your parents?"

"I'm implying you know this man. It was no random act that he chose you, so tell me why."

She swallowed hard. "I've known him almost my entire life."

"Not what I asked," Bowie said silkily, leaning in until she could feel the hard line of his powerful thighs. He planted a hand on either side of her, dipping his head until his gaze was level with hers. "Who is it?"

"I grew up with him."

"Brother?"

"Not…really." That wasn't a lie exactly.

"When you hold back information, you're interfering with an investigation."

Her stomach dropped to her knees, but she tried not to let him see her alarm. "I can't give you his name. I promised."

"You—" The vein in Bowie's neck throbbed and tension lashed the air between them. He straightened, staring at her for a full five seconds before saying slowly, incredulously, *"You. Promised."*

"Yes."

As though he were having trouble breathing, he choked out, "You promised an *outlaw* that you wouldn't tell me?"

The contempt in his voice had her lifting her chin. "Yes."

Shoving a hand through his hair, he stepped back. Stone-faced, his voice was sharp. "Why did you even come up here?"

"Because I thought you should know what I found out."

"Then tell me who you spoke to so I can do the same," he gritted out.

"I tried to convince him to talk to you, but he's been in trouble with the law before. He doesn't trust lawmen."

"Criminals usually don't," he said tersely.

"Let me talk to him again."

"If I had two minutes alone with him, I could get him to talk."

Alarm flared. "What do you mean? Beat it out of him?"

"I didn't say that."

He wasn't denying it, either, she noted. Oh, no, she wasn't letting that happen. Saul might deserve it, but she couldn't be responsible for letting it happen.

Bowie folded his arms over his broad, solid chest, his gaze piercing in the dim light. The air seemed even hotter now.

"You came up here to tell me about this person. Why won't you tell me his name?"

"I came up here to tell you that someone else could confirm Lefty's story about Hobbs."

"Why won't you tell me what I want to know?"

"Why won't you respect that I gave my word not to reveal this man's name?"

"Because that man likely murdered my parents," he snapped. "And if he didn't, that's just more reason for you to identify him. He might be able to lead me to whoever really killed my folks."

Saul might or might not have told her the whole truth about his part. Was it possible he had physically helped murder Earl and Ruby?

Bowie moved back to her. The intensity in his blue eyes had her squaring her shoulders.

"You claim my parents were your friends."

"They were." She glared at him. She felt bad enough already. "But this person is my friend, too. I just want to be sure he won't be hurt if he talks to you."

"What do you think I'm going to do?" Bowie demanded. "Draw down on him the second I see him?"

"No." Seeing the banked fury in his eyes, it didn't sound so far-fetched. "I don't know."

"I know how to treat a suspect."

"Have you ever had to deal with one in a case involving family members?"

"No. Doesn't mean I can't."

"You know I want to find out who's behind your parents' murders."

"I thought you did. Now, I'm not so sure."

"Stop trying to make me feel guilty."

"Why? You should!" A muscle flickered in his jaw and she shrank from the black fury in his face.

What if Bowie saw Saul and his anger got the better of him? He could hurt Saul or, worse, kill him. Merritt didn't want to believe that about Bowie, but how well did she really know him? Not well enough. She couldn't take a chance with Saul's life. Hadn't there been enough loss?

Torn between wanting to help both men, she reached for the doorknob. "I...need to go."

"Merritt—"

"I still plan to convince my friend to talk to you."

"I can hunt him down."

Her heart clenched. "Please don't."

If Bowie found Saul, there would be nothing Merritt could do for her foster brother. At least if she managed to convince Saul to meet with Bowie she might save his life, even though she knew he would likely spend the rest of it in prison.

"I can't believe you're asking me to let this ride."

"I'm not! I'm just asking for a little time."

He shook his head. "I can't do it."

"Not even for a few days?"

"No."

"Fine." She opened the door, glancing back.

His eyes were bleak, his jaw clenched tight.

She walked out on shaking legs. She didn't know if she was doing the right thing, but she was doing it nonetheless.

Instead of giving Bowie everything she knew and letting him take it from there, she had just committed herself to staying involved. He couldn't be any more unhappy about that than she was.

Chapter Seven

Bowie wasn't sure exactly how to handle Merritt Dixon, but he was sure going to try.

After she'd left last night, it had taken him a while to fall asleep because he'd been so irritated. And not only because of her refusal to tell him what he wanted to know.

He was irritated at himself, too. He thought he could still smell her fresh, subtle scent and he couldn't escape the image of her silky curtain of hair sliding around her shoulders. He had wanted to touch it. Touch her.

If he didn't put aside his frustration with her and this distracting awareness, he wouldn't get anywhere.

If Merritt hadn't been withholding information Bowie needed about his parents' murders, he would've admired her refusal to give him her friend's name. But right now she was a burr under his saddle and he was determined to get that name from her.

The next morning, he joined her downstairs for

breakfast. So did Lefty and Mr. Wilson, which meant Bowie couldn't talk to her. After eating, he waited around until it became apparent that Lefty was staying to help Merritt clean up the dishes. He would have to talk to her later.

He tried once more at lunch, but again they weren't alone. Soon afterward, she said she had an appointment and left. Could she read on his face what he wanted? Was she trying to avoid him?

When he stepped onto the landing of the jail later that afternoon, he saw her carrying a basket of laundry to the back of the boardinghouse. Alone.

He jogged down the steps and made his way to the Morning Glory. Easing up to the back corner of the house, he watched her for a minute, enjoying her graceful movements as she bent to gather up a wet sheet from her basket, then drape it over the clothesline.

Sunlight threaded through her dark brown hair, bringing out a glint of gold here and there. Her small hands handled the bulky sheets capably. A purple calico dress molded her trim back and waist, and made her look like a spring flower. He bet she smelled like one, too. Occasionally, he caught a glimpse of her petticoat in a swirl of skirts.

Picking up another sheet, she hung it beside the first one, turning toward him as she rolled up on tiptoe to smooth it out. Just as she finished, she saw him.

She ducked around the wet cloth, barely sparing him a glance as she bent to pull more laundry from the basket.

Four strides brought him within a foot of her and

he saw wariness in her green eyes as he approached. "Hello."

She looked away, bending to pull another sheet from the basket. "Did you need something?"

So she was still vexed about yesterday, which meant she had probably guessed why he was here. "I've been wanting to talk to you. You ran out pretty fast after lunch."

"I was at Rosa's Boutique getting a new dress fitted for the Fourth of July celebration. What can I help you with?"

Her cool tone told Bowie she knew exactly what. He debated about working his way up to the question, but he saw no reason to beat around the bush. "I'd like you to tell me your friend's name."

Despite the difference in their heights, she managed to look down her nose at him. "And I already told you no."

"Why are you protecting him?" Bowie hadn't really expected her to give him what he wanted, but he had hoped. "If he cared about you the way you seem to think he does, he wouldn't have involved you. At the very least, he would've done as you asked and come to talk to me."

"He's trying to do the right thing, *Marshal*."

He didn't like the way she bit out that last word. "Yeah, he wants to do the right thing as long as it doesn't get him in trouble."

Irritation flickered across her pretty features. "Maybe so, but his intent should count for something."

"It's gonna count for a hanging rope if I get information from someone else before I get it from him. You should tell him that the next time you see him."

She pushed the sheet aside, glaring at him. "What do you mean?"

"I mean, if he doesn't talk to me before I find him, I won't go easy."

Coming out from behind the wet laundry, she braced a hand on her hip, her mouth tightening. "And here I thought maybe you searched me out so you could apologize."

He drew back. "Apologize for what?"

"For bullying me last night. You're doing it again right now."

He barked out a laugh before he could stop himself. "I thought maybe you might have come to your senses and decided to give me your friend's name."

"Come to my senses?" Her eyes narrowed.

Was that hurt he saw in her face? Okay, maybe that hadn't been the best choice of words, but the woman made him crazy. Did she not care that she was putting herself in danger?

"You might trust that no-account friend of yours, but I don't."

Anger flushed her cheeks, turned her green eyes to deep emerald, and Bowie went stupid for about half a second. She was beautiful.

She gave him a look. "I guess you're aware that calling him names isn't the way to get what you want."

She was right. This wasn't the way to get anywhere with her. He took a deep breath, catching her sweet scent beneath that of lye wash soap. "I'm sorry, but I'm concerned about your safety."

"There's no need."

"Maybe not, but I'd like to hear that from him," Bowie said tightly. "The two men he ran with are both dead, so forgive me if I want to hear from him that you aren't in danger."

She searched his face. He hoped she was weighing his words and realizing that he was right.

"Is my safety really what you care about?" she challenged.

Yes. Surprised at her question, it took his brain a moment to catch up. He did care about her safety. Because he had grown to care about her, he realized. But he didn't say so. Since he wanted something from her, now would be the wrong time to tell her. She wouldn't believe him. "This is my town. I don't want any of its citizens to be in danger."

He thought he saw disappointment flash across her delicate features, but it was so quick he couldn't be sure. He added quietly, "And besides, we're friends, aren't we?"

She tilted her head back, shading her eyes. What was she looking for? Was she trying to judge his sincerity? He was definitely sincere.

She must have seen that because she said, "Yes, and I appreciate that, but I can't betray a confidence from another friend."

Bowie ground his teeth. Why did she have to be so stubborn? "I'm also concerned about your friend's safety. It's possible Hobbs could get to him before I do, especially if Pettit gave Hobbs the names of the men he hired to kill my parents."

She paled at that.

"Your friend would be safer with me than on his own."

She didn't answer.

"I really need to talk to him. He might say something that wouldn't mean anything to you, but it might mean something to me."

She looked conflicted, then shook her head. "He'll contact me again, and when he does, I think I can convince him to talk to you."

Bowie held on to his temper with an effort. "If your friend cared as much as you think he does, he would only want what's best for you, and putting you in the middle of this isn't it."

"Can't you just give him a chance to do the right thing?"

"I guess I don't have a choice if I want to get my information from you."

There were other ways he could figure out this man's identity. Talk to her friends, for one, but he wasn't sharing that with Merritt. He didn't want her convincing anyone not to talk to him. And, he admitted, she would not be happy if she knew.

Suspicion glittered in her eyes. "What are you planning to do?"

He shrugged and saw her mouth tighten. He thought she might lay into him, but before she could, a voice called out.

"Marshal? I have a wire for you."

Bowie turned to see a gangly boy of about twelve or thirteen. The red-haired kid hurried toward him, holding out a piece of paper. "Marshal, this wire just came for Mr. Quin, but he ain't here."

"Thanks." Bowie unfolded the paper and saw it was from Leanna. "Can you tell the telegraph operator to wire the other office in Deadwood and let the lady know she needs to wait for a reply?"

"Who's it from?" Merritt stepped toward him.

"Leanna."

The kid snickered and Bowie's gaze sliced to him. "Something funny?"

"No, sir."

But Bowie heard the kid laugh again as he ran off. He cursed under his breath. His sister was obviously still the subject of town gossip.

"What in the world?" Merritt frowned after the boy.

Bowie turned his attention to the message. Thanks to Quin's wire informing her that questions had come up about their parents' deaths, Annie was coming home. Bowie's relief and pleasure at that faded when he read she was bringing her son.

So, his sister did have a child. And he must be illegitimate or Leanna surely would've mentioned a husband. Guilt and regret sawed at him.

Merritt put a hand on his arm. "What is it? Bad news?"

"Annie's coming home and she's bringing her son." He stared out across the green hillside, thick with trees. "Do you know about that?"

"Do you mean the gossip?" At his nod, she said, "Yes. I didn't know Leanna well before she left Ca-Cross, but I'm not sure I believe she would have an illegitimate child."

"I don't want to believe it, either." Bowie refolded the

message and slid it into the back pocket of his denims. "But if it's true, it's probably my damn fault."

"Why?"

Glancing at her, he hesitated. "When the four of us split up, Quin and I had jobs, places to live. Annie and Chance didn't have that. I wasn't worried about my little brother because he can make his own way, but not Annie. I know she got a job in a saloon. What else did she have to do in order to survive?"

"You can't blame yourself for that." Merritt looked so trusting, so certain that it wasn't his fault. Annie used to look at him the same way, as if he could do anything.

"Part of it, I can." He shook his head, his voice turning hoarse. "She was always able to come to me for help. Obviously, she felt she couldn't this time. If she had to sell herself—"

He broke off.

"If that's the case, I'll never forgive myself."

Merritt was quiet for a moment. "Can you forgive *her?*"

He scowled down at her. "Of course."

"That's what matters." At his puzzled look, she continued. "She's coming home and you'll be here for her now. If she does have a child, she's going to need you and your support more than ever. The support you weren't able to give her before."

Merritt was right. He would have another chance with his sister, something he would never have with their parents. "That's true."

He appreciated her belief that he could make things up to Annie, but he was still trying to figure out what had made him run on about his family. Why had he shared so much with her? "I've never talked to anyone about this," he said slowly. "I don't know why I'm telling you."

"Thank you for trusting me. You don't need to worry that I'll repeat it."

"I guess not." He winked. "Not if you keep our conversation in confidence with the same stubbornness you have for your other friend."

He'd meant to lighten the moment, but the flash of hurt in her eyes told him he hadn't. Before he could apologize, she asked quietly, "Is that why you told me about your sister? Because you thought it would persuade me to confide in you about my friend?"

"Hell, no." He reared back. "Why would you even think that?"

"You said you've never told anyone before."

"That's true, but I told you because I wanted to." In fact, he had felt compelled. "That's the only reason."

"Okay." She shook her head, turning away.

"Hey." He put a hand on her delicate shoulder and brought her back around to face him. "Why don't you believe me?"

"I do."

"No, you don't. Why?"

Her lips twisted. "I've seen…lawmen do that before to suspects."

"You're not a suspect." It hit him then, what she *hadn't* said. "You're talking about your husband. He manipulated you into doing or thinking what he wanted?"

"Not on purpose. Or at least I don't think so. Like I

said before, he spent most of his time with outlaws and suspects. It's just the way he was."

The sadness on her face grabbed Bowie right in the chest. "But you were his wife."

"And I'm making him sound like a bad husband. He wasn't." She gave a tremulous smile.

Before he realized what he was doing, Bowie stroked her cheek. "He just wasn't there when you needed him."

The vulnerability in her eyes had his chest going tight. He wanted to kiss her. The softness in her eyes told him she wanted it, too.

His finger brushed her cheek again. Touching her soft skin, drawing in her sweet scent, Bowie knew he wasn't thinking straight. That point slammed into him when she nervously licked her lips. He wanted to do that, wanted his mouth on hers, wanted to taste her.

His senses narrowed to only Merritt. The clean, fresh scent of her, the velvety smoothness of her skin, her thick satiny hair. He wanted to undo her neat braid and bury his fingers in the dark mass, put his hands on her. All over her.

She must have seen something in his face because she did the smart thing and stepped back, just enough to move away from his hand.

It shook some sense into him. The thought that she might view him as manipulative didn't sit well with Bowie. His telling her about the guilt he felt over Annie hadn't been about manipulation. Still, he had been pressuring her.

Bowie wasn't going to apologize for doing his job, but there was more than one way to skin a cat. He'd just get his information another way.

She tilted her head. "What are you going to do?"

It took him a second to realize she was referring to his sister, not his investigation. "I'm going to wire her back and offer to send her money if she needs it. And a couple of men to escort her the rest of the way home."

"That's good." Merritt smiled.

Bowie's gaze met hers and he smiled, too. When he found himself staring at her mouth, he decided he'd better get out of there.

Looking away, she pointed to the basket of laundry. "I guess I should finish that."

"Right. Need any help?"

"No," she said quickly. Too quickly. She gave a small smile. "You go send that wire to your sister."

"I will." He started to leave, then paused. "Thanks, Merritt."

"You're welcome."

All the way across town, he thought about the things he'd told her, the fact that he had told her *anything*.

He'd gone there to get information. He'd come back empty-handed. Merritt Dixon distracted him more easily than anyone ever had. The woman would really get under his skin if he let her. He had to watch his step.

Merritt had seen a side of Bowie she never would've guessed at and she couldn't stop thinking about it. When he had received the telegram from his sister, the harsh regret on his face had tapped something deep inside her.

Even the next afternoon, it was fresh in Merritt's mind. The more Bowie had talked about Annie, the more guilt and love Merritt had seen. There had been nothing of the dauntless, purposeful lawman. For just a second, she had glimpsed the man behind the badge. A brother concerned about his sister.

He hadn't once condemned Annie for having an illegitimate child, although Merritt knew it would be an embarrassment to his family. That softness in him had led to her wanting to comfort him. And that had led to them almost kissing.

For one brief giddy second, Merritt had thought he would kiss her and she had wanted him to. What was more vexing than that was her disappointment that he hadn't. Thank goodness she had stepped back, preventing what would have been a mistake for both of them. Yet the disappointment and the moment were still with her.

She would do better to remember how he had pressured her for information on Saul, although he hadn't asked her again since their conversation. That had given her time to think, to consider what Bowie had said about her foster brother's safety and her own.

As Bowie had said, Hobbs was probably looking for Saul and he would be safer with Bowie than out on his own. She'd tried to convince Saul of that very thing herself.

Though Merritt was torn about revealing Saul's identity, she was sure of one thing. She didn't want to be involved. But she would be until she was able to convince Saul to talk to the marshal.

She would tell Bowie what he wanted to know and make sure he was made aware when Saul got in touch with her. She didn't know how much of her decision was influenced by the fact that he hadn't bothered her about it again and how much was because he had told her about his sister.

Merritt wished Bowie hadn't told her about his feelings regarding his sister. She wished she hadn't been privy to that secret part of him. It made her want to know more. It made her *want* more, period. And that was dangerous.

After supper, when she and Bowie were alone, she would give him what he wanted.

But he wasn't there for supper. Wondering where he was, she cleared the dishes from the table. Mr. Wilson helped her wash and put them away. She had just agreed to join him in the parlor when Livvy and Rosa walked in.

"Hi!" Glad to see her friends, she untied her apron and draped it over the back of a dining chair. She moved the length of the table toward the two blondes. "What brings you here? Are Ace and Lucas with you?"

"It's just us," Rosa said, her amethyst eyes serious.

"Evening, ladies." Mr. Wilson bowed gallantly.

As they exchanged greetings, Merritt noted that Livvy's gaze scanned the dining room, the entry and foot of the stairs, and the parlor.

She exchanged a look with Rosa, then said, "We just wanted to visit."

Merritt could tell by Rosa's heightened color and the spark in Livvy's blue eyes that something was going on. "I have coffee and some cake left from supper."

Mr. Wilson ran a hand over his bald head. "The cake is excellent. If you ladies will excuse me, I have an article to write for the newspaper."

Once he was upstairs, Merritt turned to the other two women. "Has something happened?"

Livvy pointed to the window across the dining room. "Let's talk over there."

The three of them walked past the long table to the opposite wall. Late-day sunlight gave way to a soft pink and gold. What was going on? Merritt had never seen her friends so secretive, so cautious.

Livvy gave one last look around, then said in a low, urgent voice, "We thought you should know Bowie has been asking questions about you."

Merritt's heart thudded hard. "Like what?"

"Specifically, he asked if I knew anything about a man you had grown up with?"

Her blood started a slow boil. He had some nerve. Even though she had asked him to give her another chance to convince Saul to talk to Bowie, he was trying to hunt down the man.

"That's what he asked me, too." Rosa pushed back a silvery-blond strand of hair, glancing over her shoulder.

"He isn't here," Merritt said. "What did you tell him?"

Livvy grimaced. "Only that I knew you had a foster brother and his name was Saul. I don't know that you've ever told me his last name. If you did, I forgot it."

"Bowie asked me the same," Rosa said. "That was my answer, too."

Merritt didn't remember what she had told her friends, either. What mattered was that the marshal hadn't gotten a full name from them. Her satisfaction at that was overwhelmed by growing anger and a sense of betrayal.

Where was he? Out trying to find more of her friends to question?

No one else knew Saul's history except her parents. Thank goodness they didn't live here. She had no doubt Bowie Cahill would've darkened their doorstep right after he'd seen the two women she counted as close friends.

"So all he knows is that I have a foster brother named Saul?"

"Yes."

"I appreciate you telling me about his visit."

"I hope we didn't make trouble for you," Rosa said.

"Not at all." The troublemaker was Saul. And Bowie.

Livvy laid a hand on Merritt's arm. "What is all of this about?"

"It's—" She broke off, realizing she couldn't tell her friends. Saul was somehow involved in the murders of Bowie's parents and he didn't want anyone knowing how they had died. "I'm sorry. I'm not at liberty to say."

Both women studied her with concern. "Are you all right?" they asked in unison.

"That's all we care about," Livvy added.

"I'm fine. I promise." It went all over her that the marshal had gone to her friends. Even if he hadn't deliberately gained her sympathy about his sister and softened her up by sharing his regret over Annie, Merritt still felt manipulated.

She had actually started to believe the man had decided to respect her position and leave her alone, but no. He had just tried a different tactic.

She should let it go. Confronting him about it could only cause problems for her. But the thought of what he'd done made her mad enough to eat bees. As did the fact that she had considered telling him what he wanted to know.

Her skin burned from the inside out. The last time she'd been this mad, it had been at a lawman, too. Seth. When he'd missed their anniversary. Again.

Livvy squeezed Merritt's hand. "You know if you need anything, you can come to me and Ace."

"Same for me and Lucas," Rosa added.

"Thanks, both of you, but I'm fine." She wasn't promising the same about Marshal Cahill.

Mr. Wilson clambered down the stairs and disappeared into the parlor. The women lowered their voices.

After several minutes spent making sure they hadn't made things difficult for her, Merritt's friends left. She found Mr. Wilson asleep in one of the chairs near the fireplace. Where was Bowie? she fumed. Drat the man.

She tried to embroider but put it aside after she tore out the same stitch for the third time. She tried to read but couldn't concentrate on the words. Rising, she walked to the window, looking out at the fat white moon hanging low in the dark sky. She felt just as pressured now as she had yesterday and Bowie wasn't even here.

Too restless to stay still, she went to the kitchen to see about the bread loaves she'd left to rise. She checked the dough and re-covered it with cheesecloth. *Where* was he?

"Would there happen to be any dessert left?" His deep voice came from behind her and had her turning in a whirl of skirts. Her anger climbed another notch at the friendly look on his face.

He swept off his hat and finger-combed his dark hair.

Her gaze slid over shoulders as wide as a wagon brace, down a flat belly to well-fitting denims that emphasized the power in his long legs. Blue eyes glinted in the light glowing from the lamp in the kitchen. Whisker stubble covered his solid jaw and his dark hair curled damply against the nape of his neck.

Heat swept her body. She wasn't sure if it was from the sultry summer temperature or from the big man standing in her kitchen doorway. Or because she was still seething over what she had learned from her friends earlier.

Merritt squashed the urge to fan herself. Though she told herself to remain calm, her words shot out, "I know what you've been up to."

He arched a brow.

Ooh, if he even thought about denying it... "Livvy and Rosa were here. They told me you questioned them."

"I did." He folded his muscular arms, looking unmovable and utterly male. A traitorous flash of desire mixed with her ire.

The unapologetic look on his face had her clenching her fists. "Don't drag my friends into this."

"If you'd tell me what I need to know, I wouldn't have to."

Of course he would put it on her. She wanted to scream. "Keep your voice down."

"Lefty's staying at the jail tonight."

"Well, Mr. Wilson isn't," she said hotly.

"He's in the parlor asleep. I saw him when I was looking for you."

"It's bad enough that I'm smack-dab in the middle of this. You shouldn't drag my friends into it."

"It's my job to find out what I can about my parents' murders, whether you like where it takes me or not. Whether I like what I have to do or not."

"Does that mean you're sorry?"

"No." He moved into the room, stopping a few inches from her. "You wouldn't tell me what I needed to know so I had to try to get the information somewhere else."

"Not from my friends," she gritted out, struggling to keep her voice low. He smelled like male and soap and the outdoors. His nearness caused her belly to quiver, which only angered her further.

"Did you tell them why I was asking?"

"No." She glared. Even if it was for a good reason, it annoyed her that she couldn't confide in her friends.

He eased closer, the steely glint in his eyes at odds with his soft words. "Rosa and Livvy weren't upset about it. Why are you?"

"Because you went behind my back to do it!"

"Behind your back?" His dangerously quiet voice had her pressing against the long counter behind her, but she refused to retreat even a step. "That's not how it works, sweetheart. I don't have to ask your permission, but if I had, would you have agreed?"

"No."

"That's right, so I did my job."

The smug certainty on his face had her chest squeezing painfully tight. "Your job," she repeated flatly.

"Yes." He tapped the star pinned to his pale blue shirt. "I a*m* the law."

She knew that! His gaze met hers and for a moment

they just stared at each other. Her gaze dropped to his mouth, tight with disapproval. To her utter frustration, she recalled their near-kiss from yesterday. And the tortured look in his eyes as he spoke about his sister.

That was really why she was upset, wasn't it? Because she had felt close to him, believed he felt the same, foolishly believed that connection would somehow influence his behavior. But it hadn't. And it wouldn't.

The rigid set of his shoulders said he was waiting for her to say something else.

Suddenly, she felt closed in, trapped. She couldn't stay in here, just inches from him, and risk him seeing how much he affected her.

"I'm…sorry for getting so upset." She sensed Bowie's surprise in the stillness of his body. With jerky movements, she pointed to the covered plate in the corner to her right. "There's a big piece of butter cake."

He frowned.

"Help yourself." She skirted the cookstove and walked out of the door, giving a ragged sigh.

The anger drained completely out of her, leaving an ache in her chest.

Bowie hadn't tried to hurt her but he still had. All he had done was his job. *His job.* He was a lawman and she would do well to remember that.

Chapter Eight

That conversation in the kitchen two nights ago bothered Bowie more than it should have. He was doing his job, dammit, and Merritt had taken it personally. Even though she had apologized for that, he didn't like that she felt he would run over her to get what he wanted. He wouldn't. He didn't think.

Maybe she was right and a lawman couldn't put a woman first. Bowie could. If she was the right woman. And Merritt Dixon couldn't be.

A big part of his frustration was physical. He could lie about it, keep pushing it to the back of his mind, but it was there all the time. An ever-present awareness of her and a dark pulsing throb in his blood. As much as he tried not to, he wanted her. He had realized just how much that night in the kitchen when he had burned to shake her silly and kiss her at the same time. That had never happened before and it buffaloed him.

Over the next couple of days, Bowie was left in no

doubt that he had crossed some invisible line with Merritt. She didn't avoid him, was polite when she spoke, but the warmth and openness he had been drawn to when they had first met was gone.

Each day, he asked if she needed help with anything and each day she said no. She said it with a smile, but it was still a "no."

Two nights after their little hen fight, Bowie offered to help her clean up after supper, but she refused. Politely. Tamping down a flare of exasperation, he followed Mr. Wilson into the parlor. The older gentleman sat in one of the chairs adjacent to the fireplace, so Bowie took the other one. To his surprise, Merritt joined them, choosing a seat next to the piano in the corner, her profile to Bowie.

While Mr. Wilson read a heavy green-bound book, Bowie cleaned his Colt. He hadn't seen Lefty in the past day or so.

Merritt settled into the straight-backed wood chair and opened the skirt of her white apron to reveal a lap full of pecans. The last of the day's sun streamed through the double windows behind him and painted the room in a soft gold, outlining his landlady's pert nose and the soft curve of her jaw.

Wearing a yellow-and-white-striped day dress, she had swept her hair up into a chignon, baring her dainty nape and the tender skin behind her ear. The only sign that she felt the summer heat was one undone button at the top of her bodice. The slight V revealed the hollow at the base of her throat and the sheen of damp skin. Bowie wanted to put his mouth on her there.

She cracked the nuts, then cleaned the hulls from

the meat and dropped the shelled pecans into a bowl wedged between her side and the chair arm.

Evening noises drifted through the open windows. Across the railroad tracks on the north side of town, the faint sounds of piano music rang in the air. Absently polishing the barrel of his revolver, he watched Merritt as she worked industriously.

She had barely looked at him all evening and he wanted to see if the cool remoteness was still in her eyes.

"That was a real good supper, Merritt."

"Thank you." She smiled, but didn't glance his way.

"Do you need some help shelling those pecans?"

"I'm doing fine on my own."

Frustrated, he dragged a hand down his face. She'd been doing fine on her own every damn time he'd offered to help in the past two days.

"Mr. Wilson, did you find the shirts I left in your room?" she asked.

"Yes, and thank you for mending them."

"You're welcome." Her lips curved in a smile, a real smile. Bowie's eyes narrowed. He rose, sliding his gun into his holster as he covered the small distance between them.

Hoping to get a reaction out of her, he reached down and lightly touched the hand that had been injured in his room. "You sure it's okay to do that? It doesn't bother your hand?"

"No, it doesn't. It's all healed up." She pulled away, finally peeking up at him from beneath her lashes.

It was hard to be sure through the hazy sunlight, but he thought he caught a flicker of irritation in her eyes. His gaze moved to her face and he reached out to feather his finger over the fading scar at her temple. "And here?"

She went as taut as a bowstring, her voice cool. "I'm fine. Thank you."

At last he saw something besides her polite, downright aggravating demeanor. He thought about running his finger down her cheek, but the rigid set of her shoulders plainly warned him off.

Too restless to sit, Bowie backed against the wall and crossed one booted foot over the other. "What are you going to do with those pecans?"

"Make a couple of pies."

He studied her, trying to figure out why she got under his skin so easily. She couldn't be more put out with him than he was with her right now. It seemed that the less she wanted to do with him, the more he wanted her. That was plumb loco.

Every night since she had come to his room, he had been dreaming about her. Hot, sweaty tangled-sheet dreams where he didn't only get to see her silky naked flesh, he could touch it.

He had tried to ignore the want, then combat it by thinking about other women. He noticed other women, even appreciated them, but once they were out of sight, he couldn't recall anything about them. It seemed there was no space in his head for anyone or anything except Merritt.

Which boiled his water because he should be thinking about the investigation more than he thought about her.

She was aware of him, too. It was there in the slight

stiffness of her body whenever he was in the room. He had tension in his body, too, but it wasn't from being near her. It was from not being near enough.

With a look of fierce concentration, she pulled open the cracked nuts and peeled off the hulls and any other parts of the shell that might be inside. After shelling the last pecan, she gathered her apron skirt to contain the broken hulls and got to her feet holding the bowl in her other hand.

"May I get anyone anything? More cake? Coffee?"

"Nothing for me. Thanks," Bowie said as Mr. Wilson nodded his agreement.

"All right." She walked out of the room, her boot heels tapping against the wood floor.

After a few minutes, he heard her start back across the dining room. Then the front door clattered shut. Footsteps sounded on the porch, then nothing.

His head came up as he listened for her. Perhaps she was just checking on something outside, but his gut said no.

Mr. Wilson was engrossed in his novel. Bowie pushed away from the wall and went to the door. The light turned to a golden haze as the sun sank lower in the sky. He saw Merritt was already across the street that ran in front of the boardinghouse.

She was headed for town. Where was she going? Why had she just up and left?

He slipped outside, careful to shut the door quietly. Maybe she had heard from her friend and foster brother, Saul, and was on her way to meet him. There had been no sign of anyone around the Morning Glory the past couple of days; Bowie had been shadowing Merritt's every move. But maybe the man had slipped her a note like he had the last time.

Bowie didn't like spying on her, but he had to find out who had killed his parents. Right now she was the closest thing he had to a lead and this was the quickest way to get to her source.

If she had told him what he needed to know, he wouldn't have to resort to this. She crossed the street at the Porter Hotel and Café, angling in the general direction of the shoemaker, the boot and saddle shop and the livery.

Bowie followed, easing to the corner of the bathhouse and pausing to watch. A quick look around showed the streets were empty, as they usually were this time of day.

As Merritt passed the shoemaker's store, Bowie moved to the next building, staying close to the structure, stopping at the corner of the barbershop.

She was between the barbershop and the shoemaker's store when a man stepped out in front of her. Bowie tensed, frowning when Merritt stopped to speak. The man's face was hidden until he stepped around in front of Merritt.

Hobbs. Without his ever-present bowler hat. A strange heat shoved through Bowie's chest. Had the ex-marshal been waiting for Merritt? Was she surprised to see him? Since her back was to Bowie, he couldn't tell a damn thing.

He didn't think she had come out to meet Hobbs, but what did he know? Whether it was planned or not, seeing her with the murdering bastard blistered him up good.

She began to walk, and the trim, dark-haired man fell

into step with her. She appeared to put up no protest. Of course, Bowie couldn't see her face or hear what she was saying, which raked at his nerves. Why was she letting Hobbs accompany her? *Why* was the man tagging along? What could he possibly want?

Bowie had to get closer. Wishing the sun had already set, he quietly made his way behind the barbershop, then to the shoemaker's store next door, where he saw Merritt stop in front of the boot and saddle shop. Hobbs stopped, too.

It didn't look as if she was encouraging the man, but she didn't appear to be discouraging him, either, which had Bowie grinding his teeth. From his position, he could finally hear.

"I'd show you a good time," Hobbs said.

On a wave of anger, Bowie's spine snapped straight. Merritt's reply was too soft for him to understand.

"Just think about it, all right, Miss Merritt? It's a week away so there's time."

She murmured something else Bowie couldn't hear.

That might've been due to the roaring in his ears, because he had just realized what Tobias had asked her.

The Independence Day celebration was in a week and the former marshal was inviting Merritt to attend Cahill Crossing's all-day festivities with him.

No way in hell. The thought shot through Bowie's mind before he could stop it. Impulse had him starting forward to warn Hobbs off, but Bowie managed to stop himself just in time.

In the next instant, that almost changed when he saw Hobbs kiss her hand. An unfamiliar heat charged through him and Bowie's hand went to his gun. He

didn't want that lying, murdering no-good's hands anywhere on Merritt, for any reason. He didn't want her
spending any time with the lowlife, either.

One way he could stop that would be to ask Merritt to
the Independence Day celebration himself. The thought
had him going still. He needed to watch her and, if he
was with her, he could watch her up close.

The idea was tempting. Too tempting. He would
only get in deeper with her and that was a bad idea. He
already had trouble staying away from her. Besides, he
would have a better opportunity to see who approached
or observed her if he weren't by her side.

She shifted, just enough to step back and shrug off
the ex-marshal's touch. She appeared to handle Hobbs
just fine, but Bowie still seethed.

She knew Hobbs was involved in the murders of
Bowie's parents. Just as she was aware that the former
marshal was probably also looking for her foster
brother, Saul. She wouldn't go anywhere with Hobbs,
Bowie reassured himself.

Unless she felt she couldn't say no because he had
told her to hide her dislike of the man if possible. She
hadn't put up a fuss about the poetry and flowers Hobbs
had brought her for that very reason.

Bowie didn't want her feeling that way. He wanted
to show himself, warn the former marshal off, but if he
did that, he would give away that he had been watching
her.

As much as Merritt had disliked him questioning her
friends, she would hate the thought of him now following her every move. She would immediately know that

he was waiting for her to meet up with Saul so Bowie could arrest him.

If she also found out that Bowie had gotten her family's last name from Ace and sent a wire to her parents, Tom and Carolyn Jensen, in Austin about Saul, she would be walking mad all over. Bowie couldn't reveal himself, couldn't give up his chance to be there when she next met her foster brother.

Bowie had no claim on her and couldn't stake one. He had a job to do and watching her was part of it. That job had never seemed as hard as it did right now.

Muscles rigid, he waited to see what she would do next.

The tightness in his chest eased when she opened the door to Ace's shop and went inside alone. For the first time in minutes, Bowie drew a full breath. He waited to see where Hobbs would go, but for long moments, the ex-marshal lingered outside the saddle shop until Bowie's patience was stretched to its absolute limit.

Tobias finally left, walking to the north side of town rather than coming back toward the place where Bowie waited. Pressed against the side of the building, he watched as Hobbs stepped into Steven's Restaurant. He appeared to have no idea he was being watched. Bowie had to make sure Merritt didn't, either.

He settled in to wait for her to leave. After about an hour and a half, she came out with both Ace and Livvy. They said their goodbyes and she began walking back toward him.

He didn't move, staying motionless against the back corner of the shoemaker's store so as not to draw attention. He didn't think she could see him from her angle, but he wasn't sure. She was smiling and looked more relaxed than she had in days. At least around Bowie.

He couldn't tear his gaze from the curve of her mouth, the sun's golden hue on her velvety skin. He stayed behind her, slipping silently along the rear side of the businesses on the way back to the boardinghouse. There was no sign of Hobbs, which was a relief. Bowie had wondered if Tobias might be watching Merritt himself, looking for another opportunity to speak to her.

After their conversation the other night, after Bowie had nearly kissed her, the smartest thing for him to do would be to leave her alone, keep her as far from this investigation as possible, but he couldn't.

If he stopped his surveillance, he might lose his chance to get to her friend. And if he kept watching her on the sly, he wouldn't be able to say certain things to her, warn her to steer clear of Hobbs.

Bowie had thought surveilling her was a good idea. Until now.

He felt like he was tied to a tree with a stampede charging him and all he could do was wait to be trampled.

The next day, Merritt was restless and on edge. She blamed Bowie. She had been fine last night until he had come over and touched her. The warmth of his hand on hers, the stroke of his finger against her temple, had sent a current of sensation running beneath her skin from head to toe. It rankled.

It had stirred her up. She wanted him and just hadn't been able to sit there any longer letting him touch her.

She had needed some air, someone to talk to, so she had gone to Livvy's.

She had already presumed her relationship with Bowie was something other than what it was, had mistakenly believed they had made an emotional connection when they hadn't. At least, Bowie hadn't.

Now, Merritt thought she'd finally gotten things straight between them in her mind. They were friendly acquaintances. She had helped him a small bit with his investigation and he had used that information to try to get more.

He was a lawman. He had never claimed to be anything else. He had never said he wouldn't contact her foster brother, hadn't agreed to wait for her to speak to Saul again. She needed to remember that man, not the softhearted one she had glimpsed when he had talked about his sister.

She needed to treat him like a boarder, not someone she fancied.

If Bowie affected her too much one way, then Hobbs affected her too much the other.

She groaned. When she had encountered the former marshal last night, he had invited her to the town's Fourth of July celebration. She hadn't outright refused, although she had thought her obvious reluctance even to talk to him would've discouraged the man. It hadn't.

When he had kissed her hand, she had barely kept from recoiling.

She didn't want to go anywhere with him and had wanted to tell him to leave her alone, but she hadn't. And why?

Because Bowie had asked her to try and put up with

the low-down snake. She resented doing it, but if it helped get justice for Earl and Ruby, Merritt would do what she could.

Still, there was only so much she could stomach and spending hours with the ex-marshal was not on the list. He had urged her to consider it and she had. Maybe if she gentled her refusal, it wouldn't alienate him. That should please Bowie.

Though she had been afraid Hobbs might come by the boardinghouse today to ask for her answer, he hadn't. That was cause enough for celebration, but she had also spent each meal with Bowie and sat with him in the parlor after supper without experiencing any more of that silly physical frustration. Thank goodness he hadn't touched her again.

Still, she was glad to escape to her bedroom when he and Mr. Wilson had said good-night and gone upstairs. A few minutes later, she closed the door to her bedroom. She peeled off her gray skirt and white bodice, unhooked her corset and sighed in pleasure as her chemise billowed away from her body.

Sitting on the edge of her bed, she unlaced her everyday boots, took them off, then her stockings. She leaned back on her elbows and wiggled her toes, glad to be rid of her shoes.

After undoing her braid, she threaded her fingers through the strands until the heavy mass fell around her shoulders. The tension of the day seeped away as she brushed out her hair. Once finished, she gathered it to the side in a loose ponytail, then pulled down her lone sheet. The air coming through the half-open window wasn't cool, but it wasn't daytime-hot, either.

She would be comfortable as long as she didn't move around too much.

Just as she bent to turn out the lamp at the head of her bed, a tap sounded on the glass.

"Merritt?" a masculine voice whispered.

Saul! She padded over to the window and pushed aside the chambray curtains. In the glow of the lamp, his hawklike features were reflected from the other side of the glass.

She raised the window all the way. "Are you all right?"

"Yes. I told you I'd contact you, so here I am."

"Good. Are you hungry?"

He nodded.

"Go up to the front corner of the house. I'll let you through the side door into the kitchen."

With a quick nod, he disappeared. After tugging on her boots, she grabbed her light cotton wrapper from the back of the nearby chair and pulled it on, then picked up the burning lamp and quietly made her way across the dark dining room to the kitchen.

She let him in, keeping the door propped open. A few minutes later, he stood over the long work counter wolfing down the leftovers from supper.

She took a half loaf of bread, a wedge of cheese and three pieces of fried chicken out of the larder and placed them on the counter with two cans of beans, two cans of peaches and the four apples she had left.

When he finished, he whispered his thanks, then turned to gather the food. He knocked a can of beans to the floor. Merritt froze at the loud thud while Saul managed to stop the other cans from falling. She held her breath as she waited to see if anyone upstairs might have heard.

After a few moments of total silence, she nodded. He scooped up the can on the floor and helped her carefully pack everything into the saddlebags he'd left outside by the door.

"Where have you been?" she whispered.

"Here and there."

She hadn't really thought he would tell her. Looking around to make sure they were still alone, she followed him outside. "Did you think about what I said?"

"About talking to that lawman?"

She nodded.

"I just don't know, Merritt."

"You know Hobbs could be looking for you," she pointed out, trying to keep the panic out of her voice. "He probably is."

"Maybe so, but he hasn't found me yet."

"If you would talk to Bowie, he could protect you. You'd be safer with him than on your own."

He looked around nervously. "I came from the direction of the jail and saw the marshal's name on the door. It's Cahill. Is he related to the Cahills who were murdered?"

She didn't want to answer. It would only give him another reason to say no to her.

"Merritt?" he asked sharply.

"Yes, but—"

"He'd likely shoot me on sight."

"No, he wouldn't. Not if you turn yourself in."

He shook his head, swinging up into his saddle. His

bay gelding stepped forward, the light revealing her missing left ear. "I'm going to leave here, ride west."

"You promised you wouldn't do that."

"Would you rather see me get killed?"

She put a hand on his leg. "If you would just help Bowie, he would help you."

He looked down at her with a sad smile, his sharp features blunted in the shadows. "I wish I were as good as you think I am."

"Saul, don't go. Just talk to him once."

He tensed and stared into the kitchen behind her.

She turned. "What is it?"

"Thought I heard something. How many people you got living here?"

"Three, including me. I have a spare room. You can use it."

"If I stay and Hobbs is after me, that will put you in danger. I'm not going to do that," he said in a low voice.

"Promise me you won't leave the area, at least not without telling me."

His horse backed up, shifting restlessly.

"Saul, promise."

His gaze shot to something behind her and his eyes widened. "I love you."

With that, he wheeled his mount and disappeared into the dark.

"Saul!" she whispered.

His horse thundered down the side of the house heading south toward the river.

She followed for a few feet, but she couldn't see anything past the moonlit corner of her house. The trees obscured any further view as did the hillside. The sound of pounding hooves grew more distant.

Why had he done that? She didn't know when she would see him again.

Frustrated and worried, she turned and walked back toward the kitchen door. A shadow fell across the soft golden light coming from the kitchen. She drew in a sharp breath when she saw Bowie standing in the doorway.

Had he seen Saul? No, if he had, he would've tried to arrest him.

"Who was that?" he demanded.

"You scared me!"

"Who? It was Saul, wasn't it?"

Nerves raw, she pushed past him, walking into the kitchen.

He followed. "I know someone was here, Merritt."

"Yes. Someone who needed food."

He grabbed her arm, turned her toward him. "It was Saul Bream. Why was he here?"

Her head jerked up. "How did you find out his last name?"

"Your parents told me."

"My parents." Dumbfounded, she just stared at him for a moment.

"I wired them, told them I was looking for him and why. That was all the information they could provide."

Of course he had contacted her parents. Merritt shouldn't be surprised. He had already shown himself to be doggedly persistent at following up on any clue, no matter how small.

He gave her a little shake. "He could be dangerous."

"Not to me."

His hands ran down her arms to bracket her waist.

Pulse hitching, her gaze flew to his.

"What if he hurts you? Or tries to use you as a bargaining tool?"

"He won't." The deep male scent of him, the heat of his body, was distracting.

"He's a wanted man, Merritt. They do desperate things."

She knew that was right, but…she didn't think Saul would hurt her. *You also never imagined he would be involved in a murder,* she thought ruefully.

"I don't want you in danger," Bowie said softly.

"You're probably more worried that I won't tell you when he contacts me again."

His eyes narrowed; a muscle spasmed in his jaw. "Would you have told me about this meeting?"

"If I'd known about it, but I didn't. Last time, he sent me a note. I had no way of knowing he was going to show up tonight."

"You could've come and gotten me."

She leveled a look at him. "If I had asked him to wait a minute, then come searching for you, do you think he would've been here when I returned?"

He didn't answer, just dragged a hand down his haggard whisker-stubbled face.

"I know you think it's your job to protect me, protect everyone, but if something happens, I won't hold you responsible."

"That isn't why I care, dammit." His gaze slid hotly down her body, making her very aware that she wore only a chemise and a light wrapper.

She ignored the sudden weakness in her knees. "Then why?" she challenged. "Are you afraid it will look as though you aren't doing your job?"

"No," he gritted out.

"Well, then?"

"This is why," he muttered before his mouth came down on hers.

She stilled for a second, then parted her lips to let him in.

Dimly, she was aware that she made a sound. He curled her tight into him and kissed her harder, demanding more.

She could feel every hard inch of him through her clothes. Both of her hands crept up his chest and slid around his neck, holding on tight. A delicious warmth spread through her like honey. Her fingers delved into his thick hair and she arched against him. His chest was solid muscle against her breasts, his body tight and hot.

She couldn't get close enough and he seemed to feel the same. He curved his palm under her hair, then cradled her skull, burying his hand in the silky mass as his mouth moved over hers.

Heat flushed her body as she felt the solid ridge of his erection. He pulled away, breathing hard, his eyes black with want in the dim amber light. "We need to stop."

Dazed, she lifted a shaking hand to her mouth. Seth had never kissed her like that.

"Merritt." Bowie's husky voice had her toes curling. He straightened, his big hand sliding from her hair.

"You're sorry," she guessed hoarsely, her heart sinking.

"No. I stopped as much for me as I did for you."

"What do you mean?"

Arousal streaked his cheekbones. "I'm not going to change who I am. What I do."

"I didn't ask you to." She stiffened, drawing away from him.

He closed his eyes briefly. "I'm not saying this right."

She stared up at him, her heart hammering against her chest as she tried to pull herself together.

"You've told me why you don't want to be involved with a lawman."

Frowning, she nodded.

"That's all I want to be."

"So you pulled away for me?" she asked, confused. Incredulous.

"For me, too."

She didn't understand, but she wanted to.

"I told you my engagement didn't work out."

She nodded.

"Clea didn't want me to be a lawman. She wanted me to take my place in the family cattle business, follow in my father's and brother's footsteps. Their well-established, very wealthy footsteps. When I said no, she broke our engagement. I didn't know she felt that way before we got involved, but—"

"You do know that about me," Merritt said softly as understanding dawned.

"Yes." His eyes were stormy. He looked as if this bothered him as much as it bothered her. "The hell of it is, I understand why you feel that way and I wouldn't ask you to change that, either. We can't get involved."

She knew he was right. She'd told herself the same thing. She *believed* it. So, why did it hurt?

She bit her lip to stop it from quivering. With more composure than she felt, she said, "So, we should be only friends."

"Friends," he repeated in an even voice.

She could read nothing in his voice, good or bad. "Unless you don't want that?"

"I do." His jaw clenched as he stared down at her. "I just don't know if I can do it."

Merritt didn't know if she could, either.

Chapter Nine

Bowie was everything Merritt didn't want and he wasn't going to change. Not for her or anyone.

He repeated this to himself every day in the week that followed their kiss in the kitchen.

There were no more kisses, no more meetings between just the two of them. This was what they had agreed on. It was sure as hell the smart thing.

The problem was, smart didn't seem to matter when she made sure he had hot shaving water every morning or kept supper warm for him on late nights or looked so beautiful.

Getting involved with Merritt would be like following a cold trail—going nowhere for both of them. It didn't matter. He still wanted her and it only grew more intense with time.

She wanted him, too. Which only made it more difficult to do the right thing. He tried to keep a distance because the farther he was from her physically, the more he was able to control his frustration.

Watching her was another matter. He was still surveilling her. Between that and being marshal, he wasn't getting a lot of sleep. That was the only reason he had heard that noise the night he had come downstairs to find her outside with Saul Bream.

Bowie hadn't had any luck tracking down the man or his one-eared bay. Even a trip to Wolf Grove to ask around about Bream and his horse had yielded nothing. It sure as hell would have been easier on Bowie if he had learned something. He might have been able to stay away from Merritt, but he couldn't afford to miss a chance at Bream if he contacted Merritt again.

Day after day, night after night, of watching her, remembering that damn kiss, sawed at Bowie's resolve to remain only friends. He didn't know how long he could hold out.

Especially when the day of the Fourth of July festivities arrived.

The flag, always raised at the town hall, fluttered in the hot breeze. The entire town had been decorated with red, white and blue ribbons. Swags in the same colors hung across the streets and marked off the planked floor that had been erected for today's speeches and tonight's dancing.

He kept an eye on her throughout the reading of the Declaration of Independence and Bowie's reading of the town charter that told the story of how Cahill Crossing had been established and named for his family.

He wasn't able to tear his gaze from her, appreciating the way the bodice of her red-and-white-striped dress gloved her full breasts and tapered into the star-studded blue sash at her small waist. He watched her through the picnic she shared with Ace, Livvy and Mr. Wilson under the arbor built for the celebration and covered with large tree branches for shade.

The worst moment for Bowie was when night fell and the temporary plank board platform became a dance floor. When she danced with Hobbs, Bowie just barely managed to keep from cutting in. He couldn't stand the thought of the other man touching her when his burning-hot dreams of making love with her just grew more intense. More difficult to ignore.

Once it was fully dark, Arthur Slocum and Ben Verden began shooting off the town fireworks.

The loud shrieking noises were followed by brilliant bursts of light against the dark blue sky. Golden light streaked up high, then burst into myriad red, gold and blue showers.

Everyone's attention was trained on the stunning display. If Bowie hadn't been watching Merritt, he would've been too amazed by the exploding lights to notice her leaving. He lost her for a moment in the crowd, then spied a flash of a red-and-white-striped dress disappear behind the Porter Hotel and Café.

Was she returning to the Morning Glory? Was she meeting someone? Maybe Bream?

Amid the crackle and pop of the fireworks, Bowie eased through the throngs of people, then strode down the street. When he passed Porter's and stepped into the street that fronted the boardinghouse, he saw her.

She hurried toward the houses on the same side of the street as her house. Why? The hair on the back of his neck stood up. Hobbs lived down that way. Was she going to the ex-marshal's place?

Bowie didn't want to jump to conclusions. Hobbs wasn't the only resident who lived in this area. But evidently he was the one Merritt was interested in because she made straight for his log house and the front porch. What was the witless woman up to?

Checking over his shoulder to make sure he wasn't being followed, Bowie jogged to the house, reaching it just in time to see the front door shut quietly. Had she gone inside?

He eased up to the window and peeked in. There she was. What the hell!

She lit a candle and began looking around the large front room, opening the cupboard on the far wall and bending to peer inside.

Was she crazy? A quick glance around assured him they were alone. He silently opened the front door and stepped inside.

She jumped, letting out a squeak upon seeing him. "What are you doing?"

"Getting you out of here."

"How did you know where I was?"

"I saw you leave the party. Anyone could've seen you."

She froze. "Do you think someone did?"

"I don't know." He bit back a roar of impatience and reached her in two strides, snagging her elbow and giving a tug. "So, let's go."

"I'm not finished."

"Yes, you are. What if I'd been Hobbs coming through that door?"

Alarm flashed across her features. Her chest rose and fell rapidly, drawing his gaze to her breasts swelling against her square-cut bodice. It was lower than anything he'd seen her wear before. In the flickering candlelight, her skin gleamed like pearls. He wanted to get his hands on her.

"Come on," he said. "Now."

"You have no right to drag me out of here."

"I'm the law, sweetheart, and you've just broken into someone's house."

"I'm trying to find something to help Saul."

"You can't help him if you're in jail." He turned and curled a hand around her other arm, pulling her into him. "Unless you want me to carry you, start walking."

Her eyes sparked with anger and she angled her chin at him.

"Merritt, don't be a fool," he gritted. "Let's get out of here."

She hesitated only a moment. "Very well," she muttered, blowing out the candle she'd brought and slipping it into her pocket.

Bowie cracked open the door and, after making sure they were still alone, he towed her off the porch and around to the back of the house, pressing her up against the rough timber wall. "What were you doing in there?"

She tugged away from his touch and he let her, but stayed where he was, keeping her in place, too.

The moonlight illuminated her features, polishing them to marble. He caught her soft scent on the hot summer air and realized how isolated they were. "I was looking for something that might prove Hobbs's part in your parents' murders."

Bowie blinked. Had he heard her right?

"If I can find something incriminating on him, then Saul can stop running."

"Woman, are you crazy?" He could barely choke out the words. All he could imagine was her hurt and bleeding. "What if Hobbs had caught you instead of me?"

"If he finds Saul, he'll kill him."

"And what do you think Hobbs would do to you if he caught you here?"

"I don't know, but I have my gun." She patted her skirt pocket.

Closing his eyes briefly, he dragged a hand across his nape, noting the pop of fireworks from town. "What would you have said if he'd caught you? You broke into his house, Merritt."

"I would've thought of something."

"That's a real good plan," he drawled.

She stared up at him, her eyes a luminous silver in the moonlight and shadows. The soft curls on top of her head were woven with a red ribbon, and Bowie wanted to rip out the pins and bury his hands in the silky sable mass.

"Are you going to arrest me?"

"If I were, you'd already be in irons and in my jail."

"What are you doing here? Did you follow me?"

"Yes, and you should be glad. Be glad I'm the one who found you snooping around Hobbs's front room and not him." He shook his head. "I don't know what you thought you were going to find."

"Have you searched his house?"

"Not officially."

"What does that mean?"

"I've been inside, looked around without it seeming like that's what I was doing."

"Then how do you know there's nothing here to be found?"

"I didn't say that. At least I have the authority to go around searching people's homes." He couldn't stop thinking about what might have happened if Hobbs had walked in on her snooping through his house. "Don't do this again. It's foolish."

She bristled. "I'm trying to help you."

"And Saul," he added dryly.

"What's wrong with that?"

"Nothing, but—" He broke off, listening closely.

"What?" Her voice rose.

"Shh." He clapped a palm over her mouth and leaned down, breathing in her ear, "I hear something."

She froze, one hand curling into the waistband of his trousers. Through his shirt, he could feel her nails raking his belly and his entire body went hard. Panic flared in her eyes as she turned her head to look in the direction he was staring.

He could've sworn he heard movement on the front porch, but after a long moment punctuated by the fading pop of fireworks and the buzz of voices from town, all was quiet.

He turned his attention back to her, his gaze roaming over the soft curve of her jaw, the dirt she must have gotten from Hobbs's door or door frame, the tempting length of her neck. He wanted to put his mouth there, find out if that was her sensitive spot.

He felt her tremble beneath his touch and removed

his hand from her mouth. The memory of the way her eyes had gone all smoky after their first kiss teased him.

Her tongue peeked out to lick her lips. "Do you still hear something?" she whispered.

He shook his head, painfully aware of the throbbing of his blood, the knot of need coiling in his gut. He'd stayed away from her for a week. A week that suddenly felt like a month. He wanted another taste.

He brushed away the dirt streaking her magnolia-smooth skin and twined a finger in a long, silky strand of her hair. "You look beautiful tonight."

"Thank you."

The huskiness of her voice made him ache. He looked down, his mouth watering at the plump ivory flesh swelling against her bodice. He wanted to run his tongue over the perfect curves, dip into the fragrant valley between her breasts.

To hell with their agreement. He had to kiss her.

He lowered his head, searching her eyes. She might not want this. She seemed to have been dealing better with their decision to remain only friends.

"I don't think I can be friends with you, Merritt. I want more than that."

Her eyes turned dark with desire, making his heart kick hard. "We talked about it."

"We did." If she said no, he would stop. His thumb caressed the delicate line of her jaw and she pressed into his touch. "And if you want to remain only friends, I'll try."

She stared at him for a long moment. "I'm not sure."

The softness in her eyes was enough of an invitation

for him. "I've been thinking about doing this again all week."

"Me, too." The whispered admission kicked off a scalding desire inside him.

He brushed his lips against hers lightly, a bare touch, testing, teasing.

She made a sound in the back of her throat and gripped the front of his shirt. Bowie settled his mouth over hers. With a soft, breathy sigh, she let him in. Her arms went around his neck and he took the kiss deeper. Even through the bulk of her skirts, he could feel her heat.

She wiggled, sending a surge of hard, hot want through him. When she melted into him, he lifted her, holding her tight to him as he dragged his lips from hers and nipped lightly at her earlobe.

The broken sound she made had him sliding his mouth down her elegant neck to the sensitive curve where her shoulder began. The velvety texture of her skin, her fresh, subtle scent, made his arousal rock hard.

Her head went back, baring her throat, her ragged sigh unleashing a primal need inside him. His mouth covered hers again and he set her on her feet, moving his hands to her waist, then up to the lower curves of her breasts.

Her breath caught and his erection throbbed. His heart pounded against his chest. Pounding, pounding. It was so loud.

He froze. That wasn't his heart. Someone was here. Walking up the front steps of Hobbs's house.

Bowie raised his head, giving Merritt a warning squeeze. She opened her eyes, dazed with want, making him ache clear to the bone. She nodded to show that she understood to be quiet.

Bowie hardly dared breathe, trying to calm his raging blood. The front door opened, then shut. Against him, Merritt tensed. He waited for the door to open again. When it didn't, he motioned for her to stay put, then sidled up the side of the house to the edge of the porch.

From this angle, he could barely see through the window. It was Hobbs. Bowie silently cursed. They were damn lucky the man hadn't found them.

Bowie had been so caught up in Merritt that he almost hadn't heard the ex-marshal arrive.

He returned to Merritt.

"What was the noise?" she mouthed.

"Hobbs."

Her eyes widened.

"He doesn't know we're here."

She nodded, looking pale and anxious. After a few minutes, when it appeared the other man wasn't coming back outside, Bowie leaned in, breathing the words, "We'd better get out of here."

"Back to town?"

"Or to the boardinghouse."

"Yes, there."

"All right." Taking her hand, they walked back silently.

Once inside the Morning Glory, she lit the lamp on the table in front of the foyer window. They both let out a big sigh.

She tugged her hand from his and walked over to sink down on the stairs in a billow of skirts. "That was close."

"Very." He opened his mouth to reprimand her again for going to the former marshal's house by herself, for *breaking in*.

"Thank goodness you found me and not Hobbs."

"You shouldn't be poking around like that."

"I'll be more careful."

He clamped his jaw tight. "I don't want you going back there. It's too dangerous. The next time you want to look for something, come to me. I can do it legitimately."

She didn't say anything for a long moment, then finally nodded. "All right."

She smiled at him and the remembered feel of her mouth kicked him right in the gut. She must've remembered, too, because she flushed a pretty pink. Which made him want to kiss her again.

"I meant what I said about being friends," Bowie said. "That isn't what I want."

She rose, chewing at her lip. "Nothing's changed between us."

"I know." Frustration and a sense of loss drummed inside him.

"I'm not sure I want to remain just friends, either."

His senses went on alert. "You're not?"

"I just don't know if there's any point to us making it more."

He'd said the same thing to himself all week. "We could take things slow, see how it goes for a bit."

"Do you think that would really work?"

He didn't know, but he wanted to try. "Only one way to find out."

"I just don't know, Bowie," she said softly. "I'll have to think about it."

Well, that wasn't a "no." He grinned. "You know where to find me when you decide."

"I do." She smiled, lighting up his whole night. "Good night."

She moved around him, going across the dining area toward her bedroom. He waited until she got inside and closed the door before he started back to town to make sure everything was still fine.

He hadn't gotten a "yes" out of her, but she hadn't pulled the reins on him, either.

Merritt felt the same way Bowie did about being friends. It wasn't what she preferred. No man had ever affected her the way he did. He made her feel desirable, something she hadn't felt since Seth had died.

Bowie's suggestion that they take things slowly and see what happened between them was tempting. Very tempting. Even so, it wasn't a good idea.

He had flat-out told her he wouldn't give up his badge for anyone and she was certain that she didn't want a life like the one she'd had with her late husband. She knew what her decision should be, but she couldn't bring herself to make it.

Especially when he had confided in her about his former betrothed. Merritt had thought about that a lot during the week leading up to the Fourth of July celebration, when he had nearly kissed her out of her drawers.

For the two nights following, she slept restlessly and was again thinking about his suggestion one afternoon as she closed the top drawer of her vanity table. There was no sign of her new handkerchief. It had been embroidered with her initials in colors to match the dress she'd worn to the Independence Day festivities.

She had searched the skirt pocket, under her bed and on top of her bureau. Maybe she had gathered it up with her undergarments when she had done laundry yesterday. She had still been floating from that kiss with Bowie out behind Hobbs's house and could barely remember washing the laundry, much less gathering it up.

She walked out of her bedroom and headed for the kitchen where she kept the large wicker basket for the wash next to the door of the spare room. Before dawn this morning, she thought she had heard someone come in and had assumed it to be Lefty. The fact that it was early afternoon and he wasn't up yet must mean he was in bad shape. She was just glad he had returned to the boardinghouse.

It had been five days since she had last seen her friend and she had started to worry. Reaching the wash basket, she turned it over, disappointed to find it empty. The door to the small room was ajar.

Planning to fix Lefty a pot of coffee and see if he needed to eat, she pushed open the door. She was surprised to find the bed empty. It hadn't been slept in. She went down the short hall to the back stoop. He wasn't out there, either. He hadn't been here.

Anxious now, Merritt decided to look for him in town. Two hours later, she'd had no luck and her concern turned to gnawing worry.

What could have happened? It was likely her friend

was sleeping off a rough night, but he had never been gone this long before. He could be hurt or—

She drew in a sharp breath. What if Hobbs had figured out Lefty was the one who had given Bowie the information that the ex-marshal knew the Cahills had been murdered?

Urging herself to stay calm, she checked the Morning Glory one more time. When she didn't find Lefty, she hurried out of the front door, past the opera house and to the jail. She rushed up the steps, catching sight of Bowie at his desk, his hat on the corner. She fumbled with the doorknob.

He looked up in surprise, his eyes crinkling at the corners. "Hi."

"Hello," she said breathlessly, closing the door behind her.

He rose with a slight frown. "Are you okay?"

"Yes." Her gaze went past him to the door that separated his office area from the cells. "Is Lefty here?"

Bowie shook his head. "Come to think of it, I haven't seen him in a while."

Her heart sank. "Neither have I and I'm worried."

"You know how he is," Bowie said gently.

"He's not here. He hasn't been at the boardinghouse." She shook her head. "He's never been gone this long."

"When did you last see him?"

"Five days ago. Three days before Independence Day. I asked him if he was going to the celebration and he said yes. But I didn't see him." Her voice rose. "What if he's hurt? Or what if Hobbs figured out he was the one who gave you that information about Hobbs knowing your parents had been murdered?"

Concern creased Bowie's sun-bronzed features. "Hold your horses. Let's not jump the gun."

"I don't know where else to look."

He buckled on his gun belt, then slid one of his big weathered hands down the inside of his thigh to tie the leather thong to his leg. "Where have you looked?"

"I asked around town, but no one has seen him. Then I went to Hell's Corner."

His head snapped up. "Merritt."

"And the Black Diamond as well as the Hard Luck," she added quickly.

He cursed violently, causing her to jump. "Those places are across the tracks. There's a bad element all around that area."

"And he goes there to drink," Merritt said tersely. "But he hasn't been there. No one has seen him at any of those places."

Bowie scooped up his hat and settled it on his head, opening the door with his free hand.

"Where are you going?" she asked.

"With you, to look for Lefty."

She hadn't expected that. She didn't know many lawmen who would have helped her look for a friend who was drunk more often than he was sober.

Tears stung her eyes. "Thank you."

He gave her a gentle smile. "You're welcome."

They made a quick pass through town with no luck. As they approached the railroad tracks, the train whistle sounded, announcing the daily arrival. They paused, waiting for the locomotive to shudder to a stop, for the iron wheels to cease screeching. A black cloud billowed out of the smokestack and the bite of coal filled the air.

When he could be heard, Bowie said, "I don't want you going over there, but I know you won't stay put."

"He's my friend."

"Right." He took her arm and guided her across the tracks. "Stick close to me."

She would. Being with him would surely discourage any unwanted attention, like the two men who had followed her from saloon to saloon earlier.

She and Bowie checked the two cafés, Landry's Boardinghouse, the billiard hall and dance hall, then Pearl's Palace. There was no sign of Lefty.

Her concern growing, she made her way back across the tracks with Bowie. Even if he was ready to give up, she wasn't.

They halted between the general store and Rosa's Boutique. Bowie braced his hands on his hips, his gaze scanning the street. "Where else should we look?"

"You're not giving up?"

"No. We haven't found him yet." He glanced down at her. "Would he stay anywhere outside of town?"

"Maybe. It can't hurt to look."

They stopped at the boardinghouse so Merritt could change into her split skirt. While she did, Bowie saddled Mr. Wilson's mare for her. Mounted on his black gelding, he was waiting in front of the boardinghouse with the mare.

They rode north, stopping along the way to call out for the missing man. They guided their mounts down a wooded hillside to a lush valley and reined up at Phantom Springs, which was less than a mile from town. Water bubbled up from a jumble of rocks and flowed across flat slabs of shale, past the rapids to slowly move southeast and supply water for Cahill Crossing.

Typically, Merritt loved it here. The murmur of the water over the rapids sounded like whispering voices, which had prompted its name. The peaceful spot never failed to bring a smile, but today she paid more attention to the surrounding hillside and a craggy rock formation some distance away along the bank.

"Lefty!" Bowie called out.

She turned her horse to face the opposite direction of Bowie's, also yelling for her friend.

"Here I am!"

A thrill shot through her as she wheeled her mount around. Stooping, Lefty made his way out from under a rock overhang.

"Oh!" Merritt cried.

Bowie was there to help her dismount and she hurried down the bank to the other man. "I was so worried!"

"I'm sorry." He sent a sheepish look Bowie's way. "Sorry, Marshal."

"Just glad you're all right," Bowie said.

Merritt looked Lefty up and down, noting sunburned skin beneath the growth of several days' worth of whiskers. "You are okay, aren't you?"

"Yes. Is everything okay with you?"

"It is now. Have you been out here the entire time since I last saw you?"

"Yes, ma'am."

"Why?" she asked softly as Bowie walked up beside her.

Lefty looked at the marshal, then back at Merritt. "I haven't had a drink in six days."

"You're trying to quit!"

He nodded.

Merritt smiled up at Bowie, who glanced around. "Did you walk out here from town, Lefty?"

"Yes, it isn't too far." He turned his attention back to Merritt, squinting. "I had to get away from the saloons."

"Makes sense," Bowie said.

"I'm so proud of you." Merritt squeezed the older man's arm. "But I don't like you being out here alone. Please come back with us."

Bowie touched her arm, silently communicating that her friend might need more time.

She nodded. "Unless you don't feel you should leave yet."

Lefty hesitated. "I think I can."

"Good." She smiled. "We'll get you back to the Morning Glory and get some food in you."

"Thank you, Miss Merritt."

She patted his arm. "I'm so glad you're all right."

The three of them walked back to the horses. Bowie lifted her into the saddle, squeezing her knee and giving her a smile that warmed her all over.

Lefty mounted up behind the marshal and the three of them headed back to town.

Unable to stop looking at Bowie, Merritt kept her mare slightly behind his black gelding as they wove in and out of the shade trees on the hillside. The man had helped her look for someone who most lawmen probably wouldn't have given the time of day. Not once had he suggested she just wait for Lefty to show up. Bowie had put aside whatever he was doing to help her. She hadn't expected that.

Maybe he was so driven by his job because his current investigation was personal. His ex-fiancée might have thought Bowie wasn't enough for her, but he was plenty for Merritt. Clea had been a fool. Merritt didn't want to look back and wonder if she had been one, too.

When he had confided in her about Clea, Merritt had felt that connection to him again. It had also made her wonder if she had ever made Seth feel like a lesser man. She hoped not. Even though his job frustrated her, she had loved her husband.

Her gaze settled on Bowie's broad shoulders and the biceps flexing beneath the snug fit of his white shirt. Thank goodness he had been the one to find her the other night when she had broken into Hobbs's house. She had no idea what she would have done if Hobbs had shown up instead of Bowie.

They reached Cahill Crossing right before suppertime. The three of them ate together at the boardinghouse, Bowie and Lefty finishing off the roast and potatoes. Mr. Wilson had sent word that he was working late at the newspaper.

After visiting for a few minutes, Bowie rose, giving her a broad smile. "Another good meal."

"I have pecan pie," she said.

"I need to get back to the jail and finish what I was doing earlier."

"Let me wrap up a piece for you to take."

"I won't say no to that."

The heat in his blue eyes had Merritt wishing he

could stay longer, but she went to the kitchen and returned with his dessert.

Lefty began stacking dishes. "Don't you worry about this, Miss Merritt. I'll clean up."

"Thank you." She walked with Bowie to the front door, stepping back when he opened it. A glance over her shoulder showed that the other man had gone into the kitchen. "Thank you so much for helping me find him. I know you were busy."

"You were really worried."

"Yes."

"I didn't like it."

His gruff declaration had her smiling. Merritt knew then that she was going to go along with his suggestion. It didn't matter that she was still questioning the wisdom of getting involved with him. She smiled and rose on tiptoe, bringing his head down for a quick kiss.

His eyes darkened, his free hand going to her waist. "What was that for?"

"For helping me find Lefty."

Mischief lighting his eyes, he grinned. "Anything else I can do to help you?"

She kissed him again, longer this time.

He groaned. "I wish this was your way of telling me you've thought about what I said and you're willing to give us a try."

"It is— Oh!"

He lifted her with one arm, setting his cloth-wrapped pie on the windowsill. His other arm came around her. "You sure?"

"Not a hundred percent." She looked into his eyes, drawing in his masculine scent, feeling every inch of him down to her button-up boots. "But I can't ignore it anymore. I need to know."

Fierce desire flared in his eyes as he kicked the door shut and kissed her until she was dizzy.

Even though being in his arms felt right, Merritt hoped she hadn't made a mistake.

Chapter Ten

The next day, Merritt awoke impatient to see Bowie and it had nothing to do with the two-hour walk they had taken by the river last night after he had finished his work at the jail.

Though she had enjoyed herself and she thought he had, too, they had been careful of each other. Merritt still wasn't sure getting involved was a good idea and she knew Bowie didn't want to rush anything, even though it had been his idea that they explore what was between them.

That, along with the hunt for Lefty, had driven all thought of her missing handkerchief out of her mind. She planned to inform Bowie this morning at breakfast, but Lefty and Mr. Wilson joined them.

Once finished, Bowie said he would see her for lunch, then left at the same time as Mr. Wilson.

While Lefty cleared the table and brought the dishes into the kitchen, Merritt began washing the bread pans, egg beater and skillet. Anxious to talk to Bowie as soon as possible, she scrubbed everything hurriedly, moving on to the dishes.

Lefty had shaved and combed his hair. Washing the china plates as quickly as she could while still being careful, she only then noticed the neatness of his brown-checked shirt and tan trousers.

"You look very handsome today."

His neck turned red as he set down a stack of coffee cups. "I got a job."

"You did?" She rinsed the ham platter and laid it on a towel covering the counter beside her. "I'm glad to hear it. What will you be doing?"

"Mr. Stokes said he would let me work at the general store. If I'm not serious about quitting the drink, I'll lose the job."

"I think you're serious," she encouraged.

"Thank you," he said gruffly.

She picked up another towel and began to dry the plates. "I'm glad he's giving you a chance." Merritt paused at the look on her friend's face, half uncertainty and half excitement. "That's good. Isn't it?"

"Yes, ma'am, and I appreciate it. Once I get my first pay, I plan to give you some rent."

"That isn't necessary, Lefty."

"I want to. You've taken real good care of me." He stacked the clean plates and took them into the dining room to store in the sideboard. "I don't want to take advantage."

"You're not. Besides, I like having you here."

Stepping back into the kitchen, he looked down. "I don't want to live on charity anymore."

Merritt could see it was a matter of pride. "All right."

"I can only afford the spare room, so I'll stay there unless you'd rather I find another place."

"Absolutely not! And I have two bigger rooms upstairs that are empty."

"If I stay in the smaller one, I can save a little money."

Merritt stopped to look at him. "You've thought this out."

He nodded, seeming to hesitate before saying, "I want my wife and family back."

Her heart ached. "Have you been in contact with them?"

"Not yet. I don't want to wire them until I can say I'm sober and have a job."

Warmth welled inside her and she gave him a quick hug. "I'm so proud of you."

He gave a sheepish laugh. "I haven't done it yet."

"But you will. I just know it."

"I'd better get going or Mr. Stokes will fire me on my first day."

"Thanks for helping me with the dishes." She dried her hands on her apron, then took it off and laid it on the counter. The older man had one foot out the side door when she asked, "Lefty, have you seen my handkerchief? It's a new one with my initials embroidered in red, white and blue."

"No, ma'am, but I can help you look."

"Thank you, but I've already looked everywhere. I'm afraid to think where it might be." She literally *was* afraid. "You go on to work and have a good day."

"You, too."

Her day would be much better if she could locate

that blasted handkerchief. Every time she thought about it, she became more convinced that she had lost it in Hobbs's house and he'd found it, even though she didn't have a single thing to back up that opinion. The idea tied her stomach in knots. She hated to think what he might do if he discovered she'd been in his house.

If he had found the handkerchief, surely he would've made that known by now. Perhaps by having her arrested for breaking in!

This was ridiculous. She was worrying herself sick. The sooner she talked to Bowie, the better.

Nerves wound tight, she grabbed a flat-brimmed straw hat from her room, putting it on as she walked across the dining area. She opened the front door. And stopped short at the sight of Tobias Hobbs.

Her stomach dropped to her feet. Why was he here?

The former marshal swept off his bowler hat, keeping one hand behind his back. "Good morning, Mrs. Dixon."

"Mr. Hobbs." Dread crept up her spine and she tried to keep her voice casual. "What brings you by?"

Her pulse was racing. All she could think was that he'd found her handkerchief. Her knees nearly buckled when he brought a bouquet of wildflowers from behind his back, presenting them with a flourish.

"I haven't seen you since the Fourth of July celebration and wanted to stop by. Looks like I just caught you leaving."

"Um, yes." Her relief over not being confronted about being in his house diminished as she tried to determine if there were any undertones in his words. Did it mean anything that he had specifically mentioned the festivities of the other night?

"I won't take up much of your time." His smile seemed genuine as he handed her the bouquet. "These are accompanied by an invitation to dinner tonight."

"Oh." She took the flowers, gripped the bunched stems hard. Earlier in the week, she had not only declined his invitation to the Independence Day celebration, but also a request to attend church with him.

She knew Bowie wanted her to treat Hobbs as usual if she could manage it. She would try. "Thank you, Tobias. Let me put these in water before I leave."

Hoping he would take the hint that she had no time to visit, she sighed inwardly when he stepped over the threshold. His dark gaze followed her as she moved to the sideboard and found a vase in the cabinet. After pumping some water into the glass container, she arranged the blooms inside.

"Did you enjoy the fireworks the other night?"

"I did." More about that? Forcing a smile, she turned.

"I don't remember seeing you after they were over."

She tensed. Was he merely making a statement or did he know that the reason he hadn't seen her was because she had been behind his house with Bowie? The mild look in his eyes didn't tell her a thing.

"What do you say about dinner?"

Wiping her suddenly sweaty palms surreptitiously on her skirts, she said pleasantly, "Thank you for asking, but I'm courting with someone."

Neither she nor Bowie had told anyone yet, but it wasn't a secret.

Surprise flared in Tobias's dark eyes as he stroked

his neat mustache. "Since Independence Day? This is recent."

"Yes."

"So, it isn't serious yet."

"No." Not yet.

He nodded, walking outside, and stopped at the porch steps.

She followed, nerves fluttering. Trying to act as she normally would, she said, "I heard you were now working at the freight office for Mr. Fitzgerald."

"Yes." He smiled. "I don't like it as well as I liked being marshal, but there's more freedom."

Having been a lawman's wife, Merritt knew that to certainly be true.

"I haven't been called upon in the middle of the night to address a problem." He was certainly handling her refusal with grace. "May I ask who's courting you?"

The man didn't appear threatening or even disgruntled. She and Bowie hadn't agreed to see only each other, but Merritt had no interest in seeing anyone else, especially Hobbs.

"It's Bowie—I mean, Marshal Cahill."

"Ah."

What did that mean? For a second, Tobias's eyes appeared to harden, but she couldn't be sure because he chose that moment to tug his hat lower on his head, shading his eyes.

"I won't give up hope. Maybe one day you will accept my invitation."

He was going to keep asking? She forced a smile. "That's very persistent."

He tipped his hat to her. "Have a good day, Miss Merritt."

"You, too. Thanks again for the flowers." She waited until he had crossed the street and reached Town Square before closing and locking the front door.

She rushed to see Bowie. She'd been plenty nervous about her handkerchief before Hobbs had shown up. Now she was even more so. He had knocked her off balance by showing up at her door. It wasn't only his visit that had her stomach in knots. It was his conversation.

She had gone from being certain that he had her handkerchief to believing he didn't to wondering if he was toying with her. By the time she walked into the marshal's office, her thoughts were a jumbled mess and her composure was frayed.

Closing the door, she glanced back, relieved not to see Hobbs.

"Hey." Bowie rose and stepped out from behind his wide oak desk. Sunlight glinted off his badge.

A light gray shirt stretched across shoulders as wide as the door, and the denims that fit indecently well showed off a flat, hard belly and powerful thighs.

His blue eyes twinkled. "What are you doing here? I just saw you less than an hour ago. Not that I'm complaining."

Anxious and now slightly paranoid, her words rushed out. "I started over here to tell you about my handkerchief, then Lefty wanted to share some news, then Hobbs showed up and I'm afraid he knows."

"Whoa." Bowie's big hands closed over her shoulders. "Slow down, honey, and tell me what's going on."

"I don't mean to act like such a goose. I just—"

She took a deep breath.

"I've lost my handkerchief."

He waited expectantly.

She glanced around his office. "Has anyone turned it in?"

"No."

"I was afraid of that," she said thickly, trying to choke back a fresh swell of panic.

"Merritt." He drew her closer, his steady gaze encouraging her to continue.

She explained about the new handkerchief that she had tucked into the neckline of her new patriotic dress. "I realized yesterday that it was missing and I meant to mention it, but I was worried about Lefty."

"Okay." Bowie remained patient. "I'd like to help you, but I'm not sure how."

"Oh, sorry." Giving herself a mental shake, she said, "The last time I had it was at the Fourth of July celebration and I lost it that night."

"I don't recall seeing it on you when we were behind Hobbs's house." His gaze sharpened. "And you think you lost it there?"

"I don't know! What if I did?"

"Maybe you dropped it in town," he offered reasonably. "It could've blown away."

"I thought of that so I asked around town. No one's seen it. My initials are on it! If Hobbs did find it, he'll know it's mine." She curled her hands into the front of his shirt, resting them on his rock-hard chest. "What if he knows I was in his house?"

One of Bowie's big hands moved to her waist. "You said he showed up at the Morning Glory?"

"Just a bit ago."

"What did he want?"

"He brought me flowers and invited me to dinner."

Irritation flickered across Bowie's rugged features. "So, he was doing the same thing he's been doing since before that night."

"Yes."

"It's hard to tell anything from that. He very well could have your handkerchief and know you were in his house, but his behavior isn't suspicious in and of itself."

"He asked if I had enjoyed the fireworks and mentioned that he hadn't seen me after the display. Why did he only ask about the fireworks? Why didn't he ask me if I enjoyed the entire day?"

She squeezed her eyes shut. "I'm being stupid, aren't I? Trying to tell if there was hidden meaning in his words. I just don't know. I thought about going over to his house—"

"No!" Bowie's hand tightened on her waist.

She petted his chest. "I remembered what you said about that, but I need to know."

"Honey, if Hobbs has found your handkerchief, he's already onto you."

"In which case, he would probably keep it, wait to see if I mentioned it. Wait to see if I might return to his house to look for it."

"That's what I would do."

She sighed. "So, I guess the best thing to do is not let on that I've lost it."

"Or that you suspect he might have it."

"I'll try."

Bowie's gaze searched her face. "I hope you didn't accept his invitation to dinner."

"No." She rolled her eyes. "I told him you and I were courting."

Bowie chuckled. "I bet he didn't like that."

"He assumed things between us weren't serious since they are so new and said that he hoped one day I would accept his invitations."

"He's not giving up."

"It doesn't appear so." She toyed with a button on the placket of Bowie's shirt. "You probably think I'm a goose for being so upset."

"No." He smoothed his thumb over the furrow between her brows. "I just don't want you to worry."

"But what if he—"

Bowie stopped her with a finger on her lips. "I'll see if I can find out anything."

"Thank you. Again."

Eyes twinkling, he pointed to his mouth. "Shouldn't you be thanking me on this spot right here?"

She laughed and brushed a kiss against his firm, warm lips. Knowing they both had work to get on with, she left, giving him one last smile before walking down the jailhouse steps.

Thanks to him, she no longer felt the edge of panic, but worry still niggled at her. And she couldn't shake it.

Bowie had tried to reassure Merritt about her handkerchief, but he wasn't sure he had. So in the week since she had told him she feared she had lost it at Hobbs's house, Bowie had secretly searched the man's house and the freight office where he worked.

There had been no sign of the handkerchief. Bowie didn't like Merritt worrying about it, but so far he hadn't been able to alleviate that for her.

He also hadn't had any luck tracking down Saul. Describing the outlaw's bay that was missing its left ear had drawn only blank stares from people. Bowie had also questioned Lefty to see if the older man might have seen Saul or his horse around the Morning Glory or while he'd been holed up at Phantom Springs. The older man hadn't been able to help, either.

Bowie was taking Merritt to dinner tonight, the second time in a week. While surveilling her, now as much to find Saul as to keep an eye on Hobbs, he had seen the ex-marshal visit Merritt three times.

He would bring some geegaw or ask her to accompany him to church or to take a walk with him around Town Square. Though she always protested the gifts, she ended up keeping them out of politeness, but she didn't accept any of his invitations. She spent a lot of her free time with Bowie.

So far, his suggestion that they take things slow was working out very well. He was a lawman and he was going to stay a lawman. He and Merritt were being smart. This gave her a chance to see if she could accept his job and to judge whether Bowie showed the same tendencies as her late husband.

After dinner at Steven's Restaurant, Bowie rented a buggy and drove them out to Phantom Springs where the hot July air was slightly cooler next to the water. He found a spot beneath a thick sprawling oak tree near the small pool formed around the rocks where the water bubbled up from the ground.

He had been looking forward to this—and Merritt—all day. She looked fresh and cool in a green-and-white-striped dress that sleeked over her full breasts and down to her tiny waist. Her hair was pulled into a loose ponytail that draped over one shoulder, revealing the elegant line of her neck and one dainty earlobe. Sunlight glittered on the water, painting her fair skin and dark hair a soft gold.

She walked to the edge of the water, then sent a sweet smile Bowie's way. "I love it here."

"It's one of my favorite places, too." He snapped open the quilt he'd brought and spread it on the thick grass beneath the shade tree.

He offered his hand and she took it, sinking gracefully to the blanket. She folded her legs to the side, causing her lightweight skirts to billow around her. Bowie shifted his holster and sat down next to her.

"We made it just in time to see the sunset," he said, pointing at the sun as it descended below the horizon. He relaxed against her, his forearm occasionally brushing her leg.

The water whispered around them, turning into a sheet of gold as the sun went down. He turned his attention to the scene in front of him. A burst of red and gold melted into the hillside beyond and washed the landscape in a fiery orange before disappearing to leave everything a soft gray.

Dusk settled over the land. Silver light etched Merritt's profile and Bowie admired the fine-grained texture of her skin. "I've looked for your missing handkerchief at Hobbs's house and the freight office."

She turned to him with a hopeful look on her face.

"I'm sorry to say I didn't find it."

Despite her obvious disappointment, she smiled warmly. "Thank you for trying. I appreciate it."

"I wish I had better news." He would dearly love to put that worry out of her head.

"Maybe you were right. I dropped it and it blew away."

Bowie knew she didn't believe that. He didn't, either, and would keep looking.

She shifted her attention to the water, now a ripple of silver in the dusky light. He studied her, taken with the way the light glided over her delicate features.

She reached over and put a hand on his thigh. "Look."

He followed her gaze to the water where the light appeared to dance on the surface.

"It looks like stars on the water," she said softly.

It did, but Bowie was more interested in watching her. As the glittering spots faded, he eased back on his elbows, wondering how long it would take to undo the line of buttons down her back. "How long were you married?"

She glanced over her shoulder, looking curious. "Six years. And I've been widowed for three, though I haven't lived here quite that long."

"What made you choose Cahill Crossing?"

"I wanted a fresh start and I'd heard about this new town that was growing in lush hill country. I thought I'd be able to make a place for myself here." She looked thoughtful for a moment. "Plus I felt lonely in Austin."

She didn't say so, but Bowie thought she'd felt lonely there even while her husband had been alive. He took her hand, playing with her fingers, and she smiled, putting a kick in his blood.

The night pulsed around them, ripe with the fragrance of trees and Merritt's fresh scent. Bowie wanted to kiss her. Get his hands on her.

She rearranged her skirts. "Have you heard from your sister again?"

"No, but I sent word to Quin that she's coming home. The telegraph office in Dodge City will hold the wire until he arrives, if he hasn't already."

"Have you had any contact with him since he and Addie left the 4C?"

"No."

She turned to face Bowie. "You know why I came to Ca-Cross. May I ask why you left?"

He toyed with her index finger. "Because of Clea. I thought I told you." He knew he had, just not everything.

"Is she the reason you didn't stay after your parents were killed?"

He snorted. "No, she was long gone by then. Ran off with some rich man's son."

"After I lost Seth, I wanted my family around me. Didn't you feel that way after Earl and Ruby died?"

He never talked about why he had returned to White Tail after his folks were put in the ground. Never had. For some reason, he didn't mind telling Merritt. He just couldn't seem to pull the trigger and get started.

Silence stretched between them and she slipped her

hand from his to curl over his knee. "Never mind. I shouldn't have pried."

"It's not that I don't want to tell you. I'm a little buffaloed that I *do* want to tell you, but I don't like talking about it because I was a jackass."

He sat up, covering her hand with his where it rested on his thigh. "When my folks were killed, Ace had left the position and I was the new marshal in White Tail. Ma and Pa were headed to Wolf Grove for the announcement that our family had sold land for the railroad and that a new town would be named after us."

Bowie shook his head, recalling the disappointment on his father's face when his second son had left the 4C to pin on a badge. "Pa never wanted me to be a lawman, and when he and Ma asked me to meet them in Wolf Grove, I couldn't face his disapproval again. I told them I had a dangerous prisoner I couldn't leave. That was true, but my deputy would've been able to guard that man just fine. I just didn't want to turn over any part of my job. And I didn't really want to see my pa."

He stared at the water bubbling out of the ground. Merritt slid her arm through his.

"Do you blame yourself for their deaths? Is that why you didn't stay after they were killed?"

"I *was* to blame. We all felt at fault for it, for one reason or another. Not one of us accepted their request to meet them. We were all off doing something else."

Merritt didn't say anything, just sat there waiting. Listening.

"The day of the funeral, after we'd buried them, Quin started issuing orders, assigning responsibilities for the 4C to each of us. I already had a job. I wasn't taking on another one, especially if it meant I would have to resign a position I'd worked hard for.

"It felt like Quin was trying to take Pa's place and it set me off like a stick of dynamite. I lost my temper, went after Quin. Annie stopped our fight before we did each other any serious damage, but she and Chance weren't any more willing to stay under Quin's thumb than I was."

Merritt gave his leg a comforting pat that also shot heat through him. He laced his fingers with hers. "We all scattered like buckshot. Looking back, I can see now that my brother was just trying to put some order back in our world, keep our family together."

"Have you told him that?"

Bowie shook his head.

"Maybe y'all can put your family back together. You're here and Annie soon will be. Do you want to patch things up with Quin?"

Bowie hesitated. "Yeah, but I said some things. I don't know if he can forgive me. Or if Chance and Annie can."

"Can you forgive them?"

"Yes."

"You should try to work it out. The only family y'all have left is one another. Don't walk away from that."

He looked down at her, surprised at the shimmer of tears in her eyes. Maybe that was why she felt so loyal to Saul. The man, outlaw or not, was like a brother to her.

Bowie's heart felt too big for his chest. Had he ever felt a connection this strong to Clea, for any reason? No.

He shifted so he could pick Merritt up and put her in his lap.

She laughed softly. "What are you doing?"

"Wanted you closer." He settled his mouth on hers.

She immediately put her arms around his neck, her breasts pressing into his chest. The feel of her against his arousal had his entire body going hard. A savage desire burned through him.

She melted into him and he took the kiss deeper, caught up in the soft stroke of her tongue against his, her sweet scent, the way she moved restlessly against him. Aching, he slid one hand into the silky cloud of her hair and cradled her head, bringing her closer. Holding her so tight he could feel the hooks of her stays through his shirt.

Nuzzling her neck, he breathed in the fresh soap fragrance of her skin, wanting to feel her bare flesh next to his. He cupped her ankle, but before he could move his hand up her thigh, a crackle sounded above them.

The noise pulled him out of his sensory fog. He lifted his head, breathing hard, struggling to focus. Looking up, he realized he had heard a squirrel or bird in the tree's branches.

The interruption served to remind Bowie where they were. This wasn't the place for what he wanted to do with her. Anyone could ride up. When he finally got Merritt beneath him, he didn't want the threat of an interruption hanging over them.

"We'd better stop," he murmured against her neck.

"Yes." The breathy word made it very difficult to put

her away from him, steady her on her feet and stand, but he did.

She folded the blanket, storing it under the buggy seat before Bowie handed her in. He climbed in beside her and clucked to the mare. The buggy lurched into motion, causing Merritt to slide against him. He liked the feel of her so close.

"Thanks for telling me what happened between you and your siblings. I imagine it wasn't easy."

"You're welcome." He took her hand, thinking how pretty she looked with the moonlight skimming her delicate features, turning her eyes to dark, mysterious pools.

The short ride back to town was made in comfortable silence. Just as they reached the wild north edge of town, Bowie reined up.

"What—"

He curved a hand around her neck and pulled her to him for a kiss.

When he drew away, they were both breathing hard. Her eyes were deep and soft with desire. Her mouth was wet from his, her loosely bound hair slightly mussed from his hand.

Anyone who saw her would know she'd been kissed. He wanted them to know she'd been kissed by him. She belonged to *him*.

The thought stunned him so much that it took him a moment to register the sounds of raucous laughter and voices coming from town followed by the crash of breaking glass.

Merritt's eyes widened. "What is going on over there?"

"There's no telling." He groaned, brushing a kiss across her hair. "I'm going to have to deal with that ruckus."

He flicked the reins against the horse's rump, the fog of desire clearing now.

He chose to drive around town rather than through it to reach the boardinghouse. Was it too much to ask that people keep the peace for longer than a day? He would have liked to have spent an entire evening with Merritt.

For the first time in his life, Bowie resented his job, resented having to leave a woman for some kind of tomfoolery.

That pulled him up short. Since when had he ever begrudged his job?

He'd been telling himself he was in control of his feelings, controlling the pace of his relationship with Merritt, both of them taking their time to figure out if things might work out between them. Control was the last thing he felt.

He had barely recovered from the shock of telling her everything he had told her about his family, and now this.

Something big and hot unfurled in his chest and he couldn't get a full breath. Whoa.

That was when Bowie knew he had raced way past cautious and straight into head over heels. It scared the hell out of him.

Chapter Eleven

The time Merritt and Bowie had spent at Phantom Springs changed things between them. She felt closer to him than she'd ever felt to anyone, including Seth. Bowie sharing with her the painful rift between him and his siblings had touched her deeply.

When he had expressed his regret over letting his sister down, Merritt had given that more weight than she should have. This time was different, not based on a feeling, but on the fact that he continued to tell her things. In particular, he talked about how he had felt the first time he had pinned on a badge. For once in his life, he had stepped out of his older brother's shadow. Been his own man.

Merritt shared with him, too. About how Saul had come to live with her family and how hurt she and her parents had been when his reckless behavior had escalated into crime.

As much as Bowie shared, there were plenty of times

that he didn't. At those times, it seemed as if something bothered him. She didn't press him to talk about it, though she wished he would.

The man was also distracted, thanks to the badge he wore. She had come to see that he was so intense and driven about his job because he was investigating his parents' murders. It was personal. How could he not be completely focused on this case?

He was dedicated to his job as a lawman. There was no denying that and he was good at it. Still, he spent time with her every night, made time for them. She appreciated it.

In the days that followed their outing to Phantom Springs, he took her to other places. To Wolf Grove to attend a horse race, out to the 4C to show her the sprawling ranch nestled between two of the three water sources that formed Triple Creek.

What meant the most to her was the time they spent talking on the front porch after Lefty and Mr. Wilson had retired for the night.

Ten days after her evening with Bowie at the springs, Merritt fixed lunch for just Lefty and her. She hadn't seen Bowie since breakfast that morning and Mr. Wilson had left an hour ago, telling her he likely wouldn't make lunch or supper.

He was going out to the Fitzgerald ranch to write an article about yet another piece of land the wealthy rancher had bought. Don Fitzgerald seemed determined to let people know each time he increased his already-vast holdings.

Lefty cleaned his plate, then reached for another

piece of ham. "Mr. Wilson and Bo sure missed another fine meal."

"Thank you."

"I like the marshal. He's a good man."

Merritt nodded, sipping at a glass of lemonade she'd made that morning.

"It meant a lot that he gave me the benefit of the doubt when I offered that information on Hobbs. Especially since I wasn't sure if I'd really heard it or if I had dreamed it."

"I like that about him, too," she said.

The older man studied her. "There's something different about you."

She lifted a hand to her hair, swept up into a high chignon. "Like what?"

"Nothing like that. You're as pretty as a picture." The older man chuckled. "It's nothing I can put my finger on. Since you and the marshal found me at Phantom Springs, I've noticed y'all have been spending a lot more time together."

"We have." Merritt couldn't stop a smile.

"I'm right glad you sent Hobbs packing."

"I didn't. He finally asked if I would ever accept any of his invitations and I said no."

She hadn't needed to explain that it was because she had fallen for Bowie. She could tell by the look in the former marshal's eyes that he knew.

"I'm glad," Lefty said.

She was, too. Although Hobbs had persistently invited her out, he hadn't been obnoxious and yet his visits put her on edge. Always stirred up her worry about her missing handkerchief.

She turned her attention to her friend. "How is your job?"

"Going well." He looked down at the table, saying quietly, "I sent a telegram to my wife."

Proud of him, she squeezed his hand. "And?"

"She wants me to come home," he said hoarsely. "See if we can put things back together."

The thickness in his voice had tears stinging Merritt's eyes. "Oh, Lefty, I'm so glad."

She leaned over to hug him. "Will you go?"

"Yes, ma'am."

"Wonderful! When?"

"At the end of the week. I told Mr. Stokes I'd stay as long as he wanted, but he said the end of the week was fine." He glanced at the mantel clock on the sideboard. "And I'd better get back to it."

Merritt rose when he did. "You let me know if I can do anything to help you."

He nodded and started for the kitchen doorway, then stopped. "If things work out with my wife, I plan to bring her here to meet you. I think you probably saved my life, Miss Merritt."

Her vision blurred. "I don't know about that."

"Which won't be worth a plug nickle if I'm late to the store."

She smiled at his attempt to lighten the moment and said goodbye.

Once she had cleaned up the dishes from lunch, she sat down again at the dining table with her sewing basket and a stack of items that needed to be mended. This room had the best light and she was in the path of any breeze that blew through her open bedroom window and the kitchen's screened door.

Mending was a chore she didn't enjoy, but it was part of the service she offered to her boarders. Since her current boarders were bachelors, they had all requested it.

Lefty's news had put a smile on her face. Thoughts of him were joined by thoughts of Bowie and she moved rapidly from one garment to the next.

Some minutes later, she became aware of sweat dampening her bodice and hands. She used her apron to blot her face and hands, realizing there was no breeze blowing through the house.

She rose, moving to the kitchen doorway to make sure the outside door was open to allow air through the screened door. It was. Turning, she walked past the dining table to her bedroom to check the window. Ah, it was closed.

She hurried over to open it, and saw a piece of paper stuck between the frame and window. It had to be from Saul. She lifted the sash, immediately identifying his signature sketch of her profile.

The note said he needed to see her and would come to the boardinghouse tonight after dark. He didn't want her driving out somewhere to meet him this time. To indicate if it was safe for him, he asked that she put a lit lantern on the back stoop.

Relieved, she refolded the message. After their last meeting outside the kitchen, Merritt hadn't known if she would see him again. Bowie had interrupted them before she had secured that promise from her foster brother.

She had promised Bowie she would contact him the

next time she heard from Saul. She didn't know how her foster brother would react if the marshal was present when he arrived, but it was best that Bowie be there.

Slipping the piece of paper into her skirt pocket, she hurried to the jail, but when she arrived, she discovered a sign hanging on the door: Back Later.

She went through town asking if anyone had seen him. Henry Stokes said that Bowie had been at the general store investigating a report of stolen goods. While there, he had received a telegram, but Mr. Stokes didn't know where the marshal had gone when he'd left.

Ace Keating might. Merritt stopped at the saddle and boot shop to ask him if he knew where Bowie might be. Ace said his friend had ridden out to the 4C, but hadn't said when he would return.

She thanked the saddle maker and made her way back to the Morning Glory. The locomotive whistle sounded, signaling the arrival of the daily train. She hoped Bowie would return by the time Saul showed up because she wasn't going to ask her foster brother to come back another time. She was afraid he might not.

Bowie hadn't expected to ever fall for Merritt, but he had and his realization about his feelings for her spun him like a top.

At first, he flat didn't know what to do so he had been glad that his responsibilities as a marshal had put some distance between them.

It hadn't been anything overt and nothing he had tried to do on his own. Different things had needed his attention and he'd been relieved to have some space from Merritt.

Although, if he had thought that would make him think about her less, *want* her less, he'd been dead wrong. His relief had lasted about two days. He missed seeing her, being with her. For the life of him, he couldn't make himself stay away from her. Or stop himself from kissing her when he had the chance.

With his schedule and people around so often, kissing was all Bowie could do and he wanted to do a damn sight more. Shucking her right out of her clothes would be a good start.

The night he'd had her all to himself at Phantom Springs seemed more like months ago than days. Bowie worked hard to keep his mind occupied with something besides her. Which was only one reason he was grateful to get a telegram one afternoon ten days after the evening they had spent completely alone. Quin and Addie were in Wolf Grove and headed home.

After following up on a report from the general store of stolen goods that hadn't been stolen at all, only stored in a place Stokes usually didn't store them, Bowie headed to the 4C.

As he reached the top of the hill where the family's stone-and-timber home sat, he spied Quin's unsaddled bloodred bay, Cactus, roaming around one of the corrals behind the house.

Bowie reined up just as his brother and sister-in-law came out of the house, looking tired and dusty.

Quin frowned. "Didn't mean for you to ride out here. Just wanted you to know we were home."

Bowie's chest tightened. Maybe Quin didn't want him here. Too bad. "Got a lot to tell you."

He dismounted and looped his reins over the hitching post.

As soon as he stepped onto the wide porch of the three-story structure, Addie hugged him. "Sorry I smell like dirt and horses."

He awkwardly patted her back. "You still smell better than any cowhand I've ridden with."

She laughed and stepped aside as Quin came forward. As Bowie shook his brother's hand, the other man's gaze lit on his badge.

Something flickered in Quin's eyes before they turned hard. "What's this? You going back to White Tail?"

"Nope." He wasn't sure how his brother would take this. "I'm Ca-Cross's new marshal."

Addie clapped. "Good! I'm glad to get Hobbs out of there, especially after he falsely arrested Quin."

Quin's face held no expression. "I knew the election was coming up, but what made you run for marshal?"

He explained how several of the men in town, including Ace, had come to him and asked. "I didn't think I'd win, but I did."

"Hmm."

Bowie couldn't tell if Quin liked it or not. Well, he'd have to get used to it. "I figured having a badge couldn't hurt the investigation."

"True." The other man studied him thoughtfully. "This means you're staying at least four years."

"Yes." Bowie tensed, wondering what his brother would say.

All he got was another, "Hmm."

Addie slipped her arm through Bowie's and half

dragged him inside. He looked helplessly over his shoulder and Quin grinned.

"Let's go in and have a seat in the parlor," Addie said. "Elda, my cook, is making dinner."

"It's worth staying for," Quin added.

"You don't have to twist my arm. She fed me a couple of times while you were gone."

"You were out here?" Quin's gray eyes darkened.

Bowie shifted, his neck burning. He hadn't meant to mention that. "Just checking on things."

His brother's face lightened, but he said nothing.

As the three of them walked into the parlor, Addie released him. Bowie took off his hat. In the extra living area across the hall, he saw the mounted longhorn head above the mantel.

He claimed a seat on the big couch in the parlor. Quin eased down into Pa's big leather chair and Addie perched on its arm. Memories of the last time he had been in this room with his siblings pricked at Bowie like arrows.

After a heated exchange, Bowie had charged Quin, who had knocked him into the chair where he now sat. He remembered what Merritt had said about forgiveness and not turning away from family. He dragged a hand across his nape.

His brother might have been remembering, too. His gaze went to the hand that still carried a scar from being cut that day by Ma's broken porcelain bowl. "You said you had a lot to tell."

Bowie blew out a breath. Placing his hat beside him on the couch, he leaned forward, resting his elbows on his knees. Where to start? With something positive.

"Annie got your telegram about Ma and Pa, and she's coming home. She sent a reply, but since you were gone, it was delivered to me."

"Good." Relief was evident in Quin's voice.

Addie reached down and took her husband's hand.

"Any word from Chance?" Quin asked.

"Not yet." Bowie wondered if his baby brother would even return when he learned their parents had been victims of murder and not a wagon accident. He hoped so.

"Are you convinced Ma and Pa were murdered?"

"Yes." Bowie's voice hardened. "As sure as hell's hot."

The other man's eyes glittered. "What have you found out?"

"The biggest thing is that Hobbs has known it was murder since it happened. In fact, he hired the three men who did it."

"I'll kill that bastard," his brother said in a quiet, deadly serious voice.

Addie leaned forward. "How do you know Hobbs was involved, Bowie?"

"Lefty Gorman."

"Lefty." Her jaw dropped.

Quin looked just as stunned. "He's usually liquored up."

"I know. Even he wasn't sure if he'd heard it or dreamed it, but he told me, anyway, and he was right about it." Bowie explained how the older man had overheard the ex-marshal outside the jail one night telling someone that there was a third party who knew the Cahills had been murdered.

"I confronted Hobbs, but didn't tell him where I'd gotten the information."

Rage vibrated from Quin. "And he denied everything."

"Guts, feathers, beak and all. But later Hobbs's involvement was confirmed by one of the men who was present when Ma and Pa were killed."

"Confirmed how? Did you catch him?" Addie asked.

"I hope you killed all three of them," Quin growled.

"Two of them are dead. Vernon Pettit, who was the man you were accused of killing. And Huck Allen, the man who told you that what happened to Ma and Pa went deeper than we knew."

"Huck Allen," Addie repeated. "That's the name of the low-down snake who used me like a shield? The one Quin killed at Triple Creek trying to protect me?"

"Yes."

"So, who's the other hood-wearing coward who got away at Triple Creek and killed your parents?"

"I'm not sure if they're the same man, but I'm starting to think so." Something he wouldn't share with Merritt just yet. "A man named Saul Bream was the third man present at Ghost Canyon where Ma and Pa died, and he's the one who confirmed that Hobbs was involved in the murders."

Bowie took a deep breath. Might as well just get it out now. "Bream also happens to be Merritt's foster brother."

Addie's green eyes grew huge.

"Merritt?" Quin rapped out.

Bowie grimaced. "I told you there was a lot."

Quin shook his head as if to clear it.

"Bream came to her with the information, saying he and Allen had been hired by Pettit to rob the Cahills. Their job was to stop the wagon. When they did, Pettit ran it off the road."

"Into Ghost Canyon."

"Pa was finished off with a rifle butt."

Quin's jaw looked tight enough to snap clean in two. "So, why haven't you arrested this Bream bastard?"

"I can't find him, but he's in touch with Merritt. She's talked to him twice. She promised to let me know if he contacts her again."

His brother stared at him as if he were a half-wit. Yes, Bowie realized how weak-kneed it made him sound that he was willing to wait for Merritt to let him know when she next spoke to her foster brother.

At his second mention of her friend's name, Addie's eyes burned with blatant curiosity.

Quin stood. "I suppose she's just going to turn her foster brother over to you out of the goodness of her heart?"

"No. She knows it's the right thing to do." And he believed she would do it, though he hadn't been completely sure until this past week.

"That doesn't mean she will."

"True. But she's the one who gave me the confirmation about Hobbs in the first place. If she were going to hide Bream or his part in this, she wouldn't have come to me at all."

"I guess so," Quin said grudgingly.

"So." Addie's deep green gaze fixed on Bowie like a dog on point. "How much has Merritt been helping you?"

"Not that much. I don't want her involved even as much as she has been."

A broad knowing smile spread across his sister-in-law's face as if she had just caught him with his hand in the cookie jar.

"Well, hell, man," Quin barked. "How involved is she?"

Bowie pinched the bridge of his nose, recalling how he hadn't been able to pry Saul's last name out of her. How he had caught her breaking into the ex-marshal's house to help her foster brother. "She's in the thick of it."

"Who else?" Quin planted his hands on his hips. "The whole town?"

"No."

"Are you courting her?" Addie asked with what Bowie was coming to recognize as characteristic bluntness.

"We've…become friends." And more. But he was keeping that to himself for now.

She grinned as Quin's gaze swung from Bowie to her, then back to Bowie. Quin frowned. "You really think Merritt will hear from Bream again?"

"Yes."

"And tell you about it?"

"Yes." Bowie got to his feet as a roly-poly woman with red hair stuck her head around the door.

"Supper's ready, Addie. Hello, Mr. Bowie. Nice to see you again."

"You, too, Elda. I'm looking forward to the meal."

"Good thing I made plenty." She chuckled as she

disappeared from sight. "Got enough for you and that bottomless pit of a brother."

Bowie grinned.

"We'll be right in," Addie called after the woman.

Quin rubbed a hand down his face, looking haggard as he spoke to Bowie. "Will we?"

"Yes. I'm starving." He joined his brother and sister-in-law and walked with them to the large dining room.

"Anything else we need to know?" Quin put a hand on the small of his wife's back to let her precede him.

"Well, I moved Purvis and Fields to Wolf Grove. The day after I won the election, I was bombarded with threats on their lives. A lot of people were het up over the trouble they caused y'all."

"Wolf Grove sounds like the best place for them," Addie said, moving to the long dining table. "I've thought about doing them harm myself."

Was she serious? Bowie thought she might be. He glanced at Quin, who nodded over his wife's head at Bowie.

Supper passed quickly and Bowie lingered afterward, talking to Quin and getting to know his feisty sister-in-law.

He'd missed suppertime at the Morning Glory. He hoped Merritt would still be awake when he returned to the boardinghouse. It was well after dark when he took his leave of the 4C.

Quin and Addie walked out with him. The lantern burning on the porch provided enough light for Bowie to see to unloop Midnight's reins from the hitching post and swing into the saddle.

"Bo?" Quin's voice rumbled from the porch.

He looked up to see his brother standing behind Addie with his arms wrapped around her. Quin looked ridiculously smitten until Addie elbowed him in the stomach and nodded her head toward Bowie.

Quin grimaced, stepping to the edge of the porch and saying gruffly, "Glad you're home."

Bowie nearly swallowed his teeth. Before he could recover from that, his brother added, "You're a good lawman, Bo. You've learned things I probably never would have."

"Thanks," he said faintly. Quin was trying. Bowie could do the same. He wanted to apologize for what he'd said to his brother the day they had buried their parents, but he saw the same apology in Quin's eyes so all Bowie said was, "I'm glad I'm home, too."

Blowing out a breath, Addie threw up her hands, giving both men a look. "That's it? Aren't you going to hug or something?"

"No!" they exclaimed in unison.

She rolled her eyes. "Men."

Bowie grinned. "Thanks for supper, Addie. And thank Elda again for me."

He urged his horse into motion.

"Come for supper on Friday night," his sister-in-law called out. "And bring Merritt."

"I'll ask her." Addie had obviously guessed there was something between him and his landlady.

"Good." His sister-in-law sounded pleased.

He heard his brother ask, "Why did you tell Bowie to invite Merritt to supper?"

"Oh, Quin," Addie said in exasperation. "Because he likes her."

Chuckling, Bowie rode off. He was a good half mile from the house before he realized he was grinning like a fool. Maybe because he and his brother had put things right, or at least started to. He hoped they could do the same with Annie and Chance.

And maybe, Bowie admitted, a big part of his good humor was because he was crazy about Merritt Dixon. No sense lying to himself anymore.

A fat white moon poured light across the hilly landscape, providing a clear view. Bowie kneed Midnight into a gallop, anxious to get home and see if Merritt was still up.

Chapter Twelve

"I've been thinking about what you said, about talking to the marshal."

"I think you'll be glad," Merritt said to her foster brother. "Bowie's fair. He can help you."

Saul had climbed through her bedroom window moments ago and now stood to the side, his back pressed against the wall. In the flickering light of her lamp, she could almost see the nervous energy radiating through the rangy lines of his body.

He eyed her speculatively. "You keep calling him by his first name."

"Yes." She still wasn't sure it was a good idea to tell Saul she was involved with the lawman. And certainly not that he was living in her house.

Bowie hadn't returned from the 4C, but she hoped he would before Saul left.

"Last night, I saw you on the porch with a man wearing a badge," her foster brother said. "You're courting, aren't you? Is that why you're trying to get me to turn myself in?"

"I'm doing that for you, you oaf. You'd be safer if you surrendered."

"What about your vow never to get involved with another lawman?"

"He's different."

Saul barely lifted the curtain and shifted his gaze, searching the darkness.

"Do you think someone's following you?" Merritt asked.

He shook his head. "Just making sure."

Seconds ticked by. She didn't say anything, hoping Saul was considering her suggestion that he turn himself in or at least talk to Bowie.

"You said if I helped Cahill nab Hobbs, he might help me out. Do you really think so? He wouldn't shoot me on sight?"

"I've gotten to know him and he's fair. You'd be safe."

"Do I have you to thank for that?"

"No." Something didn't feel right. "He knows who you are and he hasn't sent a posse after you."

"How does he know who I am?"

"When you told me that you knew Hobbs was involved in the Cahills' murders, I told Bowie. He wanted your name, and when I wouldn't give it to him, he talked to a couple of my friends. All they knew was that I had a foster brother named Saul. That led to him sending a wire to Mama and Papa asking about you."

Disbelief widened Saul's eyes. "And they told him?"

"All they could give him was your last name since

none of us have seen you for the past two years. Besides, that's the least of your worries. What you've done is wrong and you know it."

He stayed in his place next to the window. "And you still think he would go easier on me?"

"He wants Hobbs, and putting him behind bars would definitely be better for you, too. Otherwise, he'll always be a threat." If Saul talked to the marshal, he wouldn't have to keep looking over his shoulder. "If you help Bowie expose Ca-Cross's former marshal, I know he would do everything he could to help you."

"What does that mean? Keep me alive?"

"It might," she answered soberly. "Bowie knows everything you've done and he has told me he's willing to talk to you. He wants whatever information you can give him on Hobbs."

Saul scratched his head, eyeing her speculatively. "I haven't told you everything."

She went still inside, dread slicking up her spine. "What else is there?"

He snuck another look out the window and her patience stretched thin. "Saul!"

Shifting his attention back to her, he leaned his head against the wall. "That Cahill fella who was shot a month or two ago?"

"Quin?"

Saul nodded. "Huck and I sent him a note, telling him if he gave us two thousand dollars, we would tell him the truth about his parents. That they were murdered."

It took a few seconds for his words to sink in. "That's extortion!"

"We needed the money," he defended.

"Heaven forbid you get an honest job!" She thought of Lefty, who had more understandable reasons for turning to crime and hadn't done so.

He laughed shortly. "I almost didn't get the money. His woman showed up instead of him and all hell broke loose."

"Addie was there?"

"Yes. If she had just stayed out of it, tossed down the money and ridden away, nobody would've gotten hurt, but she didn't. Then before we could grab the money, Cahill arrived, guns blazing."

"You shot Quin!" Anger burned through her.

"It wasn't me. Huck shot Cahill, then Cahill killed Huck!"

"It could've been you who was killed, Saul. And you could've gotten Addie killed."

"That wildcat did just fine," he muttered, thrusting his left arm toward her. "She cut me good."

"In self-defense!" Merritt barely glanced at the healing scar on his forearm. Her chest ached as though she had been slammed into a wall. "I'm surprised there isn't a wanted poster out on you."

"They couldn't see my face. I wore a hood."

"What else?" she demanded.

"That's all, I swear."

She didn't know whether to believe him. Not anymore. Not now that she realized just how far he had crossed the line.

"So, now that you know all of that, do you still think the marshal will help me out, if I help him?"

His words ripped at something deep inside her. For the first time, she looked at her foster brother without the veil of their past and she hated what she saw. He had no remorse. None.

He was more worried about what might happen to him rather than what he'd done or the people he had hurt. If he was sorry at all, it was because he might have to suffer the consequences of his actions.

In a flash of blinding, painful clarity, Merritt realized the only reason her foster brother was telling her this was because he was hoping she would put in a good word for him with Bowie. "You don't even care that you've done wrong."

How long had Saul been more bad than good? Why hadn't she seen it?

Because she had wanted to believe her foster brother would change. But he never did. Two years ago, he and his outlaw friends had been involved in the Cahills' murders, then they had gone to prison for robbing a train. When Saul got out of prison, he hadn't come home or tried to find Merritt. He had taken right back up with those same men.

She was done looking the other way for her foster brother. Tears stung her eyes. "I can't believe all the things you've done."

What if there was more? What if he still wasn't telling her the whole truth about everything?

Enraged, her voice hardened. "I want you to surrender, put yourself in Bowie's custody."

Saul pushed away from the wall. "I'm not doing that!"

"If you don't, I'll tell him everything myself."

"You would turn me in?"

She ignored the hurt in his voice. "You've broken

the law. Maybe done murder, almost killed two other people. You can't get away with that!"

"I came here to talk to *you* about this, Merritt. Getting that marshal involved was all your idea."

"You said you came to talk about meeting with Bowie. That was a lie. You didn't come because you were sorry for what you've done. You wanted to find out if I would put in a good word for you with him."

Raw hurt slashed at her. "Why do you do things like this? *How* can you do them?"

He searched her face and what he saw had him backing toward the window. "I've never seen you so mad."

"I never knew until now just how far past the law you'd gone." Suddenly, she saw how foolish she had been to believe in him when he had no intention of changing. She was so mad, her entire body burned.

Saul's eyes hardened into a flat meanness she had never seen before. "If you're going to be this unforgiving, I can just imagine how the marshal will be."

"Oh, he'll be much more forgiving than I am."

Saul cursed and scrambled out the window, one boot hitting the frame.

She rushed to the window in time to see him vault onto the back of his horse and ride away. Betrayal, then fury, squeezed her chest until she could barely breathe. The blood rushed in her ears.

She had offered him numerous chances to turn himself in, to let Bowie help him, but he hadn't wanted to do it.

Well, if he wouldn't go to Bowie, she would. It was time for Saul to pay for what he'd done.

Wrenching open her bedroom door, she immediately

noticed the darkness of the house. The lamp she had left burning at the bottom of the stairs was out, probably thanks to Mr. Wilson or Lefty when they had retired for the night.

She grabbed the one from the table at the head of her bed and marched across the dining area, forcing herself to tread lightly on the stairs so as not to wake up the two older gentlemen.

She hadn't heard Bowie come in, but she had been so angry at Saul, she doubted she would've heard anything shy of a twister ripping through the house.

Just thinking about her foster brother brought a fresh surge of anger. She reached the top of the stairs and turned right, walking softly past Mr. Wilson's bedroom to Bowie's at the end of the hall.

Stopping in front of his room, she knocked softly. When there was no answer, she tried the porcelain knob. The door was locked. If he was here, he must be asleep.

Wrenching disappointment drove her temper higher. She needed him!

Whirling to leave, she stopped short as he rounded the stair railing and came toward her. Immediately, relief threaded through her anger.

The play of lamplight across his strong arms and shoulders made him seem even bigger, broader. He moved with a slow predatory grace that had her heart thudding hard. Impatient, trying to rein in her anger, she waited for him to reach her.

Her gaze moved over his wide chest to the gun belt slung low on his hips. She absently noted that he carried his boots in one hand. His socks glowed in the shadowy light.

He reached her, holding up his boots. "Tried to be quiet. I was hoping you'd still be up."

"Ace said you went out to the 4C." Her voice was tight, the words pinched. "Is everything okay?"

"Yes. Quin and Addie are home."

She caught the tang of his shaving soap, his dark male scent tinged with a hint of sweat and salt. "How did things go between you and your brother?"

"Good. They were good."

"I'm glad." She truly was, but it was all she could do to contain her outrage.

Bowie stepped closer, frowning. His gaze, silver in the dusky light, searched her face. "What's going on? Is everything okay? Are you hurt?"

His gaze slid down her body, then back up, sparking a different kind of heat. "I'm fine. Just…mad."

The word seemed inadequate for the molten pulsing of her blood.

Bowie dug into his trousers pocket for his key and unlocked the door, nudging her inside.

He set his boots on the floor, watching her carefully. Leashed tension coiled in her body, and her normally soft features were cold and unyielding. She was furious, but also…hurt?

She paced to the opposite wall, the light from her lamp washing his room in amber. "Saul was here!"

Bowie tensed. She'd said she was all right. She *looked* all right, so he relaxed slightly. Still, he didn't like how easily her foster brother could get within arm's reach of her. She might not fear the man, but he was a threat. To her and to Bowie's family.

As she marched back in his direction, he noticed that

she was shaking. The lamp wobbled in her hold. When she reached him, he barely managed to extricate the burning light before she stalked back across the room. He set it atop the dresser to his left.

"I thought I'd convinced him to come talk to you." Restless energy vibrated from her petite frame. "When he got here, he said he'd been thinking about it."

Bowie gathered Saul had changed his mind. Before he could ask, she spun and headed back toward him, her shoes making a soft scuffing sound on the floor. "He wanted to know if I believed you would really listen to him or just throw him in jail. I said of course you would listen!"

Bowie palmed off his hat and hung it on the peg next to the washstand.

"He tried to extort money from your brother!"

Twice, Bowie added silently, catching a whiff of her fresh scent.

"Twice!" She flashed two fingers at him, turning in a whirl of skirts to march across the room.

Whoa, she was as primed as a gunpowder fuse. She was going to wear a permanent groove in the wood floor.

Deciding to give her some space, maybe let her temper burn itself out, he braced one shoulder against the wall. Her blue-and-green-striped skirts swirled, occasionally revealing a white petticoat as she went back and forth.

"Saul was in on it with Vernon Pettit and Huck Allen. The first time they tried to get money from Quin, Vernon Pettit was killed. And the second time, it was Huck Allen. It could easily have been Saul!"

So, Bowie's suspicion that her foster brother had been the third man at those meetings with Quin had been right.

"Even though Saul wasn't the one who shot Quin, he could've been." Merritt barely took a breath. "And he put Addie in the line of fire. When your brother showed up and drew on him and Huck, they used Addie as a shield!"

From his sister-in-law, Bowie knew that Allen had been the one who had actually done that, but Merritt didn't seem of a mind to make the distinction. Sure seemed like her foster brother had confessed a lot.

"Addie cut him with a knife. On his left forearm." Fire sparked her green eyes. "Did I already tell you that?"

He shook his head at her rapid-fire words. That scar and the one on the left side of his neck would make it easy to identify the outlaw when Bowie finally caught him.

"After he told me about Quin and Addie, he asked if I thought you'd still go easy on him after learning that." Her voice rose, but she must've remembered Mr. Wilson was just down the hall because her next words were forceful, though hushed. "He just kept asking. He told me he was sorry, said he knew he needed to do the right thing."

The bewilderment in her voice mixed with anger. Pain darkened her eyes as she looked at Bowie.

She was hurt. He understood that. Her foster brother had been deceiving her for some time, maybe the whole of their lives together.

She had loved Saul like a brother for a long time, still did.

"The more he talked, the more I realized that he wasn't sorry at all." Her voice was thick as she walked back and forth in front of Bowie's bed, staring hard at the wood floor. "He was only telling me these things in the hope that I would put in a good word for him with you, convince you to go easier on him. I think he wanted me to do that whether he gave you more information or not."

Bowie had shown leniency for her before, agreed to let her try to convince her foster brother to do the right thing, but he couldn't do it this time. Now Bowie would have to *make* Saul do the right thing.

Merritt would be hurt and disappointed, maybe even feel betrayed. The thought of it didn't sit well with Bowie, but he wasn't budging.

She walked to the opposite wall. "He had no intention of turning himself in or talking to you. If he doesn't stop running and face what he's done, I'm afraid the next time I see him will be in a pine box."

He didn't want that for her, but Saul had made his choices. The sooner Bowie had Saul Bream in irons, the sooner he could expose Hobbs for everything he'd done and the better for everyone.

She slowed, her gaze lifting to his. The sadness, the loss, in her eyes had his chest going tight.

"He's an outlaw." Hurt trembled beneath the words. "My foster brother is an outlaw."

Anger at Saul rose up inside Bowie, at how badly, how often, the selfish bastard had hurt Merritt.

She wiped away a tear. "I know you've been listening. Don't you have anything to say?"

He braced himself for her reaction. Would she be indignant? Insulted? Just plain mad? "I'm just waiting for you to ask me to go easy on him. Like all the other times."

She paled and stopped dead in the center of the room. A strange look flitted across her face.

He straightened. "Merritt?"

She stood frozen, held in place by the horrible realization that slammed into her. What she had asked Bowie to do and *not* to do. Every time she had come to him with info about Saul, she had asked Bowie not to act. He had done what he had needed to, but it was no thanks to her.

She shouldn't have asked that of him. What if he'd felt she was presuming on their friendship or the fact that he lived in her house? Taking advantage.

That was what Saul had done to her. And she had done it to Bowie.

She looked at him, looked close.

He watched her expectantly. Resigned.

"I thought if I gave Saul enough chances, he would take one of them, turn his life around. But he didn't. And he isn't going to. I see that now."

Bowie's eyes widened, the hazy light softening his hard jaw.

"I don't want you to go easy on him. He needs to pay for what he's done."

"What?" He looked at her as if she had just drawn down on him.

"Saul's beyond my help, but not yours."

The big marshal just stared at her with a dazed look on his face.

"Bowie," she whispered in a choked voice as she walked over to him. "I'm sorry. I finally understand what Saul is and what he isn't. And what you are."

His eyes darkened.

"I'm willing to put Saul's fate in your hands." *And my fate, too,* she added silently.

"Why? Because you're mad enough at him to bite the head off a hammer?" he asked gruffly.

"No." It hit her then that she wasn't here only because she was angry and fed up, but because she trusted Bowie. She smiled, lifting a hand to his face, amazed at her certainty of this man. "It's because you're a good, honest man and I trust you to do the right thing."

He put his hand over hers, then brought it to his mouth, turning it to kiss the center of her palm. The emotion blazing in his eyes had her moving closer until her breasts touched his solid chest and she stood between his powerful thighs.

"And you're not going to ask me to give you one more chance to talk him in?"

"No."

Heat flared in his eyes and he lowered his head to kiss her.

She rolled up on tiptoe to meet him. It was exhilarating, intoxicating. The tender kiss quickly turned demanding and she was more than willing to give him whatever he wanted. Give him everything.

He deepened the kiss, sliding his hands into her hair, pushing off the ribbon holding her ponytail. The heavy mass slid across her shoulders in a thick curtain.

Making a noise deep in his chest, he swung her up in his arms and walked to the bed, laying her across the mattress. When he came down on top of her, he settled between her legs, holding her head and kissing her until she felt as if she were spinning.

He dragged his mouth to her jaw, her neck, up to her ear. He pressed openmouthed kisses down her neck, nibbling at the collarbones showing above the rounded collar of her dress.

Breathing hard, he lifted his head, his features sharp with desire. He pushed up on one arm, stroking her hair from her face. "I want you," he said hoarsely.

"I want you, too." This man had been there for her every time she had needed him. Whether it was about Saul or Lefty or Hobbs. Or helping her in the kitchen because of an injured hand. Calming, reassuring her, sometimes protecting her.

"Stay with me," he said into her neck, sending a shiver through her.

She had told him everything she knew. Now she wanted to give him everything, including herself. "Yes."

He kissed her again.

Restless, she tugged his shirt from his trousers and slipped her hands to the bare skin beneath. When she pushed the fabric up to his shoulders, he reached back to pull the garment over his head.

He moved his mouth to her ear, his hand cupping her breast. "I want to see you."

She nodded, her stomach dipping. Though he tried to open the small buttons down the front of her bodice, his fingers were too big.

"Here." Merritt pushed at his chest and he sat back, helping her sit up.

As she thumbed open the buttons, he threaded his fingers through her hair, lifting the mass and inhaling deeply. "Gorgeous."

Merritt's top parted and she opened it, pushing the sleeves down her arms. She felt a tug at the low neck of her camisole as Bowie tried to undo the tiny buttons there, too.

Before she could get her arms free to help, he made an impatient noise and closed his mouth over her through the muslin of her undergarment.

A ragged moan spilled out of her and she arched into him. The wet fire of his mouth set something off inside her, a desperate need to feel his skin against hers.

She pulled off her bodice and reached behind her to unfasten her skirt and petticoat as she toed off her shoes.

She went to work on her camisole, lifting up so he could pull off her skirt and petticoat, untie the tapes on her drawers and shove them off. He ran his hands up her bare thighs, and when she freed the last button on her camisole and it fell open, he froze.

The look in his eyes had her mouth going dry. Staring at her almost reverently, he traced his index finger over one blue vein from the swell of her breast to her nipple. He brushed his thumb along the inner plump curves before he lowered his head and took her in his mouth.

Her entire body quivered. He drew away, arousal streaking his cheekbones, raw desire in his face as his hands went to his trousers.

After getting rid of her camisole, she helped him undo his buttons until she could slip inside and curl her hand around him.

The muscles in his stomach clenched. Pushing his pants off, he moved her farther up the bed. His mouth found hers as he swept a hand over her hip. A work-roughened palm coasted down her stomach, then between her legs to delve a finger into her silky heat. Then a second finger.

She stroked his hot, rigid flesh, urging him to her. He rose over her, moonlight softening his jaw and the blaze of emotion in his eyes.

Holding her gaze, he slid inside and she pulled in a deep breath, curling her arms around his corded neck. She pressed into his touch, her legs tightening around him. He moved deep and sure, driving her up a dizzying peak.

He moved a hand to her lower back, lifting her into each stroke of his body, and gathered her even closer, kissing her, coaxing her to surrender to him.

When she felt tiny urgent pulses inside her, his muscles bunched and he went over the edge with her.

After a long moment, she came back to herself.

His weight pressed her into the mattress and she ran a hand over his sweat-dampened back, aware of a light breeze working through the room. His breathing was ragged, his flesh slick on hers. He brushed a kiss against her temple, then her forehead, each of her eyes.

She moved her hands over the tough sinew of his shoulders, his iron-hewn arms. He lifted up to look at her, smiling tenderly as he stroked her hair away from her face.

He rolled onto his back, bringing her on top of him, keeping her close. Pale light filtered into the room and she drew in the musky scent of his skin.

Outside, she heard the chirp of crickets and the distant bawl of a cow. Flattening one hand on his chest, she snuggled into him.

His arms tightened around her, his voice rumbling beneath her ear. "Stay."

Drowsily, she nodded, realizing what she felt was more than trust. She had feelings for this man. This *lawman*.

She knew he cared for her, too. Being with him felt right. Her decision to come to him tonight had been a good one. Not only because she trusted him, but also because she…loved him.

She loved him.

Listening to his deepening breathing, she held him tight and closed her eyes.

Bowie woke to the feel of soft fingers stroking his hair. He rolled to his back, blinking himself awake. Pale pink daylight washed over the woman sitting on the side of his bed.

Merritt. Memories of last night had him tugging her down on top of him to kiss her. She kissed him back, then laughingly pulled away.

"I have to go change clothes, then start breakfast."

"Lefty and Mr. Wilson can fend for themselves this morning."

He sat up, moving his face into the thick tumble of her hair, glad she had left it loose. He kissed her neck.

She sighed, making him want to pull her back down onto the bed. "No, I have to go."

He drew back to look at her, his gaze moving over her body, wishing she hadn't already dressed. His attention lingered on her for so long that she blushed.

"Stop."

"Okay," he said. "I'll get dressed and come down to help you."

The smile that curved her mouth had Bowie's body going hard. He traced her lips with his index finger. "I like that smile."

She nipped at his finger and stood. "I'll see you downstairs."

He grumbled, watching the sway of her hips as she walked to the door, admiring the dark satin curtain of her hair, remembering the petal-soft feel of her skin. He wondered how long it would be before he could get his hands on her again.

After she left, he lay there for a moment, thinking back over last night and why she had come to him in the first place. She'd seen Saul for what he was and trusted Bowie to do the right thing.

He knew Merritt hadn't come upstairs with the intention of sleeping with him, but he also knew she wouldn't have given herself to him if she didn't trust him. If she didn't have feelings for him.

He was glad they'd taken their time to get to know each other. Her surrender last night told him she accepted him for who he was, for everything he was, badge and all.

Alone in this bed, he realized that she belonged beside him. In bed or out. As much as his feelings for her had scared him when he had first realized them, now he welcomed them.

He was dressed and downstairs in five minutes. When he saw that her bedroom door was closed, and neither Mr. Wilson nor Lefty were anywhere to be seen, Bowie grinned, intending to slip into her room and get at least one more kiss.

Wanting to surprise her, he soundlessly turned the knob and stepped inside, shutting the door just as quietly as he had opened it. She stood next to the window, bathed in the first touch of sunlight. Only half of the buttons up the front of her blue dress were fastened and her hair swirled around her shoulders. She stared at something in her hand.

Bowie's gaze followed hers and it took him a moment to register what he was seeing. A piece of jewelry. A ruby, a silver chain. There, in her palm, lay a necklace.

His mother's necklace.

No, it couldn't be. He must be seeing things, but as he stepped closer, he knew he wasn't. That was his mother's necklace in Merritt's hand. The necklace that had been missing since Ruby Cahill's murder.

Merritt looked up then, horror and guilt chasing across her delicate features when she saw him.

All of the loss, the guilt and regret he'd carried for the last two years rose up.

Fury gathered inside him with the force of a twister and he exploded. Before he even realized he'd moved, he crossed the room and gripped her wrist. "Where in the hell did you get that?"

Chapter Thirteen

Merritt jumped at the savagery in Bowie's voice, but she understood he was probably shocked at seeing his mother's necklace. Shock that she had felt herself when Saul had shoved the necklace at her and ridden off just minutes ago.

Her blood had run cold when she realized he could have had the jewelry since Ruby was killed. Maybe even taken it off her neck himself.

Bowie's grip tightened on her wrist as he stared down at her palm, his eyes glittering with a viciousness that took her aback. "Answer me."

"Saul. I got it from Saul. I told him to give it to you himself." Some of her initial dismay was fading and she tugged against Bowie's iron grip. "You're hurting me."

He released her as if he couldn't bear to touch her, plucking the necklace from her hand. He curled it into his fist.

"How long have you had this? When did you get it?"

The sharp-edged questions flew at her like arrows. "This morning. Right before you walked in the door."

"How long was he here?"

"Less than five minutes. He rode right up to the window and apologized for last night. He knew how angry he'd made me."

Bowie stalked to the open window and yanked aside the curtains, his gaze panning the treed hillside. "Which direction did he go?"

"South. He rode for the trees. After that, I don't know." Realizing he was furious, she rubbed her wrist. "You have to be shocked. I was, when Saul gave it to me."

"Shocked." He barked out a harsh laugh. "You might say that."

Oh, yes, he was enraged and it seemed to be directed more toward her than Saul. "I told him to come in and talk to you. Instead, he pushed the necklace at me and rode off. When I saw it, I knew what it was, knew that it had belonged to your mother. I couldn't believe he had it."

Bowie turned from the window, his eyes narrowed. "Why did he give it to you?"

"Maybe it was his idea of showing remorse. He knew I would pass it on to you and probably thought it would get him back in my good graces."

"And get you back in mine?" Bowie's lips twisted.

"If so, his plan obviously didn't work," she murmured. Her astonishment—and horror—over Saul having the necklace had waned. Now she was very aware of the suspicion in Bowie's eyes. And the accusation.

"So, he's had it for the past two years?"

"I asked, but he wouldn't answer me."

"That's because he *has* had it."

As much as Merritt hated the implication, she thought so, too.

Bowie stepped back over to her, his face set in stone. "Did you have this necklace last night?"

"No! If I had, I would've brought it to you."

The brutal distrusting look he gave her cut her breath. Hurt bored in deep and twisted.

She inhaled sharply. "It belonged to your mother. Why would I hold on to it?"

"Maybe to keep me from finding out just how involved Saul really was in my parents' murders."

She shook her head, not understanding.

Bowie got right in her face. "If he has my mother's necklace, that means he had to have put his hands on her to get it. After she was *dead*."

"No!" Tears stung her eyes. She didn't want to believe such a horrible thing, but she knew Bowie believed it.

It made her sick to realize he could be right. Was that why Saul had never even hinted that he had Ruby's necklace? He knew Merritt had been friends with the woman, and if she had known about Saul's participation in the Cahills' murders, she would have turned him in herself. Something Saul knew, but Bowie obviously didn't.

"If I'd even suspected such a thing," she said, "I would've come straight to you."

He gave her a look that said she might as well try to convince him that a gelding could be hired out to stud.

She could barely force the words through her tight throat. "Do you think I've known all along that Saul did more than just witness your parents' murders? Because I haven't. I've told you everything I've learned, as soon as I learned it. Last night, I told you every single thing I know."

Bowie scoffed. *"Everything?"*

Everything except that she loved him. Thank goodness she hadn't confessed that.

Her temper spiked. "You obviously don't believe me. Why would I lie?"

"So you could protect him? After all he's done, to you and to my family, you're still protecting your foster brother."

"I told you I'm finished helping him."

"Yeah."

At his sarcasm, her stomach knotted. "You're calling me a liar," she said hoarsely.

"You've been protecting someone who likely did a hell of a lot more than stop my parents' wagon."

"Saul could've gotten that necklace from Pettit or Allen, and never laid a hand on your mother."

"Still protecting him, I see."

"No." Merritt imagined her own mother in place of Bowie's and her heart clenched.

Bowie towered over her, intimidating and dark. "For someone who was so determined not to become involved with a lawman who puts his job first, you seem to have no problem putting your friends ahead of a man you slept with. Ahead of the law, as well."

She drew in a sharp breath at his brutal words. "That isn't what's going on. What I told you last night about Saul is exactly what I just told him. I'm out of it. I tried to help him and he threw it back in my face. Just like you're doing."

If her insult affected him at all, she couldn't tell. Almost as though talking to himself, he said, "I know you didn't take the necklace from him in the past few weeks, but you could've had it before then."

"Or I could be telling the truth!" she snapped. "I saw it and found out about it only minutes ago. What do I have to do to prove that to you— Wait a minute. What do you mean, you know I wasn't given the necklace during the past few weeks?"

His eyes were hard with anger. "I had you under surveillance."

Surveillance? For a moment, she couldn't speak. Queasy, she pressed a hand to her stomach, choking out, "You had someone watching me?"

"I was the one watching you."

"Why? Because you thought I wouldn't let you know if Saul contacted me?"

"At first, yes. Then later because I wanted to make sure Hobbs wasn't a threat."

She couldn't stop a stab of hurt. "So, while you were surveilling me, did you see anything that might make you believe I haven't told you the whole truth when I passed along Saul's information?"

"No."

"Then why don't you believe me?" A horrible realization snaked through her. "You can't or won't take my word for it!"

When he didn't respond, she knew she was right. She was starting to understand. Oh, yes. "You want me to put my trust in you, but you aren't willing to do the same with me."

The pain was so sharp, it numbed her. "It's because I have no proof. That's how you judge things, isn't it? On what you can see, what you can touch?"

"Yes."

"Well, I can't do that for you. All I have is my word, which seems to mean nothing to you."

"You could tell me where Saul is hiding."

"Would it matter if I did?" she asked bitterly. "I might be lying."

"You still have to let me know if he contacts you. He's a suspect in my investigation."

She could promise till Judgment Day and Bowie wouldn't believe her. "I'd like you to leave now."

"Happy to oblige." He stalked to the door. "I'll find Saul on my own like I should've done before. If you know where he's headed or has been hiding out, you'd best start talking."

A red mist hazed her vision as anger erupted. "Why don't you put me back under surveillance and find out for yourself?"

His nostrils flared; fury burned in his eyes. He opened the door, then turned, holding up the necklace. "Would you have given this to me if I hadn't caught you with it?"

The words punched her in the chest.

"Caught me?" As if she were the one who had taken it. She hadn't tried to hide it. She had told him the truth about everything, given him *everything*. She wasn't giving him anything else. "I guess you'll never know, will you?"

His mouth tightened and he walked out.

Merritt closed her eyes. It hurt that he didn't trust her, but that pain was nothing compared to finding out just how much he didn't.

Bowie wasted no time saddling Midnight and riding out to track Bream. Fetching his brother to help him would take time Bowie couldn't afford to lose, so he started from Merritt's bedroom window and followed the trail of broken grass to the hillside behind her house. Bream had come this way, just as she'd said.

A zigzag series of bent branches led Bowie down the back side of the hill and to the South Kiowa River, where he lost the outlaw's trail. No hoofprints along the bank, nothing. He rode down to the water to talk to the ferryman. Muddy Newton hadn't transported Saul across the river; he hadn't even seen the man.

From there, Bowie headed north around Cahill Crossing and angled up to Phantom Springs. As he rode, he tried to keep his mind off Merritt. The rage that had driven him to accuse her of keeping information from him surged back on a powerful wave. And just beneath that, a sliver of doubt wiggled in.

He couldn't believe she was still protecting her lower-than-snake-spit foster brother. Bream was just as likely to be Earl and Ruby's killer as Vernon Pettit. *Had* Merritt kept Ruby's necklace from Bowie in an effort to keep him from learning the extent of Bream's involvement in the murders of Bowie's parents?

If so, she wasn't the only one at fault. It was because of Bowie that his parents had been killed to start with, because he had made the choice not to meet them at

Wolf Grove. And now, just as it had a few minutes ago when he had spied the jewelry in Merritt's hand, guilt swamped him.

Bowie reached the springs and found no sign of Merritt's foster brother at or around her favorite spot. The sun had risen steadily as he had tracked the outlaw, and sweat trickled down his spine. Lifting his hat, he dragged a forearm across his damp forehead before fishing his mother's necklace from the pocket of his denims.

With the water whispering over the rocks behind him, Bowie stared down at the deep red stone in his palm, sunlight glittering off the silver chain and delicate filigree surrounding the oval-cut ruby. Ma should've been buried wearing this, but thanks to Merritt's foster brother and two other outlaw bastards, Ruby Cahill had left this earth without her favorite earthly possession.

Kneeing Midnight into motion, Bowie continued on to Triple Creek. He knew Bream had been here on at least two occasions, but he wasn't here today. He didn't spy any fresh horseshoe or boot prints. The deep print impressions in the mud along the bank where the three creeks joined testified that the only thing that had been here lately was cattle.

After riding an area that spanned an arc from northwest to northeast of the creeks' junction and finding no sign of Bream's horse, Bowie turned back for Ca-Cross. He would form a posse with a few trusted friends and try again.

As hard as losing track of the outlaw grated on Bowie, it didn't bother him half as much as the growing and gut-twisting certainty that he'd made a mistake about Merritt.

Just remembering the raw pain in her eyes earlier made Bowie inwardly wince. He hadn't been able to take her word that she had hidden nothing from him, that the necklace came into her possession exactly when she had said it had. That she had had every intention of handing it over to him.

Last night, he hadn't had any trouble believing her when she'd come to him. The way she had hurt over realizing the truth about her foster brother couldn't have been faked. Neither could the way she had looked at Bowie when he'd been deep inside her.

She cared about him. Her feelings had been plain in her deep green eyes. He had believed her when she had said she trusted him, but he hadn't given her the same trust in return.

He loved her. He'd known it for a while, but she sure had no reason to believe that. He had doubted her the first time they'd hit a bump in the road.

Bowie cursed. He'd made a lot of mistakes in his life, the most major one resulting in the loss of his parents. He didn't want to lose Merritt, as well.

Though he wanted to hold on to his anger, he knew she shouldn't have been the object of it. He couldn't shake the memory of how she had paled, the devastation on her face earlier. Devastation he'd put there.

Seeing his mother's necklace, touching it, Bowie had been blinded by anger and loss. The thought that Saul had been in possession of it all this time had driven Bowie over the edge, straight into an emotional ambush.

He hadn't been able to put away the emotion and

listen to Merritt. To really hear her. The pain, the loss, had welled up, nearly choking him. It was like his mother had been killed all over again.

Last night, he had thought Merritt had chosen him. In her room earlier, it had felt like she'd chosen her foster brother, and Bowie had wanted proof that she hadn't.

The fact was she hadn't needed to tell him anything about Bream, ever. Hadn't needed to return his mother's necklace. Hadn't had to give herself to him. But she had done all those things.

She had been showing him that proof all along. He just had to trust in it.

He didn't deserve Merritt's forgiveness, but he was going to ask for it, anyway.

The sun was setting when Bowie, Ace and Clancy returned to Ca-Cross from another search for Bream. Bowie had given only the bare minimum of information. His friends knew they were looking for a wanted outlaw and that was plenty for them.

They split up when they reached the jail. Bowie dismounted, looking down the street at the boardinghouse. It was past suppertime. Not that he would be welcome. As soon as he washed up, he was going, anyway.

He looped his gelding's reins over the hitching post and grabbed a small square of toweling from his saddlebag before making for the pump between his office and the undertaker's salon.

After two quick pulls of the handle, he stuck his hands under the gush of cool water and washed the grime from his face. He dried his face and neck as he walked back to the jailhouse steps.

When he moved the rag to his hot, dusty nape, he looked up. And froze.

Merritt stood on the landing, watching him quietly, her green eyes shuttered against him.

His heart kicked hard as he walked up to meet her. "Hi."

"Hello." Her voice was cool and distant, her mouth tight.

Damn. "I was fixin' to come talk to you."

"Yes, I needed to tell you something, too."

Maybe that she didn't like the way they had left things, either? Hopeful, he stepped around her and opened the door. Anticipation grew. "Why don't you come inside?"

"There's no need for that." Her voice was stripped of emotion and she looked at him as if he were a stranger.

Dread hammered at him. Judging by her tone and the rigid set of her shoulders, she wasn't here for reconciliation. If he was going to apologize, he'd best get on with it. "Merritt, I—"

"I need to tell you this." She stepped closer, looking extremely uncomfortable about it.

Which irritated him. They'd been naked and a damn sight closer than this last night.

"Saul wants you to meet him after dark at Triple Creek."

"Saul." Bowie blinked. "I looked there for him. I looked everywhere today. Where has he been?"

"Not with me," she said defensively.

"I didn't think he was," he said quietly, seeing all over again just how badly he had hurt her.

She didn't respond. Instead, she fished a piece of

paper out of her skirt pocket and pushed it at him. "I didn't figure you'd believe me, so I had him write it out."

"Don't," he bit out, hating that she believed he doubted her. He edged her closer to the door. "Don't think that. Let's go inside."

"And here are the notes he left me, so you can compare the handwriting." She handed him two more pieces of paper.

Anger and hurt tightened his chest. Hurt that he had made her feel this way.

When he didn't look at the notes, she frowned. Her gaze went from them to him. "You can see he wrote them. That should be plenty to prove I'm telling the truth."

"I don't need you to prove it!" he gritted out. Taking a deep breath, he lowered his voice. "Please come inside so we can talk about this."

"We don't need to talk."

Bowie felt as if his skin was being slowly peeled off. "I know you're telling the truth. Those things I said this morning… I know better. I wish I'd never said them. I know you haven't lied to me. I know you wouldn't."

"That's good, because I haven't."

"Can you forgive me?" He stuck the notes in the pocket of his denims and reached for her.

She shied away.

His hands fell back to his sides, curling into fists. How to make her understand? "When I saw Ma's necklace, it was like I lost her all over again. I never meant to hurt you and I know I did."

Her green gaze was steady, flat. Remote.

An ache spread through his chest. "Merritt, I'm apologizing here."

"All right. Thank you." Her voice wobbled slightly. "I accept."

His relief was short-lived because she turned to walk away. Panic flaring, he snagged her elbow, refusing to release her even when she tensed.

"You forgive me, but you're leaving?"

"There's nothing else to say."

There damn sure was. "I…have feelings for you."

A flash of pain darkened her eyes.

"You feel something for me. I know you do."

She shook her head.

He lowered his head, rasping, "You wouldn't have given yourself to me last night if you didn't."

She tugged hard, pulling from his grasp. "Well, it's not enough, is it?" Her voice cracked and, when she looked at him, tears welled in her eyes. "I can't give you what you need."

"What do you mean?" He took her by the shoulders. "You're what I need."

She shook her head. "What you need is someone who can offer you tangible proof of their…loyalty, their feelings. Someone you can trust even when they aren't able to do that. I can't give you that. All I have is my word."

"Which is enough for me. This morning, I was angry. And feeling the responsibility for my parents' deaths. I took it out on you and that was wrong. I never should've said I doubted you, because I don't."

"I appreciate that, but it doesn't change anything."

She pulled from his hold and picked up her skirts, hurrying down the jailhouse steps.

The sun gilded her fall of dark hair, painted her in soft gold. The image of that glorious hair spread over his pillow, the remembered feel of her soft skin beneath his hands, had his gut knotting.

Bowie wanted to toss her over his shoulder and take her somewhere so he could love her until she believed him. That should prove his feelings. Yet she hadn't asked him to prove his feelings. She had simply wanted him to believe in hers.

He did, but it was too late.

He wanted her, but he knew she needed time to cool down. To keep from going after her, he curled a hand over the top of the wooden stair rail, his grip tightening until the skin across his knuckles burned.

Chapter Fourteen

◦◦◦◦◦◦

"*What you need is someone who can give you tangible proof of their...loyalty, their feelings. Someone you can trust even when they aren't able to do that.*"

Was Merritt right? Her words kept circling in Bowie's head.

He had lost Clea because he wouldn't give up his job as a lawman. After she had left, he had thrown himself into his work to the exclusion of all else. That had cost him his parents.

Had he become his job? Turned into someone who demanded evidence in every aspect of his life? Demanded something that was impossible for anyone to provide?

Wasn't that what he had done with Quin?

When Bowie had first returned to Cahill Crossing, he had doubted his brother's belief that their parents had been murdered because he himself hadn't seen any evidence. It was one thing to obtain proof that could be used to bring their parents' killer to justice, to prove guilt in a court of law, but Bowie's doubt had been about his brother.

There was a time when he wouldn't have doubted Quin. Before the fight that had torn them apart.

If he wanted evidence that Merritt's word was good, there was plenty. He just hadn't recognized it at first. When she didn't want or need to, she had come to him with information that implicated her foster brother. She had told Bowie everything when she could've omitted things that made Saul look bad. And last night when she had finally recognized the man for the outlaw he was, she had come to Bowie.

Why? Because she trusted him to do the right thing.

She had proved plenty to him. The only thing he had proved to her was distrust.

The thought of never being with her again, of some other man putting his hands on her, having the right to touch her, had Bowie's jaw clamping tight. The sharp edge of jealousy rode him hard.

He wasn't going to lose Merritt over the fact that he had focused more on what people could prove to him rather than the word of people he trusted.

He loved her. He needed her. There wasn't a damn thing he could do about that right now, but after he had talked with Saul and taken him into custody, Bowie would talk to Merritt. He wasn't taking no for an answer.

Turning his attention to his upcoming meeting with her foster brother, Bowie slid his Colt out of its holster. He rode into the clearing beside the junction where the three water sources of Triple Creek met. A soft breeze moved through the trees that lined the bank.

He reined up on the piece of ground that sat between two of the three creek forks. His rifle, loaded and ready, hung in the scabbard against his saddle. Having already checked for anyone who might be hiding or following him, he kept an outcrop of rock at his back.

There was no movement in the trees ahead or on either side of him. Maybe Saul wasn't coming. It wouldn't be the first lie the outlaw had told Merritt.

But when Bowie's gelding shifted uneasily, he knew that meant they were no longer alone. "Bream!"

"I'm here." A tall man wearing all black stepped out of the shadow of the trees across the creek.

Bowie fixed him in his pistol's sights. The man's sharp eyes and features put Bowie in mind of a hawk. "Let me see your hands," he said.

The outlaw lifted them, revealing a gun in his right one. "No need for the gun, Marshal. I'm only carrying the one weapon."

"Why don't you hand it over, then?"

"No, I don't think so."

Bowie wasn't going to waste time arguing. If Saul made a move, Bowie would shoot. "Are we going to talk?"

The other man's gaze darted around, causing Bowie to frown.

"Are you expecting someone?"

"No." His attention went to the area behind Bowie. "You?"

"No."

"Okay." Lowering his arms slowly, Saul stepped closer to the bank of the creek that separated the two men.

So, this was Merritt's foster brother, the man who had been present when Bowie's parents were killed. Who might have killed them.

"Where's your horse?" he asked.

Bream hooked a thumb toward the dense growth of trees behind him. "Back in there."

Bowie's gaze panned the area. He knew the outlaw was doing the same thing.

Never taking his eyes off the other man, he easily slid out of the saddle to stand beside his gelding. Saul came forward another step.

A limp straw cowboy hat covered dark, ragged hair, and the sleeves of his dusty black shirt were rolled back. He eyed Bowie warily. "Did Merritt give you the necklace?"

"She did." And it was safe in Bowie's pocket right now. His hand tightened on his gun as he remembered what he had put her through because of it.

"Good. That's good."

Bowie spied a knife scar on the outlaw's left forearm. He knew where that had come from.

Seeing no reason to start at the beginning and work his way up, he asked the most burning question. "Did you kill my parents? I know you told Merritt you were present, but didn't physically participate. You having my ma's necklace makes me question that."

After a long minute, Bream admitted, "I did more than stand around."

Bowie's spine went rigid.

"I didn't kill either of your parents, but I did take your ma's necklace from her after she was dead."

His muscles quivered with the effort not to pull the trigger. He wanted to empty his gun into the bastard. But he needed answers. And he wanted Hobbs. Right now, Saul was Bowie's best chance to get both of those things.

"My pa," he gritted out. "Who killed him? It looked like someone bashed his head in with a rifle."

"That was Pettit."

"And my ma?" The thought that Ruby may have died as violently as Earl made Bowie's gut knot up like bad rope.

"I think she was dead when the wagon hit the canyon floor. Pettit said she broke her neck, but I'm not sure. He was down there for a minute or two before Huck and I reached him."

Bile rose in Bowie's throat and a black fury threatened to overtake him. Shaking with the force of his anger, he tried to shut down the emotion, tried to narrow his focus to just the questions.

"Start talking. I want to know everything. How you came to be hired. Who hired Pettit and why. Everything. Even things you don't think relate or might be important. All of it."

The other man bristled. If he decided he didn't want to talk, Bowie had a bullet that could likely change his mind.

"All right," Saul bit out.

The throaty croak of a bullfrog sounded from across the creek as Saul began to speak.

* * *

Merritt thought she had cried herself out, but seeing Bowie an hour ago had brought on more tears. After she cleaned up the supper dishes, Lefty and Mr. Wilson left to attend a meeting of all residents at the town hall to discuss forming a fire company. Merritt didn't have it in her to go.

Instead, she was stripping the linens from all the beds in preparation for laundry day tomorrow. If Bowie didn't trust her—and it was plain he didn't—then good riddance.

So why couldn't she stop thinking about him? Wanting him? Wishing he would believe her?

She understood the shock he must have felt upon seeing his mother's necklace. And the pain it must have stirred up. She'd dealt with it herself on a smaller scale. His mother had been her friend, after all. Which made his suspicions of her even harder to bear.

Merritt knew she had hurt him, too. She couldn't erase the image of the raw pain and regret that had flared in his eyes when she had given him her notes from Saul so that Bowie could confirm her foster brother's handwriting.

She would have to ask Bowie to move out of the Morning Glory. She absolutely couldn't live in the same house with him. And even though the two of them remaining in the same town was daunting, she wasn't leaving. She'd made a home here. And unless he resigned his position, he would be here for at least the next four years.

Hopefully, it wouldn't take that long to solve his parents' murders. Saul could be the key to that. She hoped he showed up at his meeting with Bowie, or the marshal would never believe her again. Not that it mattered, she told herself. Not anymore. Things were over between them.

She repeated that to herself when she walked into his room to change the sheets. A light breeze blew through the open window. Though it was faint, she could smell the mix of his dark masculine scent and her softer one in the linens, flooding her mind with images of the two of them on the bed last night. Naked.

Her throat closed up. The way he'd touched her, looked at her, had made her believe his feelings were the same as hers and that their being together was the beginning of a future. She'd been wrong.

Earlier, he had said he had feelings for her. So why had he ruined things between them? The hollow regret in his eyes made her wonder if she should give him— *them*—another chance. But he had hurt her deeply. How strong could his feelings be if he already doubted her?

She yanked the sheets off the mattress and crammed them into the big wash basket. Just as she spread a clean one on the mattress, she heard a sound behind her.

She turned, faltering when she saw Hobbs. Sudden panic and a desperate wish for Bowie to return tangled inside her. So far, she had managed to keep the former marshal from knowing her true feelings about him, so she tried to smile. "Tobias, how are you?"

"I'm fine. I've been wanting to talk to you."

Uneasy now, she kept her voice light, pleasant. "Oh? I'm surprised you aren't at the town meeting to discuss the new fire company."

"This is more important." A dark tone beneath the words made them sound vaguely threatening.

Her thoughts raced. Her pistol was in her bureau drawer. It was a good guess that neither of Bowie's guns were here; he would have taken them to his meeting with Saul.

She didn't want to think she would need a gun, but her disquiet grew, edged into mouth-drying fear when the man in front of her pulled something out of his vest pocket and held it up. Her white handkerchief with her initials embroidered in red, white and blue.

Merritt's breath backed up in her lungs. He had found it, had kept it all this time.

"Recognize this? I know you do." His tone was almost conversational. "It was on the floor of my house."

Palms clammy, she swallowed hard. "I lost that in town the night of the Fourth of July celebration."

"Not town," he said. A sly smile spread across his handsome face. "In my house."

She started to deny it, but she could tell by the cold look in his eyes that he wouldn't believe her.

"I couldn't figure out what you could possibly be doing in there, so I began watching you."

"Watching me!" Bowie must not have known or he would've done something about it.

"Tonight, after your boarders left, I saw a man slip inside your back door, then slip back out."

Saul. She fought down a swell of panic, trying to remain calm.

"I didn't recognize him, but I saw a scar on his arm. In the exact place Addie Cahill described cutting one of the hooded outlaws that she and Quin had a run-in with. I know it's the same man. What I don't know is your connection to him."

Merritt clamped her mouth shut tight.

"I don't care what your relationship is with him, but I'm guessing you know what he's done, and therefore you know why I'd like to talk to him."

Talk? Hobbs had no intention of *talking* to her foster brother. *Kill* was a more accurate word.

"I want you to take me to him."

Her head jerked up. She was not going to help Hobbs kill Saul. "What makes you think I know where he is?"

"Oh, you know. Otherwise, you wouldn't have just turned as pale as milk. Besides, in the past twenty-four hours, he's been here three times. You know where he is."

She blanched. Just as she started to deny it, she realized that Bowie might still be at Triple Creek with Saul. If so, he could take care of Hobbs. At the very least, he could arrest the former marshal for kidnapping, and maybe keep him in jail until Bowie could prove Hobbs had murdered Earl and Ruby.

"I'm not sure where he is, but I have an idea." She didn't have to fake the unsteadiness in her voice.

The thought of going anywhere with Tobias had her nerves winding tight.

Eyes glinting dangerously, he pulled a revolver from behind his back and motioned her toward him. "I don't want to shoot you, but I will if I have to, so don't try anything."

She nodded, walking with him down the stairs. His gun drilled into her ribs as he steered her to the back door. They stepped onto the back stoop.

His sorrel mare waited patiently. Hobbs quickly tied Merritt's hands and tossed her into the saddle. She slid sideways and he vaulted up behind her, settling her in front of him. The pommel bit into her thigh.

"You struggle, make any noise, try to kick me, I'll put a bullet in your friend the second I see him."

Nodding, Merritt fought to keep her composure. She would do her part to get Hobbs to Triple Creek.

She prayed Bowie was still there to do the rest.

"So, two years ago, Hobbs hired Pettit to kill my parents and Pettit enlisted you and Huck Allen to help." Bowie wanted to make sure he had everything straight.

Saul nodded. "Yes, but we were told the job was a robbery. We were to stop the wagon. We did, but instead of holding a gun on your parents and demanding their goods, Pettit ran them off the road over into Ghost Canyon. When Huck and I got down there, Pettit had just killed your pa. Bashed in his head."

It didn't matter how many times Bowie heard about it; he still wanted to kill Hobbs. And Pettit. And the man in front of him.

Saul hesitated, then said, "Your ma was already dead. That's when I took her necklace."

"My brother Quin was falsely accused of killing Pettit. Who really killed him?"

"Hobbs."

"Why?"

"Pettit got it in his head to blackmail Hobbs for having your parents killed. If he didn't pay up, Pettit threatened to tell."

"So, Pettit wasn't the one who sent a note to my

brother offering the truth about our parents' deaths in exchange for money?"

"No. Hobbs did that. He told Pettit to meet him here at Triple Creek and he would pay him the money he'd demanded to keep quiet. Then Hobbs sent a note to your brother, offering information."

"He was planning to take care of both of them by killing Pettit and framing Quin for it."

"Yes. Pettit didn't trust Hobbs, so he wanted me and Huck to go along, hide in the trees during their meeting so Hobbs wouldn't know we were there."

Smart move on Pettit's part, Bowie acknowledged.

"Pettit went to meet Hobbs and asked what was going on. Instead of answering, Hobbs shot him. Your brother must have arrived just before we did. We came up the back side of those trees over there." He pointed behind Bowie, across the width of another creek. "Your brother was laid out, unconscious when we got here.

"Huck and I were in shock. Before we could move, we heard someone else ride up. Hobbs hightailed it out of there and so did we."

That someone had been Addie, Bowie knew. Hobbs, Allen and Bream were the three men she had heard leaving the scene when Quin had come up next to Pettit's dead body.

"Then what?" he asked. "Did you and Allen decide to blackmail Hobbs, too?"

"Hell, no. Neither of us wanted to poke that bear after what had happened to Pettit."

"So, you sent a second note to my brother, offering information in exchange for money."

Saul nodded. "We would've told him everything we

knew, except his woman showed up instead of him. We weren't going to hurt her, but your brother rode in and drew down on both of us. Huck grabbed her, using her as a shield to try and get away. As I was going for the money, your brother plugged Huck with two to the gut."

"And you ran?" Bowie couldn't keep the contempt out of his voice.

"I tried. That woman nearly cut off my hand. As it was, she got me on the arm and the neck."

That definitely matched the story both Addie and Merritt had told. "And since then, it's just been you?"

"Yes. I was going to ride on, but I couldn't. I was afraid to spend any of that money, for fear of bringing suspicion on myself."

Saul had no way of knowing that Quin hadn't told anyone outside the family about the money he had lost. It was a good thing Bowie's brother had done so, because Saul staying had led Bowie to Hobbs.

"I felt bad about what we'd done. I never signed on for murder."

"So, you contacted Merritt and confessed?"

"Yes. She gave me some food and offered me a place to stay. I should've left the area then, but I couldn't." A wistful look crossed his face. "Sometimes, I wish I could be as good as she thinks I could be."

Bowie knew all about disappointing Merritt. He hated himself for doing it. "Do you know why Hobbs wanted to murder my parents? He stood to gain nothing from their deaths."

"I don't know that the idea began with Hobbs. Pettit said someone hired the marshal, the *former* marshal, to get rid of the Cahills, but I don't know who. Pettit didn't know, either."

So, someone else was involved. Huck Allen hadn't lied when he had told Quin that he had no idea how deep the scheme against the Cahills went.

The former marshal didn't stand to gain anything directly by murdering Ma and Pa. No land, no money, no livestock. His compensation had likely been money.

"Does Hobbs have any idea who you are?"

"Pettit told him there were three of us who knew Hobbs had hired Pettit to kill the Cahills."

"And now you're the only one left."

Saul nodded.

"Your smartest, safest bet is to turn yourself in."

"I've been thinking about that."

"If you cooperate, I'll make sure the judge knows you helped me catch Hobbs."

"All right—"

Saul broke off, his gaze jerking to Bowie. "Did you hear something?"

"Voices. I thought you said you weren't expecting anyone."

"I'm not," Saul whispered.

Neither was Bowie. He looked around for cover. Both he and Saul were exposed in this clearing.

The outcrop of rock behind him was his best bet and he began to back that way. Saul retreated toward the trees from which he'd come.

"I said sometimes he comes here," said a feminine voice. "I never said he was here all the time."

Merritt! Bowie's gaze shot to Saul. The alarm on the

other man's face said he had heard and recognized her voice, too.

Why in the hell would she be coming out here? Who was she with? Whoever it was made her anxious. Bowie could read that in her voice.

He thumbed down the hammer of his Colt. He would have maybe two seconds to react by the time Merritt and her companion came around the last stand of trees before the landscape gave way to the clearing.

His muscles drew tight. Finger on the trigger, he leveled his weapon, waiting. Saul did the same.

Bowie listened closely. The movement through the tall grass out beyond the trees sounded like only one horse. Apprehension hammered at him.

Suddenly, Merritt called out, "Saul, are you here?"

Bowie sent a look to the man. *Don't answer.*

He nodded to show he understood.

Bowie registered the trembling in her voice just before he spied a horse's head. Reddish-brown.

The animal stepped into view and Bowie saw Merritt. A man's arm was clamped around her middle; the edge of a hat peeked out from behind her. A man's hat. A bowler hat.

It was Hobbs! And he had a gun drilled into her temple.

Chapter Fifteen

$Everything$ folded together in one frozen moment.

"Let her go!" Bowie yelled.

"Put down your weapon!" Hobbs bellowed at the same time. "I *will* shoot her."

"I'll drop you if your finger so much as twitches on that trigger."

"Hobbs!" Saul hollered, drawing the ex-marshal's attention.

Bowie kept his gaze steady on Hobbs, who swung his gun toward Saul and fired. Then fired again.

Saul cried out and stumbled, then fell.

Merritt screamed. Bowie hadn't taken his eyes off Hobbs, who held Merritt locked against him. He didn't have a clear shot, especially when Hobbs pulled her even farther across his chest.

The bastard ducked down behind her right shoulder and turned his gun on Bowie. Except for the arm clamped across Merritt's middle, only Hobbs's hat and eyebrows were visible.

Bowie cursed. All he needed was an inch, one damn inch, and he could blow the bastard to hell.

Hobbs fired and Bowie hit the dirt, scrambling through a nearby bush. His gelding jumped, wheeling behind the rock.

Another shot rang out, but it came from the trees at Bowie's back. Higher up than they were. Merritt screamed again. Then silence.

The acrid smell of gunpowder hung in the air. Saul was on the ground, unmoving. Why wasn't Hobbs shooting? Who the hell was in the trees?

Gun leveled, Bowie carefully peeked over the top of the bush and sighted Hobbs—who had pitched sideways off his horse and now lay motionless on the ground. On top of Merritt.

Bowie scrambled to his feet and was already running when he heard a choked sob from her.

He jumped the creek, angling for the opposite bank. One of his boots slipped, landing him in the water. He grabbed a handful of dirt and grass, steadied himself, then clawed his way the short distance to solid ground.

The sound of Merritt's sobs cut through him like a blade. Hobbs's sorrel danced nervously several yards away from her. Bowie saw her struggling to get out from under Hobbs, who lay unmoving across her hips and legs.

Bowie reached her and went to his knees, shoving the ex-marshal's body off her, then helping her sit up.

Crying, she fell against him, and Bowie gathered her

close, burying his face in her neck. Sharp relief ached in his chest. Until he felt something sticky and warm.

He looked down, not registering at first that blood slicked his hand. Merritt's blood.

His heart stopped. "Sweetheart?" he croaked. "Merritt, you've been hit. I need to look at you."

"It hurts."

"I know." He kept one arm around her waist and pulled back slightly to examine her.

Blood covered her right shoulder, plastering the light blue fabric of her dress sleeve to her arm. She gave a moan that squeezed his chest hard.

The bullet had gone clean through her shoulder. And killed Hobbs. Who the hell had made that shot?

She looked at her bleeding wound and shuddered. Bowie stroked her hair.

"I need to get you to the doctor."

"Saul? Is Saul dead?" She turned to look across the creek.

Her foster brother lay where he'd fallen and was groaning.

"He's alive." Bowie's arm tightened around her.

Her breathing was labored, raspy with pain. "You got Hobbs."

"Not me. A sniper."

At the sudden pounding of hooves traveling away from them, Bowie and Merritt both looked west.

She eased away from him. "Go! Go after whoever that is. You can catch them."

"What? No! You're shot."

"And it hurts, but I think the bullet went straight through."

Yes. The shot had been deliberately placed, right through the ball of her shoulder to hit Hobbs dead center between the eyes. Bowie didn't know anyone who could make a shot like that.

"You may never get another chance to find this person," she urged.

And he didn't give a damn. Staring down into her pale face, her pain-filled green eyes, he knew he wasn't going anywhere.

"I'm not leaving."

"Just get me to Saul. I can help him and you can go."

"Get the idea out of your head. I'm not going."

"But whoever that was might be able to help you solve your parents' murders."

"Forget it." The sound of pounding hoofbeats was fading. He cupped Merritt's cheek. "You're more important. The only place we're going is to the doctor so he can take care of you."

Bowie pulled his bandanna from the back pocket of his denims.

"Bowie—"

"No." He made a tourniquet from his kerchief and knotted it tight around the part of her shoulder that curved into her upper arm.

Every time she winced, he felt it like a cut.

"What about Saul?" she asked weakly.

Satisfied he had slowed her blood flow, Bowie brushed a kiss against her forehead. "Going now to check on him."

He jogged over to the man. Shot in the gut and upper thigh, Saul was alive, but not by much.

Bowie hurried over to the man's horse and cut off a piece of the rope looped over his saddle horn. After tying it around the injured man's thigh, he dragged him over to his mount and hefted him across the saddle.

Bowie gathered the reins and walked over to Hobbs's sorrel, hoisting the dead man facedown over the saddle.

Merritt was too pale for Bowie's liking. He lifted her onto the back of his horse and swung up behind her. Because of her injuries and Saul's, too, he was afraid to let the horses run, but he urged them to a brisk walk. He gathered Merritt against him, cursing when he felt her wince.

"Is Saul bad?" she whispered.

He ached at the sadness in her green eyes. "Afraid so."

"Do you think we'll make it to Doc Lewis in time?"

He glanced back at the man who hadn't made a sound since Bowie had loaded him onto his horse. "I don't know, honey. I'll try."

A tear fell down her cheek and she laid her head against his chest.

His throat tightened. He closed his eyes, savoring the reassuring weight of her against him. Still unsteady from seeing her with the former marshal, Bowie's frantic pulse finally slowed.

He didn't care how long it took. He would get her to forgive him for doubting her. Because he couldn't let her go. He wouldn't.

It was dark, the main part of town quiet, when they reached Ca-Cross. Piano music jangled from the saloons on the other side of the railroad tracks. Voices rose and fell. Cigar smoke hung in the air.

If people started asking questions about Ca-Cross's former marshal, Bowie might have to give more answers than he wanted. Until he knew who had hired Hobbs to kill Earl and Ruby, he wanted to keep everything as quiet as possible, especially Merritt's involvement and gunshot wound.

Bowie reined up in the alley between Doc Lewis's office and the Porter Hotel, trailing the other horses and their riders behind him.

He dismounted and lifted Merritt from the saddle, starting for Clancy's back door with her in his arms.

"Bowie, I can walk."

"I know." He looked down at her, the moonlight gilding her skin to a pearly sheen. And turning the blood on her shoulder black. "I just don't want to let go of you."

"Oh," she said softly, settling against him.

Seeing Hobbs's arm locked around her had nearly sent Bowie into a rage, but discovering she had been shot had turned his entire body numb. Only now was he able to get a full breath.

He reached the doctor's back door and tapped it with his boot.

A haggard-looking Clancy answered, letting them inside with a frown. His gaze took in the bloody bandanna on Merritt's arm and he led Bowie straight to a room set off the front parlor and to the examining table.

As Bowie settled Merritt in a chair, he explained to Doc Lewis what had happened and told him there was a severely wounded man outside. Clancy helped bring in Saul while Bowie told the doctor that Merritt had been caught in a shoot-out between Hobbs and Saul, who was her foster brother. He left out any references to his parents or the fact that they'd been murdered.

The doctor's brown eyes said he knew there was more, but he didn't ask. They laid the wounded man carefully on the exam table.

While Clancy tore Saul's shirt up the front to look at the gunshot in his abdomen, Bowie pulled a chair over beside Merritt. He ripped the seam of her sleeve, peeling it down to check her wound. He didn't think there was any lasting damage. He hoped Doc Lewis agreed.

He glanced at Merritt, who was watching the proceedings with sad, sober eyes. The doctor's already-grim expression grew even darker when he cut a hole in Saul's blood-soaked trousers and ripped them open to get a look at his inner thigh.

He stopped the blood flow with thick bandages, then bowed his head. Running a hand over his nape, he stood and walked to Merritt. "He's lost too much blood. I'm afraid I can't help him."

She stifled a sob and Bowie stroked her hair, feeling helpless.

"Merritt," Saul croaked.

Wiping her eyes, she got to her feet and went to him.

The doctor laid a hand on Bowie's shoulder. "You can have the room as long as you want."

"Thanks," he said quietly, hating that Merritt was having to go through this.

Bent low over her foster brother, she clutched his hand as he mumbled something to her. With tears streaming down her face, she called Bowie over. "He wants to talk to you."

Bowie stood across the table from her and leaned down so he could hear Saul's raspy words.

"One…more…thing." He stopped, visibly gathering his strength. When he spoke again, his words were slurred, his voice fading away. "Pettit said…Hobbs knew something. About a…Van Slyck and your…folks."

"I'll check it out. Which Van Slyck?" Bowie asked, hoping Saul could hang on long enough to tell him if he meant the father or the son.

Saul's gaze met Bowie's. "Take…care of her."

He nodded.

After a rattling breath, Saul went limp.

Merritt bowed her head, shoulders shaking. Bowie moved around the table and took her in his arms, careful of her wounded shoulder.

She leaned into him. "Take me home. Please."

"I will." He rubbed her back. "As soon as Clancy looks at your shoulder."

She sat stoically while the doctor dressed her wound. Twenty minutes later, Bowie set her on her feet beside her bed.

She stood unmoving, her gaze unfocused and distant as if she were remembering something.

The blood staining her pretty dress sent another flash of anger through him. He hated that she'd been hurt. He feathered a kiss against her temple. "Honey, let's get you out of this dress."

She nodded, watching him quietly as he unbuttoned her bodice and eased it down over her arms. At his urging, she stepped out of her skirt, then let him unfas-

ten her camisole. He took it off along with her drawers. He tried not to be affected by the sight of her bare
curves, the silky skin he had touched only this morning.

He held her nightgown so she could step into it rather
than pull it on over her head.

"I can't believe he's gone," she said shakily.

Bowie gently sat her down on the edge of her mattress and palmed off her button-up boots.

As he slid them off, her gaze met his, her lashes still
spiky from her tears, her eyes deep green. "Did you get
what you needed from him?"

Bowie frowned.

"Can you finish your investigation now?"

She was angry, he realized. At him?

Rolling her stockings down her slender legs, he took
them off and laid them on the bed. "Saul told me everything he knew, but the investigation isn't over."

"Now what?" She rose, her chin trembling. Anger
blazed in her tear-filled eyes. "Hobbs is dead and so is
Saul! He's dead, Bowie."

He stood, wanting to take her in his arms. Instead,
she hit him in the chest.

Shock held him immobile for a moment. Then she
punched him again. And again. He stayed her hand and
she let out a broken sound. Her head lolled against his
chest.

His heart clenched tight. Did she blame him for
Saul's death? Bowie couldn't stand the thought. He
knew she didn't hold him responsible for the actual
killing shots, but maybe she blamed him for Saul being
at Triple Creek in the first place.

"Why couldn't he have turned himself in? Why did he have to run with those outlaws?"

Bowie was too stunned at the idea that she blamed him to answer. He probably deserved it. If he had done his job sooner, tried to bring Saul in a few weeks ago when he had caught him outside the kitchen with Merritt, the man would probably still be alive.

But the thought that she blamed him for Saul's death broke Bowie in two. She obviously hadn't forgiven him for this morning and now this.

"I'm sorry," he said hoarsely.

She lifted her head, questioning him with her eyes.

"You probably can't wait to see the last of me, but that won't be tonight, honey. I'm staying, no matter what you say. Tomorrow, if you're okay, I'll leave."

"Leave? Why?" She clutched at his grimy shirt.

It took all he had not to put his hands on her. He clenched his jaw hard enough to snap bone. "You don't want me here. It sounds as though you blame me for Saul's death."

"No! No, I don't. I'm angry about it, but not at you."

"No?" That wasn't how it felt.

"Oh, Bowie." Her eyes softened as she reached up with her good hand and caressed his jaw. "I love you."

A hush came over him. "I love you, too, but what about this morning? You made it real plain that we were finished."

"I was angry and hurt, but before Hobbs showed up here, I had made up my mind to tell you that I forgave you. That I love you and I don't want things to end between us."

"You really forgive me?"

"Yes. I knew you valued what we have more than you do your job, especially when you refused to chase after that sniper and give up the opportunity to catch your parents' murderers. I'm sorry for saying what I did about you needing tangible evidence to trust my word."

"You weren't wrong, Merritt."

"I was—"

He laid a finger against her lips. "You gave me plenty of evidence of your feelings if I had just seen it for what it was. I'll do whatever you need me to do so that you can know your word is more than good enough for me. I want your heart."

"You have it," she said softly. "If I hadn't been sure before Hobbs grabbed me, I definitely was when I saw how you tried to save Saul. I know you did that for me."

"I'm sorry I couldn't keep him alive."

"So am I, but I also know that he lived a dangerous life."

"You should be aware that he agreed to turn himself in."

She searched his eyes as if to judge whether he was telling the truth or just trying to set her mind at ease.

He lifted her hand to his mouth and kissed her fingers. "He really did, Merritt."

Tears welled in her eyes. "Good."

"He loved you. And so do I." Bowie's hands came up to gently frame her face and his mouth covered hers.

She responded immediately, going up on tiptoe to wrap her good arm around his neck.

After a long moment, they drew apart. His smile faded to a frown when his gaze settled on her face. His thumb floated over her jaw, then her cheek.

"What is it?" she asked.

"I got dirt on you."

She laughed through her tears. "Well, that's a switch. I'd better keep you around to make sure I stay clean."

"Now that's the job I really want. For the rest of our lives."

"It's yours," she murmured against his lips.

* * * * *

HISTORICAL

Where Love is Timeless™

HARLEQUIN® HISTORICAL

COMING NEXT MONTH
AVAILABLE DECEMBER 27, 2011

SCANDAL AT THE CAHILL SALOON
Cahill Cowboys
Carol Arens
(Western)

THE LADY CONFESSES
The Copeland Sisters
Carole Mortimer
(Regency)

CAPTURED FOR THE CAPTAIN'S PLEASURE
Ann Lethbridge
(Regency)

A DARK AND BROODING GENTLEMAN
Gentlemen of Disrepute
Margaret McPhee
(Regency)

HHCNM1211

REQUEST YOUR FREE BOOKS!

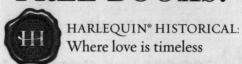

HARLEQUIN® HISTORICAL:
Where love is timeless

2 FREE NOVELS PLUS 2 **FREE GIFTS!**

YES! Please send me 2 FREE Harlequin® Historical novels and my 2 FREE gifts (gifts are worth about $10). After receiving them, if I don't wish to receive any more books, I can return the shipping statement marked "cancel." If I don't cancel, I will receive 6 brand-new novels every month and be billed just $5.19 per book in the U.S. or $5.74 per book in Canada. That's a savings of at least 17% off the cover price! It's quite a bargain! Shipping and handling is just 50¢ per book in the U.S. and 75¢ per book in Canada.* I understand that accepting the 2 free books and gifts places me under no obligation to buy anything. I can always return a shipment and cancel at any time. Even if I never buy another book, the two free books and gifts are mine to keep forever.

246/349 HDN FEQQ

Name	(PLEASE PRINT)	

Address		Apt. #

City	State/Prov.	Zip/Postal Code

Signature (if under 18, a parent or guardian must sign)

Mail to the **Reader Service:**
IN U.S.A.: P.O. Box 1867, Buffalo, NY 14240-1867
IN CANADA: P.O. Box 609, Fort Erie, Ontario L2A 5X3

Not valid for current subscribers to Harlequin Historical books.

Want to try two free books from another line?
Call 1-800-873-8635 or visit www.ReaderService.com.

* Terms and prices subject to change without notice. Prices do not include applicable taxes. Sales tax applicable in N.Y. Canadian residents will be charged applicable taxes. Offer not valid in Quebec. This offer is limited to one order per household. All orders subject to credit approval. Credit or debit balances in a customer's account(s) may be offset by any other outstanding balance owed by or to the customer. Please allow 4 to 6 weeks for delivery. Offer available while quantities last.

Your Privacy—The Reader Service is committed to protecting your privacy. Our Privacy Policy is available online at www.ReaderService.com or upon request from the Reader Service.

We make a portion of our mailing list available to reputable third parties that offer products we believe may interest you. If you prefer that we not exchange your name with third parties, or if you wish to clarify or modify your communication preferences, please visit us at www.ReaderService.com/consumerchoice or write to us at Reader Service Preference Service, P.O. Box 9062, Buffalo, NY 14269. Include your complete name and address.

HH11B

USA TODAY bestselling author

Penny Jordan

brings you her newest romance

PASSION AND THE PRINCE

Prince Marco di Lucchesi can't hide his proud
disdain for fiery English rose Lily Wrightington—
or his attraction to her! While touring the palazzos
of northern Italy, the atmosphere heats up…until
shadows from Lily's past come out….

*Can Marco keep his passion under wraps
enough to protect her, or will it unleash itself, too?*

Find out in January 2012!

*Brittany Grayson survived a horrible ordeal at the hands
of a serial killer known as The Professional...
who's after her now?*

*Harlequin® Romantic Suspense presents a new installment
in Carla Cassidy's reader-favorite miniseries,*
LAWMEN OF BLACK ROCK.

*Enjoy a sneak peek of
TOOL BELT DEFENDER.*

*Available January 2012
from Harlequin® Romantic Suspense.*

"**B**rittany?" His voice was deep and pleasant and made
her realize she'd been staring at him openmouthed through
the screen door.

"Yes, I'm Brittany and you must be..." Her mind suddenly went blank.

"Alex. Alex Crawford, Chad's friend. You called him
about a deck?"

As she unlocked the screen, she realized she wasn't
quite ready yet to allow a stranger inside, especially a male
stranger.

"Yes, I did. It's nice to meet you, Alex. Let's walk around
back and I'll show you what I have in mind," she said. She
frowned as she realized there was no car in her driveway.
"Did you walk here?" she asked.

His eyes were a warm blue that stood out against his
tanned face and was complemented by his slightly shaggy
dark hair. "I live three doors up." He pointed up the street to
the Walker home that had been on the market for a while.

"How long have you lived there?"

"I moved in about six weeks ago," he replied as they

walked around the side of the house.

That explained why she didn't know the Walkers had moved out and Mr. Hard Body had moved in. Six weeks ago she'd still been living at her brother Benjamin's house trying to heal from the trauma she'd lived through.

As they reached the backyard she motioned toward the broken brick patio just outside the back door. "What I'd like is a wooden deck big enough to hold a barbecue pit and an umbrella table and, of course, lots of people."

He nodded and pulled a tape measure from his tool belt. "An outdoor entertainment area," he said.

"Exactly," she replied and watched as he began to walk the site. The last thing Brittany had wanted to think about over the past eight months of her life was men. But looking at Alex Crawford definitely gave her a slight flutter of pure feminine pleasure.

Will Brittany be able to heal in the arms of Alex, her hotter-than-sin handyman…or will a second psychopath silence her forever? Find out in
TOOL BELT DEFENDER
Available January 2012
from Harlequin® Romantic Suspense
wherever books are sold.

HRSEXP0112